Between the Lies Revisited

PRISTINE
PRESS AND MEDIA

L.J. HARRIS

Between the Lies Revisited
Copyright © 2025 by L.J. Harris

All rights reserved. No part of this publication may be
reproduced, distributed, or transmitted in any form or
by any means, including photocopying, recording, or
other electronic or mechanical methods, without the prior
written permission of the author, except in the case of brief
quotations embodied in critical reviews and certain other
non-commercial uses permitted by copyright law.

ISBN
978-1-969642-33-3 (Paperback)
978-1-969642-32-6 (eBook)
978-1-969642-34-0 (Hardcover)

TABLE OF CONTENTS

PRELUDE

Early one Sunday winter evening, Braxton Marselle traveled leisurely on 295 South in his relatively new Nissan, heading toward Southern Maryland. He was surprised by the magnitude of the fast-approaching storm and wondered how long it would last. He drove in silence with the radio turned off and wore his earpiece in case he received a call from his wife. His mind was on the surprise tickets his friend, Dillon, had just picked up for them to see the Battle of the Church Choirs coming to a well-known D.C. venue in a few months. They would double with Dillon and his wife for a fun evening out—and he could not wait to see her reaction. Though his wife enjoyed listening to other types of music, she specially loved to hear soulful gospel and choir music. He thought about giving her a call, but things were changing so quickly that he decided against dividing his attention in any way. The sky had already turned so dark—almost black—and the temperature dropped suddenly with such considerable wind pickup that the Murano seemed to sway a bit. He felt an imperceptible chill inside the car. At first, large raindrops splashed against the windshield, but within seconds they pelted the car much harder. Five minutes later, spigots of water poured, and torrential rain drowned the area. He lightly braked to decrease his speed immediately.

It crossed his mind that he had thought his wife was being overprotective, but after one look at the murky sky, she insisted the children stay home instead of riding with him as they usually did. But now he was glad.

He instinctively squinted against the reflection from the headlights of the car behind. It followed too closely, just far enough behind for those lights to be a nuisance, then it moved closer, until it tailgated. While the blowing rain came down in buckets splashing against the car, he continued at the same cautious speed, barely able to see. The speedometer needle hovered between thirty-five and forty and he dared not go any faster. At least the traffic was surprisingly light.

Seconds later, the bright lights from the car behind disappeared and he felt momentarily relieved. But just as he checked his rearview mirror, the car hit his bumper causing the Nissan to lurch forward, but Braxton was not about to stop in this storm. Instead, he stared straight ahead. A frown creased his forehead as if he were in painful concentration as he peered through wipers thrashing quickly back and forth. He dared to slowly increase his speed enough to get the car off his bumper.

For a few moments, the car kept its distance. Then, as though the driver obviously had something on his mind, it quickly closed in on Braxton's bumper again, causing another scary, sudden lurch. He checked his mirrors and moved carefully into the right lane, just as the other car sped up until it pulled next to him. Braxton had only a few seconds to register how quickly things were turning ugly, and there did not seem to be many other motorists on the road to witness. The passenger-side window of the old, souped-up jalopy slid down enough to reveal an arm. Braxton's eyes flickered wildly from his speedometer, now almost at sixty, to the other car as it matched his speed. A hand appeared, holding a dark object. It rested on the lowered window with whatever it was aimed directly at him. He wondered what the problem was. He could not imagine that they wanted him to pull over in this weather to carjack him. He also knew that he would not do that. He forced his eyes forward but felt compelled to glance at the car keeping pace with him as he hit his earpiece and gave voice directions to dial for help. Although the object wasn't crystal clear through the rain, he knew there was plenty of reason to panic. His 911 call had just connected when the trigger squeezed. Popping bursts came in rapid succession and were muffled by the heavy rain. He couldn't respond to the voice that answered his call, startled by a small-caliber bullet that penetrated his driver-side window. The shot missed Braxton, but he instinctively jerked the steering wheel in the direction away from the other car, then adjusted too quickly when he realized what he had done. Normally the SUV handled beautifully in all types of weather, but not this time. The Nissan zigzagged crazily a few times as Braxton wrestled helplessly with the wheel in an effort to regain control. Trying to accommodate the soaked road and get away from the dangerous vehicle that had veered close enough to sideswipe the Murano at least once, there was no recovering. The car swerved recklessly on the flooded pavement, back and forth, completely out of control, before bouncing off a guard rail somewhere in the vicinity of Bolling Air Force Base. The impact threw the driver a deadly distance onto the isolated, rain-soaked highway. Braxton Marselle never knew what he hit and death was instantaneous.

1

A dull hum filled the air. Unable to determine its exact origin, the sound was surprisingly sporadic and antiquated for any machine these days —as if it was in its final days. The low, moaning-like whine that emanated was annoyingly consistent, with a weird sense of weariness that reminded Erika of how she felt. She was jarred out of her mental fog, looking for the source of the peculiar sounding machinery. The thought of something that old seemed strangely out of place considering the plush appearance of this office. Everything looked so modern, clean, and pristine.

Erika had arrived ten minutes before her two o'clock appointment at SITER, a large minority-owned information and technology research company located in Southwest D.C., where her husband, Braxton Marselle, had worked for more than twenty-five years. Here she was—back to reality once again.

"D**n him!" she mumbled under her breath, feeling instant sadness the second the words were uttered. Angry tears welled in her eyes at the thought of what happened to him. What could have been on his mind to make him drive like a freeway bandit in that terrible storm, she silently asked herself again, going over the police accounting for the accident for what seemed like the zillionth time. Of course, from what the accident reconstruction team had determined—and had been very clear about—she already had a pretty good idea why. They had described in detail what they believed happened: about the bullet hole in the

1

window, and how between that and the collision, the SUV had been knocked completely out of control in such a violent storm. With all the water and light traffic, there was little to go on. His distress call had been traced quickly but help arrived too late. The detectives had no witnesses, no motives, and no leads.

Still, she reminded herself of that bullet hole in the driver-side window and to count her blessings that the twins hadn't been with him.

Their children, Brea and Brandon, were first place with their father, who had taken great pleasure in how much they looked more like him than her. Though they were now three years old, he never tired of marveling at their surprise two-for-one deal, as he sometimes referred to them. She did too, for that matter—a son and a daughter. With such blissful luck, who would ever have guessed such a tragedy would befall them? But while the news had mentioned possibility of rain sometime over the weekend, and the weather had been threatening all that day, no one expected the tornado-like storm that finally materialized. So, at the last minute, Erika had kept her babies home, otherwise they might have been along with their father.

She wanted desperately to keep her mind from drifting to painful thoughts of Braxton right now, but she couldn't help wondering if he somehow knew what a time she was having getting his benefits finalized with SITER. Until the company got his business straight, she felt like her life hung in the balance. Glancing at the small watch face suspended from the thin chain around her neck, she sighed audibly when she saw it was already two-thirty. Her lips pursed in boredom as she shifted nervously in the oversized armchair, wondering how much longer the wait would be.

Her experience trying to get her business settled with the company so far had been incredulous. First, she struggled to reach the assigned person in the Employee Affairs, who delayed setting an appointment with her for some strange reason. She had called several different times and was passed around to different people—then was told the right person was on leave and no one else could handle it. Her frustration mounted after a few weeks of being put off until that right person finally returned her call and gave her an appointment. But when she showed up, Braxton's file had been temporarily misplaced.

"What's keeping that counselor?" she mumbled impatiently to herself. She was tired of all the waiting, just to do more waiting. There was no reason that things should not be in order after all this time. Idle time only allowed her to go inside herself again, which was not where she needed to be right now. She had slipped in and out of herself a lot since the news of her husband's death. She frequently experienced small blocks of time for which she had no memory of thoughts or activity. Her conscious mind wrestled with the shock of losing him and struggled with the unwelcome title of grieving widow. She slept without resting, waking tired and listless, and was now also the unwilling victim of an anorexic appetite.

A well-dressed, middle-aged woman wearing a black coatdress and matching suede pumps crossed the reception area toward her. "I'll be with you in just a moment," she spoke directly to Erika in a rushed voice. Erika turned in time to see the slender woman scurry past and into the room where that awful printing sound came from and wondered where Braxton's file had finally turned up. A fleeting but foreboding feeling passed through her, and a nagging twinge settled between her eyes, signaling that a monster headache was coming on.

Her gaze swept across the room, taking in the young Oriental man and another Black woman who stared dazed-like at the floor. Her mind seemed a million miles away, and Erika knew the feeling. She noticed the woman looked older with her short, tinted hair framing her delicate, fair skin that the years had been kind to, which Erika considered well preserved or good genes.

Her mind drifted back to Braxton. She pictured him, her energetic yet laid-back husband, and a sad smile pulled at her taut lips. His six-foot-one frame, with two hundred well-placed pounds, had done wonders to camouflage their twelve-year age difference. At five-foot eight, she had always appreciated height on a man.

"Mrs. Erika Marselle?" The woman stood in front of her. "My name is Katie Zimmermann. I'll be working your husband's case," she continued politely.

So, you're the woman that called? Erika thought to herself, accepting the small hand extended to her and taking in her serious expression. She silently answered her own question because she didn't think so. That call may have come from the woman she saw on her previous visit when they couldn't find Braxton's file. That woman was younger, she remembered. "What happened to the woman I saw before?" she asked with open curiosity. *Did they discover she had hidden Braxton's file,* she thought to herself.

Mrs. Zimmermann ignored her questions entirely. Instead, she motioned Erika forward with a wave of her hand. "Please, come this way," she said with a pleasant smile. "I apologize for the wait, but after a careful review of the file, I have a few questions before we begin the necessary paperwork."

Their short walk ended at the entrance of a small room that was almost empty except for a round table covered with a thick manila folder and several chairs. The folder captured Erika's attention before she even crossed the threshold. *Braxton's file,* she thought, staring at its size in disbelief. Twenty-five years of personnel actions and changes throughout his work life—how could such a huge file be misplaced, she questioned as the pressure in her head increased.

Erika spotted a water fountain just outside the conference room door and hurried to it, digging through her purse for Tylenol. She threw the pills in her mouth and drank eagerly before joining Mrs. Zimmermann.

"Please have a seat," the counselor offered, then flipped open the folder to make a few brief notes. "Mrs. Marselle, first let me say how sorry I am for your loss." Her face and voice were etched with sincerity as she stared into Erika's solemn brown eyes. "I lost my husband a few years back and still miss him terribly."

Erika stared back at her intently, wishing she would just get started. Her gaze locked onto the counselor's beautiful dress. "Thank you," she mumbled weakly. Let's just get on with this for Christ's sake, she wanted to scream.

"Did you bring an original death certificate?" the counselor asked solemnly.

"Yes." Erika handed over an envelope containing Braxton's death certificate, their marriage certificate, and the twins' birth certificates.

"Let's see," she said, reaching for her iPad. "Let's start with the insurance policy," she announced, purposely delaying any questions from Erika. "Mr. Marselle's salary was \$113,500. His insurance election was for twice his salary, making the policy worth \$227,000." She punched the figures in carefully. "In addition to that, the company pays up to fifty percent more of the salary for accidental death, depending on the circumstances. That's another \$56,750 added to the \$227,000—for a total of…oh my, \$283,750." She whispered the sum almost as if talking to herself. "Hmm," she remarked, looking pleased before turning the calculator for Erika to see. "As the full beneficiary, you stand to receive a handsome sum."

After the insurance papers were signed, Mrs. Zimmermann fell silent, and Erika eyed her impatiently. While she was certainly more than pleased with the insurance benefits and was looking forward to receiving them, she was taken aback at the woman's hesitation to start on what she considered the main benefits. "And what about the company shares, the leave pays, and retirement?" she prompted.

Mrs. Zimmermann fidgeted with the edge of the papers in her hand. Now she had difficulty facing Erika as she deliberately looked downward toward the file and spoke in a voice filled with hesitation. "We will get into the shares and leave momentarily, but…" She cleared her throat noisily and made an awkward attempt to meet Erika's stern gaze. "Mrs. Marselle, we've discovered someone else's name on Mr. Marselle's retirement papers," she delivered as delicately as she could. There was no easy way of saying it. "Were you aware of that?"

A blank stare covered Erika's face for several seconds before she responded, "What, someone else's name!"

"I'm afraid so."

"Like who, for crying out loud?" she asked with exasperation. "The file has been missing…maybe there was some mix-up," she offered, resisting the urge to snatch the file from the table and see for herself.

Understanding the full gravity of her confusion, the counselor ignored the new edge in Erika's voice and proceeded with compassion. "Silvia Marselle. Could this woman be…the mother or a sister, perhaps?"

"Why would Braxton name anybody else for his benefits when he has a wife and children?" Erika questioned with a measure of annoyance she was trying unsuccessfully to suppress. This was not helping her headache. "And why wasn't I told about this bombshell earlier?"

"Mrs. Marselle, we were only recently able to locate your husband's file, and this discovery came to light just yesterday. In fact, I went through it again just before your appointment to be sure. I felt it was best to wait the extra day until you were here in person to hopefully shed some light on the situation. We will need to, you know," she emphasized, "before we can do the rest of the benefits." Mrs. Zimmermann paused at Erika's indignant expression. "Please accept my apology if I made the wrong decision by not letting you know all of this beforehand," she seemed compelled to add.

Awgh! Erika screamed silently inside, and her expression read loud and clear. Why was this happening? She was in no condition to deal with this right now. And this woman, as pleasant as she tried to be, was only making things worse. She didn't want to hear about more problems. "What does that mean for me and the other benefits?" Erika asked as kindly as she could.

"Mrs. Marselle," the counselor started.

"Please! Just the bottom line," she interrupted, more sharply than she intended. Her patience was gone. "You do realize that my husband had been gone for a few months now? It's taken me weeks just to get to this point. But I'm sure you know that already," a distraught Erika said emphatically.

"It is unusual for anyone other than the spouse to be of record on the retirement form, unless the employee is single, of course. This person *does* have the same last name. Now, what this means is that the person listed must be contacted before this matter can be resolved, since she has not come forward on her own. I am so sorry to have to tell you this."

Erika's eyes filled with hot tears. She tucked her lips tightly together, trying to maintain control, and shook her head in dismay. "So now everything is held up again." Disbelief filled her voice. "How will you find her? And how long do you think it will take? Because this whole thing is making me sick, and if I don't have everything over with soon, I'm going to—" her voice tailed off as she wrestled her emotions.

She stood up slowly, wincing in pain from all the counselor had told her. Erika was not in a good place at all right now. Braxton's death had hit her hard. Over the past few months, she had struggled to wrap her mind around her sudden loss—with no answers from the police and lack of sleep and appetite that resulted in feeling tired and listless and a marked weight loss, growing concern for the twins, especially Brandon, frequent headaches and constant episodes of her mind drifting to nowhere and difficulty concentrating on her job. She felt like she had entered a losing battle and her chances were not looking good.

Mrs. Zimmermann, taking the cue, stood as well and spoke in her most sympathetic tone. "I don't know, but we'll have to. I think I understand just how you must feel. We'll get on this first thing on Monday and I'll call you as soon as we get anything, anything at all. But I must warn you that this could take as long as a few weeks."

No, you don't understand anything, Erika wanted to scream. She looked straight at the counselor, pain written all over her face, and rattled off a series of rhetorical questions. "Mrs. Zimmermann, did you have problems getting benefits from your deceased husband? Like an appointment runaround, missing files, being misinformed, uninformed, or waiting to be informed? How long did it take you to get your benefits?" she quizzed bitterly. "Was it even a month? Bet it wasn't. You have any children at home? Probably not," she hissed through clenched teeth, guessing that any children Mrs. Zimmermann might have were most likely grown. She pursed her lips again as only she and her sister could. "As you know, I have two," she concluded before leaving the room quickly. God! She didn't mean to act this way, but she just couldn't seem to help herself.

As Erika exited through the waiting room, she sighed with relief at the sight of her friend, Tamarra Wilson, coming through the door. Although the two women hadn't seen much of each other since Braxton's death, Erika was glad she had accepted Tamarra's offer to pick her up. Her face cracked visibly, as if it might break into a million pieces at any moment. She made several quick gasps to catch her breath and regain control. Tamarra, looking younger than her thirty-four years, had her ash-blonde hair pulled into a ponytail. One glance at Erika's face and she scrunched her own in sadness, her clear blue eyes following her friend's moist brown ones intently with deep concern. She stood at the door, holding it open, before pulling Erika into a tight embrace.

"Hey, what happened in there? Are you alright?" she asked, gently leading her toward the car.

"No! I'm not," Erika whispered, shaking her head. "I may never be alright again. I feel awful and I just want to go home and crawl into a hole somewhere."

"You want to talk about it," Tamarra asked softly.

"I can't. Not right now. Maybe later, okay?"

"Girlfriend, I just wish there was some way I could help," Tamarra said sympathetically as she looked into Erika's face. She knew Erika hadn't been the same lately, and whatever had happened with SITER only seemed to make things worse. At least she was there to drive her home, and maybe she could be of more help later.

"Yeah, I know. But Tamarra, there is one. You could do me one huge favor—if it's not too much trouble," she frowned, reluctant to ask.

"Oh, come on, Erika. It's no problem." Indeed, she would do almost anything to ease Erika's pain partly out of friendship and partly from guilt over how she had abandoned her during her time of need. "You know I'm willing to help any way I can."

"Would you drop a few things off to Nana's for the twins on your way home?"

"Consider it done."

The ride to Erika's house was mostly silent. Tamarra made several general comments that elicited the most minimal of comments from Erika. For the most part, Tamarra honored her friend's desire for quiet. Thirty minutes later, Erika was trudging up the stairs toward the twins' room, Tamarra following. Nana had insisted on keeping them for the weekend so Erika could take care of her business and hopefully get some rest. Nana had been their sitter since they were six weeks old, when Erika returned to work. Now that the twins were in preschool, Nana provided before- and after-care since the school was close to her. Erika and Braxton had even considered enrolling the kids in elementary school near Nana for the same reason. Now, Erika was unsure what she would do. The list she had received from the County Social Services had provided information on licensed sitters in Southern Maryland. Nana was a senior woman who was so wonderful with the children that she had proven to be a godsend. She was more like the grandmother and extended family they never had, and they loved her, too.

"Can I use the phone?" Tamarra asked.

"Sure, you know where it is," she pointed in the direction of her bedroom.

Moments later, Tamarra hung up the phone after several repeated calls, staring at it feeling confused, thinking she must have simply misdialed. The man that answered each time had said Shonnasy Mercedes. The first two times she had simply apologized for having the wrong number, but she redialed purposefully a third time. Shonnasy Mercedes, the same voice answered, sounding irritated now.

"I'm sorry. I guess I still have the wrong number," she stammered, feeling as badly about the repeated as she sounded. "I'm sorry I keep misdialing, but where exactly am I calling?"

"This is the dealership waiting room, ma'am, at Shonnasy Mercedes," the man added with more patience. "Who did you want to speak with?"

"Well, I thought this was a residence," she explained.

"No, ma'am," he cut in. "This is a public phone at Shonnasy Mercedes."

Tamarra thanked him and hung up with mixed feelings of relief and embarrassment over her discovery. *What's going on here,* she wondered. She was calling a public phone. She didn't even know there were any of those left, with everyone and their grandmothers having cell phones these days. The poor man must think she was a complete idiot for misdialing three times. This didn't make any sense to her. She checked the number on the paper Dorsey had given her but dared not dial again.

If this was a joke, it wasn't funny, and she definitely was not laughing. She was well acquainted with the dealership and its location because that was where she had purchased her previously owned luxury car, and it was where Dorsey worked. They had met there several months earlier and began dating soon after.

As soon as she made Erika's delivery and said her good-byes to Nana and the twins, Tamarra found herself on a mission of her own. Her sporty Benz moved swiftly along the Beltway, headed to Largo, weaving in and out of traffic smoothly, speeding at times, and forced to creep at others. The onset of rush hour was evident just the same. She suppressed her urge to press full speed ahead to satisfy her curiosity as quickly as possible.

She checked her mirrors as she approached her Beltway exit near Capital Center so that she could slide into the right lane. A glimpse of something flashed, scaring the bejeebees out of her, and her reflexes instantly took over. She heard the short screech of tires and the long squeal of her own stressed brakes that nearly startled her into cardiac arrest. Instinctively reacting, she laid on her horn and gritted her teeth as her car jerked to a sudden stop.

She watched in frenzied disbelief as a Pathfinder, not exactly living up to its name, darted crazily down the exit ramp like a demon, barely missing her. It had caused her heart to almost leap from her chest. "Don't you know that two things can't occupy the same space at the same time!" she yelled out, but of course he could not hear her since he was already gone. "Jerk-a** son- of-a-b****," her voice trailed off in hot anger. *Drivers in that much of a hurry shouldn't bother with cars,* she thought, in renewed amazement, at how many motorists seemed perfectly willing to risk an accident rather than see another car in front of them, especially if it wasn't travelling at the speed of light. And of course, he was holding a cell phone to his ear. *People like him ought to just sprout wings and fly,* she thought angrily. That was too close for comfort, and she became even more worked up.

She felt the need to sit there for a few seconds to collect herself, but her car was on the exit and a trail of cars had already formed behind her. She had been all but run over and now some inconsiderate motorist was laying on his horn in irritation for her to keep moving. Tamarra's already rapidly beating pulse quickened more as she reluctantly drove the last few blocks to the dealership where she figured Dorsey probably was at this hour. But seeing him was definitely not her reason for this particular trip.

When she finally pulled into the parking lot, she wanted nothing more than to jump from the car and dash all the way to the waiting room but instead forced herself to walk in calmly and behave rationally. She opened the door quietly, and peeked in first. She searched around before she walked inside like she shouldn't be there. She eased past the service desk trying not to look conspicuous, while looking around from her purview. She sighed with relief that the guy at the desk was not Dorsey, though seeing him there would not have surprised her since he was a manager with his own private office. Her entry had been quiet and gone unnoticed. The young Black guy sitting on the edge of the desk with a phone cradled between his head and shoulder, flipping nervously through a huge stick of papers, never even turned around.

Tamarra scanned the room for the pay phones that hung on the far wall across the room. Except for faint voices from the wall-mounted TV and the soft rustle of a newspaper, the room was quiet as she made a beeline to the other side of the room. Eagerness propelled her so quickly that she power walked. Only one thing was on her mind: the number she expected to find would match the one Dorsey had given her. She found exactly what she was looking for. When she saw that the number matched those scribbled on the paper, she felt a knife-like sharpness pierce her inside and her heart skipped a beat.

"I'll be d***ed!" she exclaimed aloud. "I don't believe this," she grunted. "Here I go again." Her emotions covered the range between anger, confusion, and disappointment, all competing for her attention at the same time. Now she was sorry she came.

2

Erika could hear the telephone from the twin's room. Her first thought was that Tamarra was calling. She rushed downstairs to reach it by the fourth ring, rather than picking it up from her bedroom for some unknown reason. But something told her it was more likely her sister checking on her again. Moistness still clung to her swollen eyelids, yet she was too outraged to actually cry.

"Hello!" she spoke tersely into the phone almost before she had it to her ear. "Hello. Hello!"

She was too late. They were gone, and that was just fine with her. She held down the button for a second and listened, putting the receiver to her ear again. It was beeping to let her know that there was a message. Maybe she could handle talking with people more easily when she had some good news to tell. She retrieved the message reluctantly.

The high-pitched voice belonged to a work colleague, Persia Prentice. She was curious about the SITER visit, which was fairly obvious by the excitement in her voice. But Persia was the last person in the world she needed to talk with right now, Erika thought as she moped through the room. Persia, as well-intended as she tried to be, was the type of person who usually saw the glass half-empty, regardless of what it contained or what the situation was. While from Erika's perspective, if the content was something good or positive, the glass is considered half-full, and anything bad or negative would make the glass, gratefully, half-empty.

And although Erika was sure Persia never meant any harm, oftentimes her remarks came across sounding insensitive or inappropriate, as if they were not always fully thought out. Yet most of the time, she was pleasant enough and somehow drawn to Erika. Feeling instant relief at not having to talk with anyone for the moment, she climbed the flight of stairs to her bedroom as if weights were strapped to her feet. She had no idea why she had rushed down the stairs in the first place to get the phone, especially since the ringer on her bedroom phone was only turned off. That was her state of mind. Mental and physical exhaustion took over as she sprawled wearily onto the king-size bed, slumping face-down on her stomach, fully dressed.

The firmness of the mattress was wonderful against her body, and she felt like she could sink into a slumber forever, but she didn't. A frustrated moan escaped loudly. She was relieved that the twins were with Nana, sparing her the guilt of feeling she might be neglecting them. That was the only way she'd get some rest and find time to go through more of Braxton's things. Hopefully, this wrinkle would be ironed out soon so she could treat her kids to one of the animated or *Harry Potter* movies before they left the area. She needed to do something to bring Brandon out of that shell he was disappearing into. They all loved movies and were long overdue for a cinematic break.

In the meantime, she needed to find something to tell her who Silvia was. Yet, as fate would have it, the distressing SITER matter flashed into her mind and refused to leave. She could not understand why her name was there. A woman she had never once heard him mention. This whole thing sounded crazy, almost more than she could bear. Fear, anger, and frustration fed into a ball of pain buried so deep inside her that she wondered how long it would be before she completely lost it. There was no real attempt at sleep for the moment.

Her thoughts raced, and Erika found herself reminiscing. It was difficult to fathom that Braxton's employer had played even a remote role in their meeting and the happiness they shared—but it had. SITER, Inc., had a sizeable Information Systems department that had provided technical support to the Federal government, including the agency where Erika had worked for years. Braxton was one of the company's most experienced systems analysts assigned to a major project, and for a while he was stationed onsite, where they eventually met.

She could not say exactly when she became aware of him. Her recollection was, one day he was not there, and then, almost like magic, there he was—a tall, shy-looking stranger working only several cubicles away. Although there had been no initial physical attraction on her part, after frequent office chit-chat, his serious and intellectual personality sparked something in her, and a meaningful romance slowly developed. His low-key manner impressed her the most. For more than a year, he dined, and charmed her thoroughly and so persuasively that when he asked her to share his Maryland duplex apartment, she was unable to refuse. They shared space for two years over her sister's constant, well-intended objections before they made it legal. Two years later, the twins were born, putting a strain on their finances and cramping their space.

It was clear that the timing was perfect to take advantage of the downturn in the housing market, but they also knew they would need a hefty down payment because of the new, stringent credit requirements. So, for the next year, even on their combined decent income, they doubled up on savings, curtailing all forms of recreation and socializing. Erika worked overtime as often as she dared after having the twins, and Braxton gave up cigarettes. And, the following year, the world was made right again when Lydia found them a fantastic deal on a prize home in the much sought-after Parisian Park housing development. Their dream house was straight from heaven, she had thought. It was only eight years old, detached, well-designed, and immaculate: four bedrooms with full amenities and, of course, a nice level backyard for the kids. What more could she ask for? The colonial all-brick mini mansion covered a sparse one-quarter acre of land only miles outside of Washington, D.C. in very nearby Prince George County, Maryland.

Her thoughts were interrupted by a barrage of musical gongs and chimes in the distance from the grandfather clock downstairs. She listened and counted without meaning to. It was almost four o'clock. Blankness crept through her head. Within seconds, she was out. Erika had finally drifted off. She did not dream.

Hours later, somewhere far off, a bell jingled softly, getting closer and louder until it seemed right in her ears. Her body twitched and shifted as she fought subconsciously to determine the source of the insistent noise. As the sound penetrated her sleep, she awakened with a jerk. The room was dark. Still lying on her stomach, she scooted across the bed half asleep and reached for the phone. She answered through dry, parted lips, like she had slept all night.

"Hey Rikki, how are you today?" Lydia's voice was filled with expectant curiosity.

Now that Braxton wasn't around and nephew Jackson was out of town, she was the only person who called her that. "You asleep?"

Erika licked her dry lips and fumbled for the lamp switch. She saw through the partially opened blind that it dark outside and wondered what time it was.

"Happy birthday," she said in answer to her sister's question. Her voice was low and gruff with sleep. She yawned and pulled herself up to lean against the large headboard so she could clear out the cobwebs and stretch. "You get my card?"

"Yeah-yeah. It's beautiful, along with its contents. Thank you! I called a while ago, trying to catch you when you first got home. Sounds like I woke you up, huh? I sure didn't mean to do that. I know you need all the rest you can get. We can talk tomorrow if you want."

"No, no. It's okay, I'm awake now. What time is it anyway?"

"Almost nine."

"Wow, I can't believe the whole evening got away from me. I was really zonked. So, how did things go today with the Ash-man?" Erika asked quietly because she certainly didn't want to talk about SITER.

"It didn't…he was a no-show."

"Say what! Lydia, he is such a jerk. Have you heard from him at all?" she questioned suspiciously, trying to cover her utter disgust for the man. Though Erika was sad for Lydia and knew she didn't deserve such shabby treatment, there was a part of her that was actually glad that he had dared to act so blatantly thoughtless. Perish the thought that she would ever voice her true feelings, but she always hoped that his latest antic would prove to be the proverbial camel-back-breaking last. And, by grace, be out of her sister's system for good.

"Yes, he is. Nope, not today, but he was supposed to be here hours ago." She paced absentmindedly around her own bedroom, glancing out the window. "I don't want to talk about him right now. How did things go at SITER?"

"I was hoping you wouldn't bring that up. I'm not sure how to answer that." It certainly didn't seem like it was getting much better, but she didn't want to have to tell Lydia that.

"So, what happened?" Lydia wondered why she was being so evasive about something that in her mind, should be relatively simple—just processing paperwork.

"Nothing really," Erika answered, realizing there was probably little chance of that happening, but she would just hope that things worked out sooner rather than later.

"Rikki, come on, this is me, okay? What happened?"

"Okay, okay. Well, the paperwork is a little complicated right now."

"Complicated how? What's up? Is it finished or not?"

"Yeah, well, sort of." This was not coming out well. She didn't want to tell Lydia about this.

"We got through the insurance paperwork, and the check will take a few weeks."

"That's good. And…?"

"They need to review some other paperwork in Braxton's file. Look, once everything has been verified, I should be good to go. Now, can we please talk about something a little more pleasant? Like your day and how it feels to be forty."

"Well, you probably should've let me go with you like I wanted to."

"What kind of sense would that have made?" Erika asked, remembering that, after the way things had gone, she was grateful Tamarra had insisted on picking her up.

Lydia sighed thoughtfully. "I feel the same as before I guess," she said, ignoring Erika's question. "Why…how am I supposed to feel?"

"I don't know. I just asked. I heard that forty is one of those turning point, milestone birthdays, and just wondered if you felt any different. Like empowered or something," Erika said with a smile.

"Look, I got to go," Lydia said quickly, her voice edged in a way that caught Erika by surprise. She definitely was not feeling empowered or anything else except pissed off every time she thought about how she had pretty much wasted her day. They were talking specifically about Ash, but they might as well not have been. "I'll talk with you tomorrow, okay?" She tried not to sound too brusque.

"Yeah, talk with you later," she said, hoping Lydia could tell that she understood.

Moments later, Lydia sat on her loveseat, staring at the TV that was on most of the time, and switched to the OWN station, feeling pretty lonely. She went to retrieve what was left of her favorite wine.

"He's never on time for a d**n thing." Frustration filled her as she talked to herself.

She caught her image in the portrait-sized mirror over the small sofa. Sad brown eyes, glistening with unshed tears, stared back. She had hoped that they would at least make it to Rips for a decent dinner. Well, that was out the window.

She raised her glass with a fake smile, a trace of one deep dimple appeared in her cheek, and toasted, looking forlorn at her reflection, "To me." She sipped from the wine glass and paced.

Nearly as tall as Erika at five-eight, Lydia had smooth, fresh-looking brown skin. It was the type of skin that needed little or no makeup. As a woman who took great pride in her physical appearance, she always took special care with the clothing she wore and how they looked on her. It was no surprise that for her day, she wore an outfit that reflected not only her fondness for fashion, but her individual taste and style. Her dark, silky hair was cropped at the top and sides, and draped the neck in a modified shag style.

"He should've at least called by now," she snapped, wishing she had someone she could call to check on him. He was always late, but never this bad. She had called his cell phone, but it went straight to voicemail like it always did. He never answered her calls anyway when he was at home or at work. "Why do I keep letting him do this to me?" she mumbled, glaring at the phone as if willing it to ring.

How she hated waiting. She had always credited herself for never giving in to those strong, sometimes crazy, urges to blow up his phone, especially after she had a few glasses of wine. Whenever she got too twitchy, she either busied herself or called someone else to regain her control. The knock at the door startled her. Her heart skipped a beat, and she exhaled nervously.

"Ashton," she whispered his full name rather than the shortened nickname she usually called him. His name fell from her lips with built-up hostility. "Who is it?" she snapped though she knew full well who it must be. She wondered how he managed to get into the building without calling her first. The security had been pretty good until now.

"It's me, babe. Ash."

She took a quick glance though her peephole, then opened the door and stared at him in complete disgust as he peeled off his sunglasses and waltzed past her. One glance at her face told him that she was ticked, and he immediately became defensive.

"How did you get into the building, Ash?"

"Someone coming in recognized me," he threw up his hand and quickly moved on. "Look, babe. Sorry I'm late, alright? I got tied up. But you know I got here as soon as I could." He talked fast and breathed almost as if he had been running.

She had always thought that he carried an erotic appeal about him—a way that was sexy as hell—until now. That special something she called 'street cool' was a characteristic she had been surprisingly drawn to back then. He was always stylishly dressed, and his smooth body language was somewhat flirtatious and had always been a turn-on. He had the habit of sprinkling his conversation with macho, slangy words that she thought made him sound cleverly slick. Whatever the right terminology was for it, today, it was annoying. He looked just plain slick standing there, neatly dressed as usual, in a collarless ivory shirt resembling the priest look he wore so well.

But she saw no sign of a gift and felt more disgust when she noticed he wore the herringbone neck chain and matching bracelet she had charged on her account for him. He had promised to reimburse her when the bill came, but she mentioned the due date to him twice—still nothing, so she sent her payment in already. And he had yet to say a word. Typical Ash.

She pushed the door so hard it slammed shut, then glared at him with hostility. She tried to stave off the raw emotion trying to bubble free, but that proved as difficult to control as an Aruba trade wind. *He's not going to ply me with his lies tonight,* she thought. "You're a real, bona- fide, honest-to-goodness-a**hole, you-know that?" she lashed out, shoving past him, almost knocking him over. She pushed the remote on the silent TV, and it went off. She returned to her wine.

"Okay, alright?" he shot back, raising his voice, acting confused at her attitude. "What's the problem? I'm here, ain't I? Something came up unexpectedly, okay?" He stared back at her, stretching his eyes, speaking with emphasis on each word as if to say, *now, get off my back and just be grateful I got here at all, and end of subject.*

Lydia slammed her glass on the table so fast some wine spilled. She paced in front of him, trying to calm her nerves for her own sake. Then, she decided to hell with calm and assumed a battle stance, looking squarely into his sexy, light-brown eyes with contempt burning in hers. She was madder than she ever wanted to be.

"You told me you'd be here hours ago. I don't know where the hell you've been all day but you've a lot of damn nerve walking in here this late like Prince Charming. You've conveniently forgot that us being together today was your idea." She rested her hands on her slim hips and talked through even, white, clenched teeth. "But, Ash, it is my birthday. My fortieth, in case you forgot. And like a damn fool I've spent the evening sitting around here waiting for your sorry a**. You know I've no real way of reaching you because you never answer that damn phone. The least you could've done was have the decency to call—to say happy birthday, you couldn't make it, or would be late, or even dog, 'kiss my foot.'" Though it was pretty obvious that none of those options was acceptable to Lydia today. "Do you realize what time it is?" she asked emphatically. "The day is gone, wasted. It's after nine and you just show up when you get damn good and ready. You know a call was the least you could do." Her voice rose and fell with naked emotion.

In all the time they had been seeing each other, he had never heard her speak like this. She was really fired up. Reading her body language and feeling the depth of her fury, he had the sense to back down.

"Babe… babe, hold on. Just hold on a minute," Ashton pleaded in vain as he stepped closer to embrace her, but she moved away. "You got me all wrong."

"Oh," Lydia accused in renewed amazement. "I know…I know. You have a good excuse, Ash. You always do. But I'm not interested. That's alright. You've disappointed me for the last time. You're always trying to act as nice as pie after you mess up, but I have to remind myself that I can't count on you for anything," she admitted sadly. She watched Aston's hands go up in helpless defeat before he ambled toward the door, shaking his head in exasperation.

"Babe, believe me. This has gone all wrong," he whined. "I can understand that you're upset this time." He stopped and turned to face her again. His mouth opened and shut a few times, but no sound came out at first. "I know I'm wrong," he said finally. "I have no defense, much less a good one, and probably would've stretched the truth a little, if you gave me a chance. And I swear, if I could, I would conjure up at least a birthday card right this minute."

"Ashton!" she interrupted tersely. "Stop. I told you I don't want to hear it." She lifted her hand and turned away for another sip of wine. "You know you really hurt me today. More than I ever thought you could."

"Look—it's your birthday, but I can make up for it." His tone shifted as if he was pleading a case. "I was up late last night arguing with Benette about where we're headed. I overslept because she left this morning without waking me, so things didn't start out so good for me. After work I ran into an old buddy of mine downtown, and he invited me for a beer. We got to exchanging a few lies and laughs," he added nervously. "And, and anyway, the time got away. I just plain lost track of it for a while, I swear."

"I don't care about what happened between you and Benette or anyone else, darn it," she yelled as her moist eyes stared at him, looking dejected and feeling somewhat drained. Pathetic as his reason sounded, it was probably closer to the truth than any other line he might have given her.

A soft knock stopped them both in their tracks.

"Now, who could that be?" she asked rhetorically as she marched to the door.

"Lydia, it's Flo," came the reply softly. Her neighbor stood transfixed with an inquisitive look about the shouts that cut from Lydia's place to hers. The truth was, she had keen eyesight and hearing and was always more attuned to Lydia's comings and goings than with the other tenants. In her own way, she had gotten used to looking out for Lydia and her son. Florita Rollins was an astute senior citizen who lived across the hall, and though she was seen as the building's resident den mother, she didn't take to everyone. And, as one of the few remaining original tenants to occupy the building long before Lydia moved in six years ago, she was known to everyone nearby simply as Miss Flo.

She silently assessed the situation, taking all of Ashton in. "Happy birthday." Her eyes moved to Lydia now. "Just a little somethin' for you," she whispered, placing an envelope into her hand. "I see you courtin' right now. Stop over and see me when you get a chance."

Lydia hugged and thanked her kind neighbor. "You didn't have to do that," she said in a hushed tone, fighting back tears.

"That's the joy of it, because I didn't have to."

Lydia turned toward Ashton with a look of overt contempt that even her neighbor remembered her birthday. When Miss Flo hesitated to leave, Lydia sensed some concern. "Did you hear us across the hall?" she barely managed to whisper.

"Umm-hum," she said, with her eyes fixed on Ashton.

"Well, trust me, everything is okay here. My friend and I are finished talking anyway." Sarcasm dripped from her every word, hoping that no one else had noticed. Lydia's eyes narrowed when she looked at Ashton again. He stood with his weight on one leg, one hand resting on a boney hip, and his head dropped with that hang-dog look. She could tell he was going into his act now, but she was fed up, and it was not going to work. Lydia was glad Miss Flo was there. It made her next words easier.

"In fact, he was just leaving. And call the next time."

An expectant gaze from both women fell upon Ashton, prompting him to step from the apartment into the hallway. "I'll talk with you later, after you calm down," he announced with a defeated expression on his face.

"Yeah, yeah," she mumbled as she and Miss Flo watched him walk the few feet to the elevator and push the button.

"Call if you need me. I'm just an earshot away," she said, smiling at Lydia as she returned to her apartment.

Lydia mouthed a silent thank you to her neighbor. Once her door was shut, she froze in disbelief. She might have been embarrassed with Ash in front of her neighbor if she wasn't so angry. But she didn't know whether to be relieved or regretful that Miss Flo heard enough to come over. To say that lady didn't miss much was indeed an understatement, but she also knew that Miss Flo was looking out for her. So, to be honest, although her neighbor was sometimes a bit too alert for her liking, Lydia decided she was probably more relieved than anything at her timing. There was no telling how far things would have gone. Better that it was her than one of the other neighbors. Years of pent-up frustration over their situation had crashed down on him. And he still got off easy. Ash, pressing his luck, was slow to get the message that she was not in the mood to be played today, and even if he was inclined to be more truthful about what he had been up to, it was a too little, too late. Lydia closed her eyes and felt a strange sense of relief and mild satisfaction. She opened them, feeling as if a burden, to some extent, had been lifted, at least for the time being.

Her mind drifted back to that fateful day Ashton had walked into her life during her days as a realtor, while she was on floor duty. He had acted interested in buying a house. The sign at the home he inquired about was barely posted, but he had spotted it that first day while driving by, or so he said. He questioned her extensively regarding the specifics and possible financing before asking Lydia to show him the

property. The interest and excitement in his voice had seemed quite genuine and rather convincing, though a small part of her still wondered if he had ever really been serious.

An appointment for Ashton was squeezed in between Lydia's other showings the following Saturday afternoon. Sure, she had a live one. Lydia did her homework and volunteered an honest explanation regarding the poor upkeep. The property was from a divorce situation and was headed for foreclosure. The grass was tall and unkempt, and there were several minor disrepairs inside that would certainly factor into negotiations.

Though Ashton seemed mildly satisfied with the property, he was reluctant to make a commitment. And, of course, Lydia had not pressured him. But when she questioned his seriousness, he cleverly put her off, saying he would give it some thought and get back with her in a few days if he wanted to move forward. A very familiar and evasive tactic to Lydia—but she left him with a card.

Those few days turned into several months. Weeks after the attractive handyman special settled and while on duty at the office, she received a call from a man with an unmistakably sexy baritone voice. It turned out to be Ashton. Without making any real mention of the home— other than to inquire if it had sold—he said how terrible he felt about wasting her time and offered his apology. She had simply written him off anyway and tried to explain it was no big deal and that he was under no obligation. The matter was as simple as that for her, but he wouldn't let it rest. Instead, he insisted on appeasing his conscience by inviting her to lunch, cocktails, or something—her choice. With patience, she heard him out. She smiled broadly, amusement plastered fully across her face as she waited to turn him down, until the magic words came from his mouth.

"I hope you like seafood…" he said smoothly. "…because I'm a seafood fanatic. I was hoping we could grab something at this little spot in Silver Spring." There was still silence on the other end. "Crabbfields, do you know it? It's a small place, but their seafood is some of the best around. What do you say, Ms. Matthews? Will you help me out on this?"

Lydia knew Crabbfields. What seafood-loving person living in the area for any length of time hadn't gone to or at least heard of the place? She recalled showing only a few seconds of surprised hesitation before ignoring the warning bell clanging so wildly somewhere inside, because she absolutely loved good seafood and never missed an opportunity to indulge herself. After all, what he'd done was pretty inconsiderate. And he was trying to apologize— redeem himself—and it was just an innocent invitation, nothing more. Oh, what the hay, she rationalized. Lydia accepted, hoping she didn't appear too eager.

The first time, they shared a few hours of get-acquainted conversation that was primarily about astrological signs, birthdays, and age, revealing something she never suspected: he was almost five years younger than her. Lydia remembered his strange remark about being a typical red-blooded Pisces. He was also proud of just turning thirty that year and considered himself a responsible guy who was just coming into his real manhood, so to speak—whatever that meant. It hadn't made a lot of sense to her then, and it wasn't any different now, but she was more into the food and wine at the time, so she didn't press him. He had come across as a nice enough guy.

After several phone conversations over the next few weeks, another dinner stretched for hours, filled with wine as well as stimulating and flirtatious dialogue that worked like an aphrodisiac. Yes, she was strangely attracted to this young fellow. She felt like she really wanted to know him better. During that outing, as Ashton watched Lydia's obvious pleasure in her sumptuous meal, he remarked, "It looks like I might be making all the right moves," his eyes roving over her body suggestively. "You think I can get a little streak going?" he asked, giving her a sexy smile. "It's important to me that you feel the sincerity of my apology, and I'm not convinced yet that you do." It all sounded pretty corny, but she didn't really mind.

Ambiguous, erotic expressions were covertly—and sometimes overtly—batted back and forth. Innuendo and visual lingo teased, challenged, and stroked the curiosity on both sides. Amply plied with wine, they finally returned to Lydia's place, and their after-dinner session was more incredible than either had expected or hoped for. It stirred a feeling in Lydia that had lain dormant pretty much since her divorce. And she was experienced enough to know that Ashton felt the passion too, though she did realize that the feeling was pure lust more than anything else. As almost an afterthought, his conscience kicked in and he felt compelled to tell her something, before things went too far, as if they hadn't already, and because he really liked her—that he had a wife. It came out more like an explanation for why he had to leave and couldn't stay. He felt Lydia had a right to know.

As time went on, Lydia continued seeing him mostly for the meals and sex, convincing herself that she had everything under control. That she was the user and not him. She went along with the seemingly never-ending arrangement they had fallen into, thinking that it was at her pleasure. Now, more years had gone by than she cared to admit, and they had gone quickly. Had she, deep down, believed there would eventually be more? She didn't know. But she remembered the moment she heard he had a wife. A single shiver of sheer disappointment had crawled from her throat to the still-flaming spot between her legs, and her heart had fallen to the floor, where it had remained all this time.

She should have wrung his scrawny neck back then and been done with him, but she hadn't. Instead, she talked herself into believing that she was mature enough to handle whatever the situation brought. It had never been her intent for things between them to drag on this long after learning that he had a wife, especially when she was already very aware of their age difference. She had heard about the cougar-relationship craze out there now, but she never really placed herself in that category. And she did have an impressionable teenage son to think about, she reminded herself.

Her image—and the respect of Rikki and her son—were very important to Lydia. But somehow, she had become trapped anyway. That first outing had intrigued and excited her so much that it served as the beginning of some crazy addiction…or maybe it was sheer loneliness. At the outset, she occasionally dated others, but none of the guys was as great a catch as Aaron had been nor as interesting or mysterious as Ashton appeared to be. Soon she stopped.

3

In the dark hours of early Monday morning, Erika found herself in her front doorway, wearing only a granny nightgown and footies. She strained to see something through an unusually thin, cloudlike mist. She wasn't sure what it was or why she didn't feel the coolness of the night air as she squinted for a better look and even tried fanning the fog away with her hand. Inching closer, uncertain of what was out there, she still couldn't see clearly. Then, an indiscernible dark figure loomed nearby that seemed to move backward with every step she took forward, so that she just couldn't get close enough for a good look. She didn't understand why it looked so vague when the surrounding area was clearing up and becoming brightly lit.

She heard her heart beating rapidly as the foggy mass dissolved and a blurry figure came into view. A tall, slender man stood with legs slightly parted and hands together as if in prayer. His suit was dark, and the tie was outrageously colorful, yet the outfit seemed vaguely familiar, but the reason escaped her. The wide, crooked grin on the handsome face of the dark stranger had an endearing look of patience. It offered comfort from somewhere in the distant past that reminded her of someone. If only she could get a closer look, she felt sure she might recognize this man. As she moved forward, she was shaky and felt like her legs might give out. Erika was certain she was on the verge of matching the face with some deeply repressed memory.

The man was silent and continued his retreat and she needed him to stop, but her words didn't come out. Why was he there at this hour? Why did she want him to come back? She didn't know.

As if he had heard her thoughts, the lighting changed, and the man was closer now. Their eyes locked; he still didn't speak but smiled broadly. Her heart stopped, and she felt the coldest chill all over her body. She was suddenly freezing but tried to run toward him. She tripped on the nightgown, stubbing her toes, and cried out. In place of the expected pang of delayed punishment to her toes, a knife-like pain caught in her lower abdomen, and she heard a low groan before she dropped heavily to the walkway. She held her stomach with one hand and pulled the material of her gown over her burning toes with the other. A deep sadness permeated her heart as she looked up to see the stranger moving swiftly away. Why didn't he stop? Why didn't he come back and help her?

Desperate to stop him, she screamed at him. His image changed, and suddenly she saw something different: a lighter complexion, fuller and coarser hair, a thicker body, and baggy clothes. His fragrance made her think of Old Spice; a scent she was surprised she knew of. She could not believe her eyes. Was this for real? "Daddy, Daddy, is that really you?" she yelled at the top of her lungs at the man moving into the shadows of nothingness. "Wait, don't go. Please don't go." Her small cries echoed after him, but he was gone.

Erika's body jerked spasmodically at the sound of her own sobbing before she shot straight up in bed, looking wildly wide-eyed and disoriented. Her breath came short and quick, like her heart might pump right out of her chest. Her PJs clung damp with perspiration, and she realized she had to go to the bathroom badly. Her tear-streaked face confirmed one hell of a nightmare. She knew she had dreamed but couldn't hold the images long enough to remember them. Perhaps that was for the best, considering everything else going on in her life.

She tiptoed to the doorway of the twins' room and watched her son for a long moment. The night light revealed the soft shadow of Brandon's sleeping face, while Brea lay sideways in her bed, curled into in a little ball under the covers. Their low-grade snoring was a clear sign that Nana must have been well prepared for the active duo and managed to wear them out completely. Erika desperately wanted their lives to feel as close to normal as she could manage and for them to stop being so worried and distracted all the time. They needed to be with her on the weekends, doing fun things rather than being with a sitter, although she knew they loved being there.

When Erika returned to bed, she caressed Braxton's empty side as she did every night, she awoke like this. Sleep came easily most times but abandoned her during the wee hours. She expected that insomnia would set in for the night. Her hand smoothed the cool sheet, feeling the deep sorrow of losing a loving mate usually brought. She felt sick with loneliness for Braxton. The heaviness of her heart hurt like hell as tension rose inside and exploded into her head with a soft, thumping beat in her ears that grew louder and louder. She couldn't make it go away and wondered if this was the start of some sort of breakdown. Eyes squeezed shut, she mumbled aloud in prayer because she was scared.

"No, please God in Heaven, make it go away," she prayed. Her eyes felt warm and tight. Seconds passed before her tear ducts filled again and tears spilled over. The water slipped rapidly down her face and the thumping beat continued. "Don't let me fall into that pit of hell, that black hole," she begged an invisible higher power. "Please lift me up for my kids' sake, if not for my own?" Her hand fumbled for the touch lamp and grabbed a thick, white Bible that someone had given her at Braxton's wake. Opening it, the first lines her eyes fell on were:

'Come unto me, all ye that labour and are heavy laden, and I will give you rest. Take my yoke upon you and learn from me; for I am meek and lowly in heart; and ye shall find rest unto your souls.

Her eyes had fallen upon the book of St. Matthew, chapter 11, verse 28. Erika pleaded to her Lord and Savior with a heart screaming for solace from the agony threatening to absorb her very being. She wiped the tears from her burning eyes with the top sheet and read on. She had never considered herself a religious woman, but she had always believed in God—accepting Jesus Christ years ago as her personal Savior and counting herself a Christian, a hearer and doer of the Word.

She and Braxton had attended Bible Way Baptist Church with the twins so often that no one seemed to notice they weren't members. But she had missed church a lot lately, especially since Braxton had left, and knew that it was past time for her and the kids to return.

Now, she quietly recited the large, easy-to-read text in the Bible, finding comfort in its words. Eventually, she became calmer and the thumping in her head that echoed in her ears subsided, leaving her too drained to even get another tissue to blow her stuffed-up nose. She used the top sheet once again. When the thumping was gone and the tears had stopped completely, Erika was sleepy. A few residue tears of relief and gratitude rolled down her face, and she hugged the book to her chest. She stayed that way for a while, savoring the relief as she curled into a tight ball on Braxton's side of the bed. She wondered if the police would ever find the thugs responsible for his death. She wanted to believe that whoever it was would be punished in life and that she held no grudge in her heart. Yet she was mad as hell that Braxton was gone. She clung to the hope that someday soon, through some incredibly remote tip, the police would solve the case and link a suspect to the shooting. Braxton should still be alive, but at the very least, they both deserved some level of closure for such a wicked deed. Yet she had some sense of the number of murderers still walking free in the Washington Metro area and the number of unsolved crimes. And that was not encouraging. Hell, while she was hoping, an explanation for this Silvia mess would be nice too.

"Thank you, Dear Father, in heaven for caring and sparing me for the sake of my children. I thank you in Jesus' name. Amen," she prayed. Every muscle from head to toe had been tense, so she continued, repeatedly reciting the 23rd Psalm until her body relaxed and she finally drifted off.

A short time later, the relentless ring of the alarm sounded loudly until the twins bounded into the room, jostling her roughly as they pounced onto the bed. Through tight, puffed eyes, she saw that ten minutes had elapsed on the clock as she slept through the buzzing alarm. The twins slipped in, snuggling close to her on either side, forcing her to drag her weary body barely close enough to slap at the snooze button before slumping back down as if the bed were a magnet.

She fought the urge to drift back into a sound sleep since getting the twins ready, while dressing herself had become a bear of a chore lately, especially with the little rest she was getting. Erika maneuvered her body into a sitting position with her eyes still closed, and the twins scrambled off to start getting dressed. Her first conscious thought was of Mrs. Zimmermann and SITER, a thought that was her primary motivation this morning. Her Bible had fallen to the floor during night. She stared at it and thanked the Lord again for the power of prayer as she remembered the night before, then she returned the book to its place on the nightstand.

Despite her wearily rough night, Erika looked forward to the possibilities of the day. This was the day she hoped SITER could get some answers even if they were just getting started. As she closed her eyes and stretched, a fragment of remembrance tugged at her mind and escaped before she could grasp hold. She felt sure it was related to the night before. But it was thoughts of her conversation with the counselor that energized her almost ten minutes later when the clock read five-fifty.

Lydia's phone sounded as if it would ring right off the hook. It begged her to answer. And as always, the time she allowed herself to dress in the morning never seemed enough, so she silently willed it to stop while she rushed to get ready for work. She knew the voicemail would pick up if it rang too long, but the ringing was drowning out the meteorologist's report of the day's forecast anyway, so she decided to answer it. One of her two TV interests in the mornings was the weather—cool, damp, with a chance of showers today and traffic—backup on the beltway.

She hoped the call just might be Jackson but thought it could also be Ashton. Lydia had spoken with her son a few times since the New Year, and their last conversation, as short as it was, had been the best since he left to live with his dad. She could accept that it might be a while before he forgave her for loving him enough to send him to his father when he had got out of control but hoped one day he would understand and be grateful. He probably remembered her birthday and chose this time of morning, as inconvenient as it was, to call because he was a kid calling his mom, and the time didn't matter to him.

Lydia held the phone and stood in front of the closet until she spotted an outfit appropriate for the weather and her somber Monday morning mood.

"Hello." She spoke in quiet expectation.

"Happy birthday Lydia. I'm sorry for calling you before work. I know you must be trying to get ready."

She recognized this friendly voice immediately. "Sondra. Thank you. How are you doing, girl?" A smile filled her voice as she eyed the clock. *This was not a good time,* she thought. *But whatever it is, hopefully, it won't take long.* "It's okay," she lied. "Your timing's good. Any later and you would've gotten the voicemail. So, what's up with you?" she asked in a voice tinged with both curiosity and anxiety. Any call from her was welcomed. But this early on a workday was pushing it as far as social calls went. She pondered between long calf-length skirt with a coordinating tunic with skinny belt and a knit double-breasted pantsuit.

"You know me. I'm either hanging or rolling," Sondra sensed Lydia's scrambling and got straight to the point. "I called Friday night but didn't leave a message. I just finished a short buying trip and got back too late last night to call. I have another run this weekend. How about getting together sometime this week? I thought I should catch you while it was fresh on my mind and we can coordinate early."

"Oh yeah," Lydia said absently, remembering the whole ordeal with Ashton. "As it turned out, I wasn't much in the mood for celebrating anyway."

"Is everything good with you?" Sondra asked with concern.

"Oh yeah…things are under control," Lydia assured.

"Speaking of celebrating, that's why I called. I know it's after the fact now, but I still want us to do something to recognize your day, even if it's wrong," she joked and chuckled at herself. "I know what you like," a smile filled her voice. "We can do dinner, happy hour, or both. My treat, of course," she added in a low tone as if to tempt Lydia. "Wherever you want to go. Today, if you'd like," she teased. "I'm just sorry I wasn't here for the weekend."

"Look, you don't have a thing to be sorry about. Friday was supposed to be booked up anyway, but it didn't work out, and that's another story. Besides, we always manage to do our thing with each other, don't we, sometime or another?" She reached for the lingerie lying neatly on the chest at the foot of the bed, maneuvering with her free hand. "So, this is all good, Sondra. Your offer sounds too good to pass up. I'm looking forward to seeing you."

After all, she and Kassandra 'Sondra' Kope had been fast friends from their first meeting at the mall more than three years before—over fashion. Lydia was shopping at the department store where Sondra was then a senior manager, though she has since been promoted to buyer. The outfit she wore became an instant conversation piece for the two fashionistas. Sondra was impressed with her elegant style and the fit of her outfit on her model-like figure. The first conversation between the fashion bugs lasted about fifteen minutes, and Lydia knew she had met a true fashion comrade. She was equally struck by Sondra's flair and creative style, and her name seemed to fit her perfectly. There was no doubt that she presented herself as a woman of a particularly discriminating style, and she recognized Lydia's taste as being akin to her own.

They exchanged phone numbers, and a few weeks later, Lydia was flattered and pleasantly surprised to get a call from her. Would Lydia be interested in modeling in a fashion show the store was sponsoring, she wanted to know. There would be a special store discount incentive for her participation.

Lydia did the fashion show more for Sondra than anything else. From then on, the two women kept in touch regularly, though they seldom saw each other more than a half dozen times a year because of Sondra's work schedule.

"How's Thursday?" Lydia quipped joyfully. "…my favorite day of the week."

"Sounds like a plan to me," Sondra chuckled with pleasure. "Now decide on a time and place, and we'll be cooking with hot sauce, as the saying goes.

"Okay. I'll call you tonight and if you're not in, I'll leave a message."

"That's fine. I'm looking forward to it. We have some catching up to do."

Now, that was a worthwhile call, Lydia thought as she dressed hurriedly. She appraised herself in the full-length mirror on the wall facing her bedroom. Satisfied with the total look she had decided upon—Hepburn-style high-waist knit slacks and a silk tee beneath the matching knit double-breasted riding jacket—she managed to leave on time.

Hours later, back at work, tired and preoccupied, Erika slipped into a small, empty cubbyhole space inside the ladies' room for some much-needed respite, hoping to stave off another time-out episode. Her trip to *la-la land* had lasted only minutes this time before an onslaught of uncontrollable tears brought her back to conscious reality. She laughed aloud with relief to see that only a few minutes had passed. Grateful for any semblance of immediate privacy from the curious yet sympathetic gawking of well-meaning co-workers, Erika prayed long and hard to the

Almighty for the mental fortitude to make it through another workday. She thanked Him for the strength to regain control so quickly while at work and for protecting her from prying, curious eyes.

Pieces of her dark, forgotten dream lingered at the edges of her mind, leaving her with the nagging sense that she was forgetting some important incident—or had something urgent to say stuck on the tip of her tongue. These same feelings were frequent after her mom passed—a time in her life so long ago that it sometimes seemed more like a dream. Between Braxton's sudden death and the Silvia situation looming so threateningly, it was no wonder that these fretful feelings were recurring. She felt her only way she could make it through all that was happening was through diligent prayer.

Her lunch hour was over, and she needed to get back to her desk, but she waited until the soft snatches of conversation and flushing commodes coming from the main restroom area had all ceased before making an exit. She would just die if anyone saw her like this. Sustained concentration was a questionable zilch these days, and as much as she wanted to be productive, work was the furthest thing from her mind. The Silvia mystery was taking over her every waking hour.

In the six weeks since she returned to work, gaunt and noticeably thinner with that spaced-out air about her that grew into daydreaming trances, the strange, knowing glances from just about everyone had not diminished. She wondered what they had heard, since no one said much about it. The reactions of coworkers and colleagues ran the gamut from a few probing questions about what happened to her husband to polite, overly sympathetic gestures and stares reeking of pity. Other times, there were careful conversations to the complete, nonchalant business as usual attitude with no acknowledgment at all. Only her long-time acquaintance, Persia, seemed the exception. Somehow, she didn't quite fit into any of those categories.

Erika inspected herself in the mirror. Through her eyes, she looked terrible. She could almost hear Braxton's voice chastising her about her appearance. *'Come on, Erika, you've got prayer on your side. Pick yourself up and be somebody,'* he would say whenever she was down about anything.

Even with an outfit carefully selected to camouflage her noticeable weight-loss—a longer jacket with an unconstructed style and a skirt with an elastic waist– her weight loss was obvious. And though, under normal circumstances, she was viewed as getting better-looking with age, today, there was nothing attractive about her. She flexed the tightness around her reddened, brown eyes that ached as she opened the door and headed out. Maybe there would be a call from SITER waiting for her.

Excitement stirred at the sight of the message slip left on her phone, but disappointment set in when she saw it was from Persia. Erika dialed the phone, waited, and wondered. She decided that Zimmermann was a mouthful to keep repeating in her mind. Was it a bad sign that Mrs. Z hadn't called yet, or was she just being too impatient? That woman had to know how upsetting all this was for her. They probably wouldn't do squat unless they were badgered to death. She didn't want to get nasty with anyone, but she would if she had to.

"Good afternoon, SITER Corporation. May I help you?" a crisp voice answered.

"Hello. This is Erika Marselle. Mrs. Zimmermann, please."

"I'm sorry, but she's not here at the moment." The voice was polite and pleasant. "May I take a message or have her return your call?"

"Do you expect her back anytime soon?"

"Ma'am, she just stepped away for a few moments. She should be back anytime. I can have her call you."

Erika reluctantly left a message, fully intending to call again before leaving work if Mrs. Zimmermann didn't respond. She busied herself as best she could to pass the time, though her mind was nowhere near her tasks. At three-thirty, the call finally came.

"Hello, Mrs. Zimmermann. How are you?" Erika greeted her, sounding hopeful.

"I'm fine, thank you. I just wish there was some good

news for you, but I'm afraid something else has come up that we need to discuss. Can you come into the office tomorrow?"

Erika tried to press for more, but the other only revealed that there had been contact with Silvia Marselle. She felt excited because she was cautiously optimistic and dialed her sister immediately.

"Lydia, it's me, Rikki," she whispered in a hush that Lydia could barely hear.

"Hey, Me, speak up. Why do you sound like you're in a cave? What's going on with you?"

"Can't. I'm at work. Listen, I just spoke with Ms. Z. I've been waiting for her to call all day. Now, she wants me to come in tomorrow afternoon." Erika tried to sound enthused rather than scared like she felt deep down.

Lydia understood immediately that she was referring to the counselor and had given her a nickname. "Okay. That sounds pretty good. This should finish everything up, right?"

"Well, she wouldn't go into details over the phone, but I hope so." Mrs. Zimmerman had only said they had contacted Silvia. Now, as much as Erika wanted to keep the details of the matter closed, she knew it was time to fill Lydia in on the irregularities just in case, and Lydia was all ears.

"I don't know. Somehow this doesn't exactly sound like good news to me, or she would have given you more of a hint over the phone. Did she say specifically why they need you again?" The apprehension in Lydia's voice was clear, and she hated to voice gloom and doom, but she did anyway.

"Not really, and at this point, I don't care." Erika tried not to snap. "I just want to get this whole mess over with. It's probably just more paperwork." She absentmindedly doodled the names Braxton and Silvia while she talked. "It's a load off my mind if they found this woman. I'm pleasantly surprised it was so quick. I'd love to hear her story."

"What time is your appointment?" Lydia prompted.

"Three o'clock. I'll just leave here early."

"Want me to go with you? I can meet you there."

"No, that's okay. I just wanted to let you know what's going on. Besides, it shouldn't take long. I'll be alright. I have to get used to handling things myself, right?"

"Yeah, but it doesn't have to start tomorrow. You could probably use a little moral support on this one," Lydia pointed out.

"I have to go," Erika interjected, realizing she hadn't done any work at all. "I just wanted to give you the latest scoop, okay?"

"Rikki, promise you'll call later if you feel like talking."

"Promise," Erika whispered.

Moving across the large reception area of the condo complex, Lydia opened her mailbox with thoughts of Ashton occupying her mind. A large pink envelope that bore Jackson's scrawling leaped out at her and made her smile inside. Her baby hadn't forgotten her birthday and excitement had mounted by the time she reached her unit. She checked her phone as she sometimes did, ignoring the beeping until it occurred to her that maybe Jackson had called. But the message was from the credit union where she had her VISA bank card, so she set it aside.

She tore impatiently at the envelope, unable to free the card fast enough. "Oh my," she squealed with the delight of a schoolgirl at the beauty of the delicate white roses on the front, bold script that read: *'For a Very Dear Mother—children do not realize.'* Her eyes traced he inside. *'Happy Birthday, Mother.'* Her heart filled with joy and her eyes with tears while they followed the message.

Until we've grown up, we never realize how sweet and kind our mother is.

How gentle and how wise—We simply take for granted from day to passing day. Each sacrifice she makes for us in her own loving way—

But then we grow up and finally learn, the way that children do How much her love has really meant— how thoughtful she's been too.

And so, this comes with all the thanks that you deserve and more, for there's not a dearer Mother than the one this greeting is for.

It was signed: *With all my love. Jackson PS. Be talking at you soon.*

Warm tears streamed down her face and she wiped at them halfheartedly, pressing the card to her chest. Maybe this meant Jackson understood why she had to do what she did. Why she couldn't let him continue as he was. Why he needed time out in a different, hopefully slower paced, surrounding under the guidance of a positive role model like his father.

The phone rang and she picked up on the second ring. "Hello," she answered, her voice still thick with tears.

"Hey, Mom." His deep voice came through loud and clear.

"Jackson… my baby!" she squealed. Excitement filled her voice, and she laughed and cried at the same time.

"Yeah, it's me, Mom." His voice was different—more mature, deeper, and happier. "How are you?" he asked with a chuckle, ignoring that she had called him baby. "I'm sorry I didn't call Friday. I was trying to wait until you got your card. I picked it special for you. Besides I figured you'd expect a call on your birthday, but I wanted to surprise you." He heard her muffled sniffling. "Mom, you're not crying, are you? You okay?"

"Yeah, better now. I just finished reading your lovely card, is all. Thank you so much. Getting such a wonderful card from you means the world to me, and I love that special message." She tried to hold back the tears of happiness stirred by the words on the card and the sound of his voice almost at the same time.

"I was hoping it would get there by at least Saturday. I mailed it kind of late and wasn't sure. Sorry, Mom. I should've sent it sooner."

She was delighted to hear him take responsibility, though she really didn't mind. "Hey, it turned out to be perfect timing for me." A few silent seconds passed between them. "You sound really good, Jackson. Is everything going well between you and your dad?"

"Yeah, we do alright. Dad's real cool. We've been

spending a lot of time kicking it, talkin' about a lot of things, you know." He refrained from mentioning that they had even talked about her.

Lydia wasn't sure but could guess. But she understood enough about Jackson's new jargon to translate, that he meant *things* were better than he expected. "Things like what?" she prodded gently.

"I don't know, just stuff," he whispered bashfully.

"You mean 'men' stuff?"

"Yeah, I guess, that too. But we talk mostly about school, sports, and some of that crap that went on up there. I connect with my boy Kevin sometimes and he fills me in on the happenings. Sometimes, I run it by Dad."

"I see. Are you using that Facebook or Tweet thing to talk with your friends here?" She was hoping his answer would be what she wanted to hear. She knew that Aaron had insisted that Jackson have a phone since he was in high school but had limited minutes with a condition to keep his grades up.

"Just Kevin, Mom. We use Facebook and text sometimes. Dad has me on a strict limit, so I can only do so much."

"So, what about school?" She had to ask. "You like it better?"

"No, hate it." He sounded serious before bursting into a quick chuckle. Just jeffing with you, Mom. It's chilly. Dad bought me a laptop for homework. But what you really want to know is my grades, right?"

"Well, I didn't ask, but if you're volunteering, I'm

waiting with bated breath," she smiled.

"They're better than when I was home. And I've been working hard on them and Dad's been staying on me pretty good about studying too. No D's this quarter, alright?" he said with finality and obvious pride. "Mom, how are you doing up there without me?"

"Jackson, I'm okay…managing. Believe me, you are my main concern. I miss you like crazy, but I'm just fine and a lot more at peace knowing you're doing well with your father. I hope you understand that. Besides you can call whenever you like to check on me."

"You got it, Mom, because I worry about you too. What's up with Aunt Rikki and the twins these days? I miss them a lot."

"Well, Rikki's trying to get back into the swing of things, taking it one day at a time. Some days she seems so tired and preoccupied, other times, she's rather alert and on top of things. But I'm keeping my eye on her. And…of course the twins miss their father."

"Yeah, I know all about that."

"You should give them a call. I'm sure she and the kids would love to hear from you."

"Okay, Mom, I will. Oh yeah, one more thing—are you still seeing that dude?"

Jackson's question caught Lydia by surprise, and she wasn't sure how to answer. The last thing she wanted was to cause him to worry about what was going on between her and Ash.

"Not really. We haven't seen much of each other lately. Why, did you want me to say hello for you or something?"

He snorted. "Yeah, right, you've got to be stone cold jeffing with me, Mom. I just asked."

"Jackson, you just remember that I love you."

"I love you too. Take care, okay? Hold on, Dad wants to speak with you, and I'll talk at you again soon."

Erika and the kids had just sat down to dinner. She was coaxing Brandon to eat his green beans—no small feat these days, especially when her own appetite was so poor. She was tempted to give in to their whining and treat them to McDonald's, but decided instead to fix their meals; they needed to eat more vegetables. When her doorbell rang and she spotted Persia's car at the curb, she instantly regretted not being at McDonald's.

"Hey, Persia." Erika tried to smile, yet she was puzzled by this unexpected and unannounced visit.

"Hi." Persia smiled back awkwardly. "I hope you don't mind me stopping by," she said, regarding Erika's appearance closely. "I'm a little worried about you." She gave Erika the once-over with sympathetic eyes, as if her meaning should be crystal clear. "…and we've been missing each other at work. I just wanted to see how you're doing."

"Well, as you can see, I'm fine," Erika smiled patronizingly, motioning her inside. "We just sat down to eat. Do you want to join us?" she offered politely, heading toward the kitchen, fully expecting that Persia would decline.

"No." Persia faltered as if she wasn't sure. "I didn't come to stay. I've just been thinking so much about you and wondered how you're coping with everything," she rattled on. "I know you said you finally got an appointment. It just seems like it's been dragging on a while," she smiled broadly waiting for Erika to say more. "I just had to check on you."

Relieved that she had at least declined the invitation—and with no intention of persuading her, Erika paused just outside the kitchen, where the kids were hopefully busy eating their dinner.

"Oh yeah, I did meet with a counselor after they finally found Braxton's folder, and we've got the ball rolling." She feigned relief. Erika rationalized that it wasn't entirely untrue; the insurance was being processed.

Persia peeked around the kitchen doorway to glimpse the chattering twins. "Hey, kids, how're you doing?" she asked pleasantly and smiled with amusement when they answered in unison. "That's great." She returned her attention to Erika. "Because I could tell you some real horror stories about the things women find out after their husbands pass," she offered with a nonchalant wave of a limp wrist, as Erika looked on silently, knowing full well she could.

"And don't think I don't appreciate you sparing me," Erika looked her straight in the eyes. "…because, believe me, I've had about all the horror I can take," she added honestly.

Persia embraced her quickly and shook her head. "No, we definitely don't want to go there. I'm so glad things are working out for you—I can see what a toll this delay has had on you. Look, Hon, I hate to run, but I'm meeting Calvin at that restaurant off Branch Avenue…uh…uh…"

she hesitated searching for the name. "…the Red Lobster." She grasped at the words, scrunching her face into a frown and grinning coyly. "He's being so nice. I'm beginning to think he's feeling guilty about something."

Persia's friend, Calvin Maxwell, was a CPA and senior financial manager for a large corporation. He wasn't much for talking and worked more than he should. Yet, from her own admission, whenever he wasn't working, she had first dibs on his time. He often surprised her with tickets to her favorite activities, plays, concerts, and weekend getaways. She knew all of this because Persia didn't miss a chance to share it. They didn't live together, and anyone would question why not since she was always at his place, even when he wasn't there.

"Oh girl…stop! Just enjoy it!" Erika chastised, probably more sharply than she intended. "I hope you don't really believe that because he seems more like Braxton than any other guy I've met. And if you even find yourself thinking otherwise, please don't let him know," she advised sincerely, unlocking the door for her to leave. "From what I see, the man is good to you. Be happy you have him—and be good right back." She held back the obvious thought: she'd thank her lucky stars if she could have Braxton back, even for a moment, regardless of the circumstances.

"Yeah, I know you're right. It's just that sometimes he's almost too good to be true," Persia whispered. She blew Erika a kiss before rushing off to her date.

Erika was always confounded by the irony in Persia's pessimistic mentality despite the fullness of her relationship and her life. At a luscious thirty-one, she was an attractive, well-dressed, and unassuming vixen, who evidently made a comfortable salary and had a man who obviously thought more than a lot of her. Yet, she never seemed as pleased as one might expect. He could never do or give her enough. She only gave him as much credit as she did now because Erika called her on it. Although Persia never mentioned marriage, Erika wondered if that was at the heart of her discontent.

Lydia stood at her neighbor's door, charged up and on top of the world, still energized by how well Jackson had sounded. And, although she was proud of the way she had handled herself with Ashton so far, everything seemed quieter and duller without the energy his presence brought.

"Come on in, chile," Miss Flo urged immediately upon opening the door. She must have checked the peephole. Lydia followed her into the brightly lit, good-smelling kitchen. One of the cooking channels hummed on the TV in the background, but it was the fresh pan trout, hot off the stove, and the bowl of buttered, crackling cornbread that caught her eye. The sight made her realize how hungry she was. She deliberately refrained from staring at the large, crisp-fried, browned-just-right pieces of seafood, but it was on her mind as Flo talked on because it smelled delicious.

Her friend chuckled. "I was hopin' you'd get a chance to come over." She clicked the remote and the sound from the TV was gone, walking lightly around the kitchen, piddling—wiping this and clearing that. "I got that recorded on the DVR, so I can always go back to it later. As the new technology goes, it's the best thing ever for someone like me. I just love watching everything," she mumbled as she moved around. "You came over just in time."

"I had to thank you again for the gift and for remembering my birthday. You chose the perfect department store," she beamed. "In fact, I have a good friend who works there."

Lydia was referring to the gift card for SAKS that was surprisingly generous in amount. "That was thoughtful and more than what one person I know did," she cracked cynically with a smile as she embraced the woman. "You're so sweet. What am I going to do with you?"

Florita grinned knowingly. "Oh, chile, you're more than welcome. I can see you got good taste and like nice things. It's just a little somethin', since I don't get out much to shop these days with all the robbin', shootin' and kidnappin' goin' on 'round here," she mumbled half under her breath. "Hate to think what the world done come to." She moved around the room, passing Lydia a plate. "I hope you hungry, 'cause I got plenty. Get yourself some fish and cornbread over there and sit down with me for a few minutes." She motioned to the stove.

Lydia's plan had been simply to thank Miss Flo for the gift and leave before anything about Ash came up. But she was thankful for Miss Flo's unexpected invitation that quickly changed her mind. And she didn't have to be asked twice, although she would have preferred a plate to go, since she had a feeling that Ash would be tonight's topic after what had happened the other day. He was the last thing she wanted to discuss with Miss Flo. She wondered how much this wise woman had already guessed.

"There's some iced tea lemonade in the refrigerator if you want," she motioned casually. "Yeah, get somethin' to wash that down with," she encouraged, placing a glass on the table. Lydia saw that there was an ice maker on the refrigerator and went about preparing her meal.

"So, Lydia, how's your boy doin' these days? Does he like livin' with his daddy?"

"Yes, ma'am, he does. He's doing better in school too. I think he likes being down there. And his attitude has improved along with his grades. His dad thinks he's adjusting really well—and that he may even want to stay, though he doesn't want me to know it yet. He was more than a little put out with me for sending him to his father, but I believe he's coming around."

"That's just wonderful…because I know you was getting worried about where he was headin'. Now that his head is clearin', he's probably worryin' about leavin' you by yourself."

Lydia's sixteen-year-old…soon to be seventeen, had changed so drastically last year that she thought the boy was possessed. After too many alarming calls to his father, with whom she kept in touch and still nursed warm, unreconciled feelings for, she had reluctantly given in to her ex-husband's suggestion to send Jackson to him in North Carolina.

A number of disturbing and upsetting factors played into Lydia's reluctant, heart-wrenching decision to let Aaron take over with their rebellious son. The tremendous peer pressure Jackson faced daily accounted for much of the drastic change in his attitude, behavior, and grades. The boy who started his sophomore year as a fun-loving, sensitive kid on the honor roll—who once cared deeply about his mom's opinion—ended it as a moody, hip-hop-spouting, arrogant adolescent barely earning passing grades, and thought nothing of lying and talking back.

First, he blatantly abused his cellphone privileges by using up all their shared minutes talking with his boys until she finally took it away. Calls would sometimes come in too late at night for any teenager. Then it got to the point when she could not trust him on the computer because of the unsavory sites he visited without her permission. Since she knew it was excellent for doing homework, she moved the desktop from the spare room to her bedroom, where she could keep a better eye on them.

Then, he grew increasingly argumentative and disobedient. Frustrated teachers frequently called over cut classes, forged notes, and disruptive behavior, frazzling Lydia's nerves to no end and left her wanting to drink. Also, Jackson harbored an overt, slow-brewing hostility toward Ashton. He had always regarded Ashton with suspicion and had never really taken to him, snidely referring to him as a young Casanova. That unvented anger had been brewing ever since Jackson entered his teens—like a blistered sore ready to spill its ugly infection at any time.

But the frightening clincher regarding her son was the foul and unpredictable company that drew him like a magnet. They were an idle, yet fidgety bunch of four that dressed like they didn't have homes, their mouths filled with constant profanity. She suspected that one of the homeboys, as he called them, carried a gun. And with all the violence in the schools, that had done it. She was skeptical that issues with drugs and petty crimes would surface any time at the rate he was going. For Jackson, it was shipping time! So, she announced the sad tiding to him during Thanksgiving break: following Christmas break, he would start the school year with his father. Of course, he lashed out and vehemently refused. But, in the end, he went.

"Yeah, we talked about that. I assured him I was doing fine. And he knows I've got Rikki here with me, and we have always taken care of each other." She believed that Jackson could see that she was managing as long as he himself was doing well.

Lydia managed to make it through her impromptu meal and conversation with Miss Flo without giving too much away. She was relieved when their focus stayed on topics like Jackson, her favorite TV programs, and anything Miss Flo heard about the former—and the first African American president before returning to her unit. It came as no surprise that a slightly older woman such as Miss Flo had been completely enthralled with the reality of a Black man as President and remained what Lydia would describe as "smitten." She openly fawned over the former First Lady, Michelle, and that book she wrote. But tonight, Miss Flo voiced concern with some of the rumors she'd heard about his role in matters related to Social Security and Medicare—for obvious reasons.

4

Tamarra watched her usual cable stations on the kitchen TV set while waiting anxiously for her call from Dorsey. When the phone finally rang, she waited for three full rings before picking up. *This is it,* she thought. The entire weekend she had avoided seeing him, dropping clues during their phone conversations about the number, waiting in vain for an explanation. He had said nothing. He was his usual affectionate, happy-go-lucky self. At times, she was torn if she should just drop it altogether. But she was really burned about what he'd done, and unanswered questions about him nagged her. He always called her, yet they never went to his place. What was his life outside of the dealership and The Club?

Now her nerves tensed at the thought of him purposely giving out a public phone number as his own. Still, she was willing to give him one last chance to acknowledge it and explain why. She was tired of men getting over on her. What exactly was he trying to hide?

"Hello." She forced a casual and calm greeting.

"Hey, sugar. What are you doing? Sorry, I couldn't call you earlier—been kind of busy today."

Tamarra detected something in his mood. On any other day, between work and home, her phone would ring several times—between his wake-up calls, their mid-morning talks at work just to touch base, and evening check-in calls during his break time at his part-time job as a bartender. Usually, she thrilled at his constant attention, but tonight things were different.

"Catching up on the news," she managed politely. "You are working tonight?" she asked softly, knowing he usually didn't drink if he was going to bartend.

"No, not if I have something better to do. I mean, they want me to, but I don't have to. You got something in mind?" he asked in a voice that indicated he hoped she did and that her plans matched his.

The lovebirds had been dating every chance they got for the past few months since they met. Her car was towed to the dealership for a major warranty work, leaving her waiting around for a good part of the day. He happened to be out of his office and struck up a casual conversation. But he was immediately disarmed by her down-to-earth demeanor and gave into an inexplicable urge to bait her during their interaction. She surprisingly took his flirtatious remarks in stride, and he pressed on. Before she left, Dorsey had her phone number and gave his word to keep in touch—a promise he eagerly kept.

It seemed clear to him before long that there must not be a special someone in Tamarra's life. She was always available whenever he called, and he would be a fool to pass up a chance with her. Most women he met at the dealership, especially the White ones, were aloof—what he called stuck-up, too formal and they didn't turn him on—but he sensed something different about her. She didn't stand on ceremony, and though she wasn't what he would call beautiful, she was attractive, and there was something exceptionally endearing about her. She had a head full of silky whitish-blonde hair, which he considered sexy, and her dreamy blue eyes seemed to see right through him. He liked that. It felt like she really saw him when they spoke. She had a bit more curves than the rail-thin women he had found himself with in the past, so he still wasn't sure what exactly the attraction was beyond her attitude, but the jury was still out.

To be truthful, his initial interest stemmed from the connection they made the day they met. Afterwards, he was motivated by how far he thought he might get with her. Once she agreed to become his guest at the bar where he worked, things moved quickly. His bartending job offered an opportunity, and he took full advantage. He allowed her to enjoy the 'happy hour' drinks of her choice with his compliments. Soon, Tamarra began going to the club most nights he worked.

That paved the way to a special closeness earlier than he had expected, despite her subtle reluctance at first. She always held back and purposely put him off for as long as she could, which wasn't as long as she thought. He refused to acknowledge the least resistance from her, chalking it up to coyness on her part. Her behavior only excited him more and drove his desire soaring, and he had to admit that after the first time, a girl had a lot of flavor, potent enough to make him want more. She was worth whatever short period of waiting she thought she was putting him through.

"I need to see you tonight. Are you up for that?" she asked in a soft, sexy voice, knowing he undoubtedly was.

"You know I am. That's just the kind of talk I want to hear. So, you got something on your mind?" His heart pounded with excitement at the thought of being with her again, and his body reacted immediately. He lowered his hand, massaging himself while they talked.

"I said I need to see you, didn't I? What do you think? How soon can you be here?"

"I'm a magician, baby. Close your eyes, count to a hundred, and I'm there."

Almost true to his word, barely a half hour later, the glare of headlights from Dorsey's old Saab signaled his arrival as she watched from the foyer window. He was not in his demo Mercedes tonight. He'd either already been behind the wheel or broke the speed limit all the way. She grabbed her jacket and ran out the door before he could even park. Whatever she had to say could be handled outside and shouldn't take long. There would be no jumping any bones tonight, she told herself. She charged down the short flight of stairs leading to the street, almost running head-on into her neighbor, Jaite. His name seemed more like a nickname since it was pronounced Jay-Tee.

His hands shot out instinctively to steady her as she made her beeline toward the street, but her sight was so concentrated on her steps she didn't see him. He turned to hear her mumble something he guessed was an apology and wave and continued running toward a waiting car.

The locks popped, then she opened the door and slid into the passenger seat. She was barely in the car when Dorsey caught her by her shoulders and pressed his thick, too-wet lips onto hers. Her body stiffened as his mouth relaxed on hers and his tongue sought an opening between rigidly unresponsive lips that remained closed. Her first instinct about him had been right. The alcohol was strong on his breath.

Tamarra hadn't yet closed the car door so through the soft lighting from the car's dome she felt that Jaite might be watching and there was no way for him to know she wasn't receptive to Dorsey's aggressive slobbering. He was all over her without even giving her a chance to breathe. Actually, Jaite had looked on momentarily in quiet astonishment, wondering what her mad rush was about. And he lingered just long enough to witness how the driver was all over Tamarra before she was completely settled in the car. That caught him off guard, and he imagined that sparks must really be flying.

Although Jaite harbored no special resentment toward African Americans—or any other race, for that matter, there was no mistaking the surprise in his eyes at the scene in the dimly lit car. The man came on like an animal in heat, and Jaite felt disappointment that his behavior wasn't more discreet, and that Tamarra seemed to accept such treatment.

There was no way for him to know that she was in fact self-conscious about the possibility of him seeing this little display of lust. She managed to put a few inches between their lips. "Dorsey!" she admonished, settling into the seat and turning far enough to steal a glance in Jaite's direction, but he was already gone. Oh, darn it. Now she wished Dorsey hadn't done that.

"Will you just chill the lovey-dovey here, all out in the open? How'd you get here so fast, anyway?" she asked in annoyed amazement, without daring to look at him.

"You know I'd fly cross country to get to you, girl," he stared at her with a confused frown on his face. What difference does it make? 'You wanted me and now I am here,' his eyes seemed to say.

Her street was dark now and quiet as usual, and the music in the car played a ballad from one of the popular singers she wasn't sure who, maybe Mary J. Blige or Stephanie Mills. Dorsey looked expectantly into Tamarra's face waiting for her next move. While she remained silent, he had a wide grin over his mouth like a Cheshire cat and raised eyebrows that seemed to ask what she was waiting for—an expression like he had really done something great by laying that drooling, too-wet, sloppy kiss on her.

With the slow music playing in the dark car, she felt the hot vibrations emanating from him and his love signals darting all round her, but she purposely ignored them— as she usually tried to do. That stupid 'let's-get-it-on' smirk plastered on his puss and that overzealous clumsy attack on her mouth, against the syrupy love music, was a bit much. None of his message had escaped her, except she was in no loving mood this night.

He made another attempt to embrace her since she wasn't getting his message, but she roughly pulled way. "Come on, Dorsey, stop it, alright," she scolded, resisting the urge to wipe the first kiss off her mouth.

He cocked his head and cut his eyes at her. "So, what's the matter with you? You got me all the way over here for this? Why are you out here anyway? You want to go somewhere or something?" he asked, noticing that she had not even given him a chance to pull into a space.

"No, I don't want to go anywhere. Just ride up the street a little, around the corner or something, and park so we can talk. I need to ask you something."

His eyes narrowed and he froze thoughtfully. "For what…aren't we going inside?" Disappointment filled his voice as he stared at her in amazement.

"No. I want to go up the street or around the corner and park. Is that alright?"

His mouth tightened and his eyes questioned her. "So, are you going to tell me what's wrong?"

"Can you just do like I asked, please? Just drive and park," she directed more emphatically, while her calm façade slowly faded and tension mounted imperceptibly in the car.

She sat in the stillness while the car crept down the street and pulled into a space. Dorsey pushed his seat back as far as it would go and turned to face her. Her expression was sadly serious, and he cut the music to give her his undivided attention.

"So, I ask again—what's got you so upset? What's happened in the short time since we spoke on the phone?" His tone sounded a lot more patient than his expression indicated.

She was not sure how to approach, only that she couldn't keep pretending she hadn't uncovered something upsetting. "Do you have anything you want to tell me?" she prompted, staring ahead through the windshield into the night.

"Hmm…do I have anything to tell you?" he repeated, looking thoughtful with feigned amusement for a full few seconds as if he was actually considering her question. "Is that a trick question? That's what's on your mind?"

Now she faced him, wanting to suppress her anger and frustration just a little bit longer but not sure she could. "Yes. Just answer the question. Do you?"

"Like what, Tamarra?" he said slowly with all the patience he could muster. "What's this about?"

"Do I need to rephrase the question for you?" *A**hole*, she called him in her mind. Her face showed she was perturbed, but he looked dumbfounded, as if he had no inkling of what was going on. "Is there something you may have done and forgot to mention before that you would like to tell me now?" she pressed on. "Because this is your chance. And I'm not going to make it any easier for you than that."

He looked at her without expression. "Oh. So that's supposed to clear things up for me? Come on, quit playing. I don't know what you're talking about and don't feel like guessing. If you want to know something, just ask? Don't keep beating around the f***ing bush." His loving mood quickly drowned under the assault of her arresting body language and sudden mood swing. "I hope this isn't what I broke the speed limit for. Just loosen up, girl, and tell me what's up in plain English."

"Dorsey. You'll miss out on the last chance I'm giving you to tell the truth on your own. If I say any more…" she warned.

"Whoa. Wait a minute. Tell the truth, about what?" he questioned, looking stunned. His hands went up in frustrated impatience in response to her willful silence. "Well, you'll just have to let me in on this one because I don't know where you're coming from. And…no I don't have anything to tell you. So, I suggest you just spit it out. We're only wasting time like this."

The nonverbal sparks heightened, igniting the tense atmosphere enveloping them. "Tell me this… why haven't you ever invited me to your place?" She started out emphatically slow, as she glared into his eyes searching for the truth.

"Maybe it's because I'm never there. I do work two jobs, and the place isn't as neat as I would like it to be." He almost yelled, lashing back in exasperation at being attacked off-guard. "Look, just say what's on your mind or drop it. Hell, I didn't come over here for this. I'm going back to work," he mumbled. "This definitely isn't getting us anywhere."

"Or, maybe it's because you've been lying the whole time," she piped in. "And, if I have to tell you, that's it. It's over. I mean it."

The finality of her words caught his attention, but he only looked straight into her eyes with raised eyebrows, hunching his shoulders. "I'm not lying. I am at a loss is what I am, at what you're so pissed off about. So go ahead. Enlighten me, please?" Icy pricks flicked from her crystal blue gaze, slashing through the darkness to give credence to the saying, 'if looks could kill,' for sure, Dorsey should have dropped where he sat. "Remember this?" She pressed the wrinkled paper toward him with attitude. "Your beeper and *home* numbers," she spat out angrily. "I tried calling you this morning. But guess what I got?"

Dorsey stared into space like a deaf mute for an instant before his mind's eye saw the blaring light that came on. As a mental picture of what must have happened when she called the number became clear, his face fell in despair. "Aww man!" He pounded the steering wheel once with his fist. He groaned as if in pain while his body rocked back and forth with regret. Damn, damn, damn!" he exclaimed. He held up both hands in front of his chest so that his palms faced Tamarra. "Listen, just let me explain. It's not what you think. Just let me explain," he begged."

I got what I needed just now when you couldn't think of a thing you wanted to tell me. You must really think I'm the fool I felt like the other morning. I tried to surprise your black a**, and found out I was calling the waiting room, of all places!"

He winced at those last words as if she had thrown cold water in his face. "Come on, Tamarra; don't get racial on me now. She may not realize that was the wrong button to push and he would try to ignore it this time because of what he had done. He realized it was an immature thing to do and didn't know what could have possibly been on his mind at the time to pull what he saw right now as a petty high school stunt. "I told you I can explain if you'd just calm down and listen." But, he wondered, could he really come up with a reason that would satisfy her?

"You also said that was your home number, but that's not true. And I believed you. Dorsey, I've tried to give you the benefit of the doubt—several chances to tell me on your own, but you got your a** up on your back, being all impatient and annoyed. 'No, I don't have anything to tell you,'" she mimicked in a mock-masculine drawl, "Like I'm the one with the problem. Why would you pull a low-down dirty trick like that on me? I thought I meant more to you than that, but you sure proved me wrong." Her voice cracked from the hurt she felt, and her hand slid to the door handle.

"Are you going to let me explain or what?" he questioned in resigned patience. During her electrifying outburst, he had pinpointed the indescribable attraction to her that had eluded him until now. As crazy as it was, it was her assertive behavior. She had a way about her that surprised him, her being a White woman, certainly the first he had ever been with, and it pulled at him. That too-rational, analytical-type attitude was more typical of his Black sisters, who remembered everything you ever said and did, where you were, what the weather was, sometimes even what you planned to say next. They forever asked pertinent questions and expected, even demanded, a logical answer. But he was just now discovering how very much he liked her.

"Or what?" she shot back. "You want a chance to insult my intelligence again, am I right?" Her eyes shot daggers. "I'm not interested now. What you did was the same as lying and the way you did it stinks! To me, that's a big deal. It is over," she shouted, staring into the windows of his soul so he could feel the depth of her heated anger. "You can take your d**n explanation and stick it for all I care." As she bolted from the car, he called repeatedly for her to wait, but she ran down the street toward her townhouse without as much as a brief look back.

At three ten in the afternoon, Mrs. Zimmermann sat at the same table across from Erika as before, holding Braxton's file. She studied a silently anxious Erika before choosing her words with care.

"As I mentioned, Mrs. Marselle, we have been in touch with Silvia Marselle. I need to correct that—she got in touch with us. As a matter of fact, she was in the office on Friday as well."

"She was in here the same day I was?" Erika asked in surprise, racking her memory of who she might have seen. The counselor hadn't mentioned this during her visit, so she concluded it must have been after she left. Unspoken questions flooded her mind, one after another. *Who was she to Braxton? What time was she here? Why hadn't she shown up before? Did she know about her and the kids?*

Mrs. Zimmermann did not respond immediately. Instead, she pulled the open file in front of her and stared down at the papers for a long pause, then raised her eyes to meet Erika's waiting gaze. When she continued, her voice became quieter, giving the young widow time to settle.

"Perhaps I should've mentioned that little detail when I spoke with you yesterday. I found her in the waiting room after you left. But I prefer dealing with such sensitive matters in person whenever possible. It cuts down on miscommunication. I hope you can agree with me on that," she added politely.

This piece of information sent Erika's mind reeling back to the other people in the room while she waited so impatiently. She was too upset to really notice who was in the room when she left, but the image of the woman she saw came to mind immediately. "So, what did you find out? Who is she?"

"His wife," Mrs. Zimmermann blurted out with no particular measure of finesse. There was just no easy or delicate way of doing this.

Erika looked as if someone had suddenly slapped her. And though part of her feared of something crazy like this, she wasn't fully buying it. This felt more like the beginning of a nightmare while she was awake. Braxton had lost his parents early and grew up in several foster homes. Fortunately, he was a bright kid that excelled naturally in school and thanks to a few scholarships and hard work, he got into a field he loved—information technology. He had no family other than her and the twins that she was ever aware of. She had secretly hoped this woman might turn out to be a long-lost half-sister, aunt, or something—better yet, some already deceased relative. Now, here it was. Her worst fear realized.

"I don't believe that for a second," Erika said adamantly. "Does she have proof?" *And where the hell had she been all this time? God, what if she has kids too,* she thought with disdain.

"Yes, she provided a marriage certificate dated more than twenty years ago. She said they separated legally about a year after the marriage."

"Are there children?" Erika asked robot-like.

"No."

Thank God, Erika thought, still feeling let down and disappointed about the situation. Somehow, without children on Silvia's end to consider, Erika felt better about waging whatever fight it took to validate her own claim. "Presuming the certificate is authentic, did she happen to mention why she still thinks they are married—how she knows what happened or why she waited so long to come forward?" She worked hard to calm herself, but the more she spoke, the more disturbed she became.

"Not in a lot of detail. Only that, an old friend told her about the accident, and she took a chance that he still worked here. She's named as his beneficiary during his early days with the company. There are no updates since."

"It sounds like she has an answer for everything. Did you tell her about me and Braxton's kids?"

"Under the circumstances, Silvia Marselle has as much right to know the details of this situation as you."

"I'll take that as a yes," Erika remarked with sarcasm now. "What was her reaction? I mean, what exactly did she want to know?" she asked intently.

"Mostly about any benefit what she wouldn't receive. She seemed surprised—and somewhat intrigued. Even a bit amused, I'd venture to say. She was a bit curious about you too." A faint but quizzical smile played innocently at the corners of the counselor's mouth as she recalled Silvia's behavior. "Look, you should know that she has requested that the annuity and other benefits be processed for her immediately based on the paperwork in Mr. Marselle's file and proof of her marriage to him."

"Oh, Lord, no!" She fidgeted in her chair. "Wait a minute

here. Excuse my language, but that's a lot of d**n nerve." Her hand slammed down heavily on the table, finding it difficult to stay still. "I'm sorry… please excuse me. But how can she do that?" Erika rose from the chair in protest to match the pitch of her voice. Wrinkles materialized full across her brow. "You all made me wait for weeks just to get to this point, but she just sails in here out of the misty blue after my husband has been deceased for over two months armed with an old marriage certificate to rob me and his kids. And she wants her benefits processed immediately? Just like that, huh? Give me a break! Whose side are you on anyway?" She felt her emotions getting the better of her once again. "You know that's not right."

"Mrs. Marselle," Mrs. Zimmermann interrupted. "I admit at this point that I can only image how upsetting this whole matter has become. But hear me out, please!"

"I'm sorry—I need you to tell me something better than what I'm hearing, or I don't want to hear anymore. This mess is driving me crazy. You never said where she's been all this time." Although Erika knew that it did not really matter in the full scheme of things, if she proved her marriage to Braxton. She believed this woman was up to no good. "I guess it's too much to hope that she mentioned a divorce?"

"No, I'm afraid she didn't. She claims quite the contrary. There was no divorce, only a legal separation." The counselor studied several sheets of paper that did not look like a part of the folder. They rested next to the file folder on the conference table. "She says that at the time of your marriage to Mr. Marselle, he was still legally her husband and refers to your union with him as common-law. She also asked about other assets that SITER is aware of."

"Oh, that woman is full of bull—" Erika caught herself before the word popped completely out and she fought to avoid using profanity. She patted her palm against the table and turned her face away from the counselor, fighting the urge to scream. "I wonder what other assets she expects you to know about," she asked rhetorically, searching deep within herself for composure. "Isn't she trying to get enough already? I'm common-law?" The words hissed through clenched teeth. "Lord…help me, PLEASE!" she mumbled under her breath, then lifted her face toward the heavens momentarily with her eyes closed. "This just keeps getting worse. I cannot believe this is happening."

Erika stared at the woman in disbelief. "I know none of this is your fault, and I hope that you'll excuse my behavior, but this woman sounds like a real piece of ugly work. I hope you don't plan to just take her word and marriage certificate and process her claim, because I have one of those too," she reminded, shaking her head in total disbelief. "No-no-no. We can't just sit by and let this happen." The accusatory words cut at the counselor while Erika stared at her in total exasperation.

Mrs. Zimmerman sat in silence watching Erika vent before raising her head so that their eyes met. Erika's gaze was stern. "I understand your frustration, fully… really I do, but our leeway in this case appears limited. After all, she's named in the file and her certificate predates any paperwork listing your name—regardless of how many years ago it was. She also produced a valid D.C. driver's license confirming her identity as Silvia Marselle. On paper, she has met SITER's requirements to satisfaction."

When Erika tried to speak again, Mrs. Zimmermann raised a hand to stop her. "Yet, I recognize and agree the circumstances merit a more comprehensive closure for this rather messy case. I asked you back to make sure we have all the correct dates pertaining to you."

"I still would like to know whose side you're on, Mrs. Zimmermann," she pressed. "I just don't get the feeling it's mine."

"I'm sorry you feel that way. I'm not on anyone's side, but for what it's worth, I do hope this matter works out in your favor, especially for your children. I am just trying to do my job."

Erika wanted so badly to believe her. "Well, will you work with me a little on this, please? Can you tell me anything more about this woman? I would like to do some checking myself."

"Sharing personal information would violate the privacy act. I can say that she's local…Northwest, D.C. I believe."

They briefly reviewed specific papers in the file that were dated after Braxton's marriage to Silvia, while Erika identified paperwork that documented events that occurred during their marriage, such as records of various assignments at different locations, promotions, and transfers. The form designating Erika as sole insurance beneficiary was in chronological order as were health benefit forms that listed her and later the addition of the twins. Only a crucial form changing spousal designation from Silvia to Erika was missing—a document that affected all other benefits except the life insurance.

The short but disconcerting exercise left Erika fatigued and, in more despair, than ever. "What else do you need from me, Mrs. Zimmermann?" Erika asked tiredly. "You have all my paperwork. I mean, what happens now?"

"Well, although this situation is very unusual for us, we will investigate all discrepancies fully…and since this requires contacting the Bureau of Vital Records for verifications and confirmations, we can delay this claim until we have fully confirmed what Silvia has provided. That may take as long as a few weeks—I'm not sure. I will then, of course, need ample time to review everything and document the circumstances in writing for management, so they understand what they are approving. In the meanwhile, if I hear or turn up anything at all, I will call you. Right away, next time. If you come across anything that questions the credibility of what we have, let me know as soon as you can and nothing will go forward until we have looked at it closely as well. And I do appreciate you coming in again. Mrs. Marselle. Do you understand all that I am saying to you?" Mrs. Zimmermann tilted her head to the side ever so slightly, as she made eye contact with Erika.

Erika was not immediately aware that tears had trickled down her face. She just could not seem to control herself. Her emotions were all over the place these days. Staring straight into Mrs. Zimmermann's eyes, she managed a weak smile and simply responded, "Yes, Ma'am, I believe I do."

Thirty minutes later, Erika walked into a small, plain-looking building in downtown N.W, D.C. From the outside, she thought the place looked more like a clinic than office space for the District's Records Bureau. She did not have much to go and was not sure how she would get the information she needed, or if she would recognize it, if she was so fortunate.

She recalled the attractive woman she saw in SITER's waiting area on Friday. She looked older than Erika…even older than Braxton, for that matter, so Erika had no way of knowing if that woman was Silvia, though she felt likely it was. Mrs. Zimmermann would part with only her full name, year of marriage and separation, and a general Northwest, D.C. address, so she really didn't have much.

She walked in and approached the screening area in the small lobby. A man in a guard's uniform walked over, shaking his head with a big smile, as if he was amused by some silly folly on her part. "Sorry, Miss. You won't get any help around here this time of the afternoon. Too close to quitting time." He threw a glance at the large wall clock that read 4:25. "We close at four thirty." He looked around at the people scrambling out the door. "Everybody's leaving or gone already. If you need something try back tomorrow. We open at eight," he said, still smiling.

"Right." She nodded in acknowledgment. That made sense, she remembered as soon as the words were out of the guard's mouth. No wonder he had that silly grin on his face. Where was her head, racing down here like a moron this late in the day? "Thanks." She flashed a smile and bolted as if she couldn't get out the door fast enough. Even if she had gotten in, she doubted there would be enough time to find anything helpful.

En route to Maryland that day, not even the thick rush-hour traffic penetrated her mood. A song on the radio that reminded her of Braxton made her aware that she was close to home. She had stopped at the one red light that seemed to last forever and remembered she had to pick up the twins from Nana's. Her mind had been moving faster than her car for the past half hour, retracing the same thoughts, trying to figure out what to do next and how to do it. She needed more information on Silvia. Some of Ms. Z's words kept coming back like a broken record.

Lydia moved as effortlessly as any model on heels, sounding loudly against the cement walkway leading to her condo building. She glanced around casually, searching her surroundings out of habit, and leaned in against the brisk evening air. It was almost nine, and she was relieved the entrance lights provided adequate brightness upon approach. The weight of her tote bag hung heavily from her shoulder and she held a pile of clothing from the cleaners. Bags from the *CVS* were clutched in her free hand. She would be beyond happy if underground parking was available again, supposedly within the next few months.

The onset of her monthly difficulty made a long, hot soak with some bath salt a must tonight. Her red flag was a welcome sight every month, but a most blessed one this month. She was so thankful that one night of passionate, unprotected sex with Ash the month before hadn't cost her, especially after how things had gone down with him. All her body wanted now was to get inside and relax.

A short distance away in the apartment parking lot, the black sports car rested between two larger cars, trying to avoid notice. The driver listened to a CD and watched for Lydia's arrival. Though she did not see him and had not so much as glanced in the direction of his car, there were always listening ears and watchful eyes somewhere lurking, when and where least expected. So, the obscured presence of that dark, devilishly looking vehicle did not escape the keen eyes of Lydia's friend and neighbor, Miss Flo. She recognized the little Beamer and the driver immediately.

Much of her day was spent pacing or patrolling her apartment from the living room to the kitchen to the bedroom, where she kept a relentless vigil on the parking lot and street below. Her sporadic watches provided frequent breaks from the TV and a reason to get up. Had there been carpet rather than the large scatter rugs she favored, a path would have been blazed throughout the rooms long ago. The neighbors had taken her constant sentry in stride, who felt Ms. Flo was being maternal and alert to compensate for an inactive, rather reclusive lifestyle. But she was convinced of the wisdom of being watchful of the goings-on however you could. What with so much happening nowadays, she felt one couldn't be too careful. Anyway, she was old enough not to care much about what people said or thought about her.

The lot was situated toward the right of the building on her side and spanned the length of two neighboring buildings. She had an excellent view clear up to the next building, which was about where Lydia's friend had been parked long enough to be tired of sitting there, she thought. She had witnessed him doing the same thing over the weekend. On Sunday night, she watched his car bypass empty spaces close to their building and opted instead to park closer to the next building, behind a car large enough to partially block it from view, like tonight. Whenever she saw him come, she waited just so she could watch his lean, muscular body glide rather than walk to the building. Though her favor was not with him at all, she could not deny he was a well-dressed hunk. She didn't see herself as too old to still recognize and enjoy a fine, scenic view when she could but had the wisdom not to dwell on her pleasure.

Tall, dark, and real easy on the eyes, this one was just the way she had always liked her men, not to mention that smooth, athletic swagger in his walk. Yeah, watching him was a thrill that took her back some years to her more spirited younger days—a time when she had known a couple of humdingers who had moved like that. Despite the obvious enjoyment she received from watching Ashton, his presence in the car he parked and never left, and his sneaky arrivals and departures left her more watchful than ever. Oh, she knew what he was doing. She didn't need to be a 'rocket scientist,' as they say, to figure that one out. That little ruckus at Lydia's place a few weeks ago came to mind whenever she saw that car now.

Flo's initial intuition about the relation between the two was confirmed by Lydia's behavior. Romance was not an easy subject to approach with Lydia. *That chile was really careful not to breathe a word about her friend and made it clear that personal talk was off limits,* she thought. "Uh huh, you are a sly, handsome rascal… with all your creepin'. I know what you're up to," she mumbled insightfully. It was as plain as the nose on her face that his curious behavior was because of the big blowout. He probably thought Lydia might be preparing for someone else to come on the scene. It was as if he suspected she was getting out of his control, or worse, that the thrill might be just plain gone. She was saying good-bye without his permission.

She could tell the young fellow was a ladies' man because she knew the type, and that Lydia had a problem freeing herself for a more desirable type of relationship. She had probably believed this good-looking rascal would someday magically change into all she had ever hoped for in a man. That she had allowed herself to be taken in by his charm and good looks, among other things, was typical of a lot of young women since the beginning of time. Though Lydia skillfully avoided the subject of intimacy with her like a deadly virus in any conversation they had, Flo had her suspicions about their setup. She was more than a little familiar with how sexual desire and romance can become the driving force that hands a somewhat naïve woman of limited experience—like Lydia—over to the bondage of a one-sided arrangement. It was obvious to her that Lydia gave far more to this man than she ever received. Flo wasn't too old to remember that good sex had been the making of some otherwise unlikely and, later, even regretful bedfellows in her heyday, while she moseyed back to her spot in front of the TV, in time to catch the show finale.

A sixth sense of sorts had attuned her ears more and more with each passing year to hall movements and doors opening and closing on her floor. She convinced herself that her acute awareness of her surroundings accounted for this. She heard a faint but discernible reverberation of the distant slamming of the door, the familiar sound of metals meeting across the hall—and she knew that Lydia was in.

Outside, Ashton waited for something or someone. Flo was doing her last watch for the night at the darkened window and was about to give up when his car door swung open. Her eagle eyes widened and became fixed for the show. He began his athletic stride toward the building like he had all the time in the world. His tall, lean physique was unmistakable, even in the shadows created by the height of the buildings. His movement was confident and casual until he turned to watch a car a short distance up the lot as it drove toward the far end of the next building. This prompted him to walk quicker and with more purpose.

Inside her apartment, Lydia listened attentively to an R&B CD that included music by artists such as Ray Charles, Otis Redding, and Johnnie Taylor and even some light jazz—the sweet sound of Kenny G, the saxophone man. She never questioned why, but nothing she heard in the current music genre sounded quite like the older R&B to her. It took her way back to a time that she wished she could visit. Preparing her bath, she got into music while she rolled her hair and pulled out nightclothes. She just needed to make one call before she soaked in the tub and allowed the scented bubbles to relax some of the stress away—so she quickly dialed the phone.

"Hi, just calling to check on you. Everything going good?"

"You know. I don't even know how to answer that. I don't want to say what comes to mind. How about you?" Erika asked.

"Like a dog that's been run over. In a word, beat! My brain is fried, so I'm getting ready for a nice hot bath, so I didn't call to talk. I just wanted to find out how your meeting went."

The insurance check's in the mail, so to speak, but they must check Silvia's marriage out," Erika briefed. She could tell this was not the best time to talk to Lydia about the details of the mess, but she was glad Lydia had called. Hearing her voice reminded her that someone was on her side. She understood that her sister's job was more tiring and stressful since she became the financial manager at a large real estate company shortly after the sale of her and Braxton's home. The housing recession had proven too unreliable for her.

"Unless you need to talk, I'll probably see you by the weekend. I know it's a tall order but try not to worry."

"That's fine," Erika readily agreed despite her deep concern about Silvia.

Lydia's attention was diverted by a soft tapping on her door, so she only half listened when Erika signed off. "Rikki, I have to go; someone's at the door." She did not get many visitors during the week and hoped it wasn't who it usually was.

"Don't you have security to let people in?"

"If you're coming from the outside, it might be Miss Flo from across the hall."

"Be sure to ask who it is before you open the door," Erika cautioned as she hung up.

Lydia did not bother to remind her that she had a peephole. "Who's there?" she asked softly, fully expecting it to be her neighbor, until she looked through the oversized hole in the door while pulling her long robe tightly around her. The peephole was so large she always felt that the person on the other side could probably see her too. A response didn't come, and she saw why. She backed away from the door swearing. "Darn it, how does he keep getting in here without calling up?" she whispered. "Who's there?" she repeated curtly, though she could see it was Ash. She was determined to make him answer before opening the door, if she decided to open it, even though he had to know she was staring into his face. When he still didn't answer, she was tempted to just ignore him but instead called out once again, more insistently.

"Lydia, it's Ash," he answered, perturbed because she had forced him to say it was him.

She had a good mind to make him talk through the door, but Miss Flo had already heard more of her business than she cared to share. Lydia moved the hanging chain into position before she cracked the door only wide enough for them to glimpse each other.

"Ash, why are you here? You know I don't like you showing up unannounced? You think you're smart by dodging security, don't you?" she admonished in a low tired voice.

"I know, I know." He could see she was still upset, though she sounded rather calm. "This is the only way I can get you to listen to me. If I had asked to come over, would you have said yes?" He felt like he knew the answer to that. Desperate situations sometimes called for selfish measures was more like what he meant. "Since I'm here, can I come in and talk to you for a minute? I promise not to be long."

He stood with his most effective hangdog look—hands in his pockets, shoulders slumped, and head hung low enough to almost touch the floor. He had no inkling that for a quick invitation into Lydia's apartment, he needed only the threat of talking loud enough for Miss Flo's to hear if she didn't let him in, and he would have been, as the saying goes, in like Flint before his fist could hit the door.

Why tonight? She cried inside. She did not have the strength to deal with him now. "Look, I'm a little out-of-sorts tonight, and I know what's on your mind. Maybe we can talk some other time." Her eyes pleaded for some consideration, but he didn't take the hint.

"Babe, please. You think you know. Just give me a few minutes… five. Just five minutes, okay?" He removed a hand from his pocket and put it up, spreading his fingers to signal five. "And I'm gone."

Reluctantly and silently cursing him, she opened the door and stood aside to let him through, checking across the hall before easing the door shut. There was no stir, but Lydia was sure Miss Flo had probably already taken all this in and was waiting within 'earshot' as she had promised before. They stood awkwardly saying nothing. He looked at her while she stared at the carpet in silence, waiting. Then, she looked at him intently.

"Alright...five minutes. You promised. And I'm holding you to it."

She led him into the kitchen, away from the front door, where she made a point of letting him see her note the time. He pulled a package neatly wrapped in red metallic paper and gold cording from his pocket and passed it to her. She stared at it speechless.

"No," she said, resisting it at first. He had even taken the time to have it wrapped. "I told you it was alright. A gift is hardly necessary at this stage of the game. You haven't heard anything I've been saying, have you?"

"Come on. Don't be so hard. I'm trying. This is my way of saying I'm sorry, Babe. I had to do something to show you how serious I am. That I really care." A smile tugged at his lips.

Still at a loss for words, she found herself accepting the small box in a daze. She walked to the sofa and sat on the edge, staring at the box. Her growing curiosity motivated her to remove the elastic gold cording. And, as the tiny wrapping fell to the floor, he watched in anticipation, waiting to see a gleeful expression of forgiveness and gratitude appear on her face when she saw the content—a look that did not come. Confusion and disappointment showed instead as she held up the tiny box for him to see.

"Ash," she said with open skepticism. "This is nice, but what's it supposed to be?" The small, pear-shaped blue topaz sparkled from its blue velvet box about as much as a topaz could. For a moment, she even seemed captivated. She walked slowly toward him. "What's this?"

"What does it look like?" He chuckled self-consciously. "It's your birthday gift. Try it on. I bet I got the right size."

Lydia looked away into space, feeling winded. She placed the beauty of the ring in the palm of her hand. "Gifts like this have never been your style of apologetic expression," she whispered sarcastically, looking at him with suspicion as she tried the ring on a finger on her right hand. It didn't fit.

"Try it on the other hand," he encouraged, and she looked reluctant. "Look. Don't make it into a thing, okay? I know I hurt you and I'm trying to make up is all. You know how much I care about you. I just can't always be what you want me to be."

Protest flashed into Lydia's eyes as she shook her head in adamant denial. She was not trying his gift on the ring finger of her left hand. "No. I don't think this is a good idea," she strongly protested, trying to give the ring back.

Ashton wouldn't accept no for an answer. He headed for the door quickly.

"No! No! It's not that simple, Ash. This is beyond a gift," she countered, her voice rising against his retreating back.

"Goodnight, babe. Thanks for listening." He walked out the door.

Lydia ran behind him in time to catch the heavy door before it slammed and watched him stride smugly toward the elevator as she called out in a harsh whisper.

6

When Tamarra got home later than usual that evening, the chill had set in and daylight was all but gone. The afternoon rain had chased the sun away hours ago and turned into a light drizzle. Her usual space was taken, and she had to park a little ways down from her unit. A dark car was double-parked a few spaces down, right about where she and Dorsey had been the other night.

Though she noticed the car, she couldn't make out the make or who was in it. Yet, there was something ominous about it lurking innocently in the rain that caught her eye as she made her way up the unit stairs. Despite a feeble attempt at playing off the discomfort, the muscles in her stomach contracted and lurched. The neighborhood residents were mostly professional working-class people like Tamarra and her bachelor neighbor, Jaite, with a few retired folks, so the community was quiet. There was rarely any unusual activity, so the street appeared safer than most. At least that's what Tamarra told herself as she tried to push aside the creepy, uneasy feeling of being watched. She mentally chastised herself for coming in so late and chose to ignore the warning that prickled over her body, and she readied her key with a shaky hand, listening for sounds.

From behind the windshield, a pair of eyes followed Tamarra, catching her in the rear- and side-view mirrors— merely watching as she left her car carrying an umbrella and grocery bag. Tamarra couldn't understand her nervousness since she could not get a good look at the car or its occupant.

How did she get herself into situations like this time after time, she wondered. Her heart raced worse than the day she saw the number on that payphone, but now the cause of her apprehension was different.

Dorsey had phoned her at work the day before as if nothing had happened, and she reminded him rather harshly that they were through and then refused his other calls. She knew he was riled up after that, but she figured he had it coming.

Tonight, as she got closer to her door, fear made her second-guess her decision to shut down his efforts to explain. She wondered if she should just go back far enough to see what the car was but decided against it. As close as it was, it seemed too far. Besides, then he would know that she saw him. She also thought about approaching him to find out what he was doing there. *No way!* Something inside her screamed. Instead, she took the stairs leading to her neighbor's door and knocked hard several times. Jaite's unit appeared as dark inside as the night, and she could feel the cold rainy air penetrating her thin leather trench, even with an umbrella. She could tell no one was home.

Tamarra held her breath as she moved carefully down the short flight of stairs toward her door and carefully inserted her key into the lock. Her hand trembled as she pushed the door and let the wet umbrella fall to the ground outside. She stumbled across the doorsill, feeling more nervous than ever. Inside, she sagged against the locked door and released a shaky, unabated relief, surprised at the height of her fear. *Goodness,* she wondered, *what's wrong with me? What was that all about?*

She kicked off her damp shoes, emptied the grocery bag, and went to the window facing the street to peek out.

She could barely see that far down, but it looked like the car was gone. Relief flooded her body. A short while later, she was comfortably clad in a robe and socked slippers when the sound of her doorbell startled her. Partly because in light of how things had gone this evening, the ringing sounded strangely shrill tonight, and she was not expecting anyone. She hesitated, wondering if she was being plain silly, even a little paranoid. She reasoned that it really didn't matter who it was as long as it was not Dorsey. She pushed the intercom button.

"Who's there?" she asked over the intercom.

"It's Jaite from a few doors away. I hope I'm not disturbing you."

"Oh yeah, Jaite," she whispered in surprise and exhaled easily. "Hold on. Be right there."

"Hi," he said softly with a faint smile. His bluish-gray eyes glanced down at her robe, and he ran his hand across one side of his neat, close-cropped beard.

"Hi," she answered, feeling awkward and shy.

"Locked in like Fort Knox, huh?" he joked seriously. "That's good," he responded to her cryptic smile. "Did you forget this?" He held out her umbrella all neatly folded up.

"I sure did, completely." She took the umbrella from his hand, though she was sure it would have been fine outside the door overnight.

His eyes fixed on her as if something was on his mind. "Well, I noticed it lying there on my way in. You might need it in the morning, step outside, and find it gone, you know."

"I can't imagine that anyone would want it," she grinned. "But you might be right. Never know these days. Thanks," she said flatly, smiling briefly and waiting for him to leave.

He watched her for a moment with a plaintive expression. "Hey, that's what neighbors are for. Goodnight."

Tamarra closed the door and flipped the locks back, wishing for the first time that she had taken Erika's advice and invested in one of the alarm systems like Braxton had installed for them—the kind you armed and disarmed with a code number and had twenty-four-hour service that included immediate contact with the police, medics, and fire department. The idea was more appealing now that she was behaving like a nut. She tossed the umbrella on the floor near the door and headed for the kitchen to pick up a wine cooler. Next stop, the Jacuzzi.

She soaked for about twenty minutes, analyzing how her thirty-four years had left her with more bitter than sweet memories of failed relationships over recent years since the breakup of her bumpy, too-long marriage. She wondered if the right man for her even existed. Were they worth all the effort? Before long, the soothing contents of her drink pushed Dorsey from her mind, and she tried to think of something more pleasant, like her next vacation. Maybe she should think about taking a Carnival cruise to the Bahamas.

She eased into the large tub while reflecting on her amazingly uncanny talent not only for attracting the wrong men, but also for actually choosing them. She couldn't have made worse choices in men if she were paid to. This bad streak started with Avory Wilson.

He was a good-looking, dark-skinned police officer she fell for right away. She disobeyed her parents to marry that hunk. He was solidly built with a pair of the prettiest long legs she had ever seen on a man. They tended to make him look taller to her than the five feet ten inches he claimed, and he was a consistent jogger. He said it strengthened his overall body condition and gave that extra edge needed for the swimming test required to qualify for his scuba-diving assignment at the D.C. police department's Harbor Patrol.

And Tamarra had loved him shamelessly, just as she thought he had loved her when she was all but forced to choose between him and her family. Avory was sweet, kind, considerate, and free-hearted— everything she thought she wanted in a mate. And she was convinced she had his heart, and for a few years they were fine. Then he began working long stretches of overtime without discussing it with her, and he spent more time away from home—at work, he claimed—and they drifted too far apart. During those last few years, their passion had subsided substantially, and their love life dwindled to nothing. That was probably the reason she had never conceived, which turned out to be a blessing in disguise now that they were divorced. She took a long swallow from the bottle.

Her thoughts drifted to Andre, who came along probably too shortly after her marriage ended. He was a happy hour hookup while she was out with a few co-workers. After several weeks of meeting at various spots to eat, taking in a movie, or having cocktails, she thought they might be making some personal progress. He was always talking about the money and things he had. Unfortunately, a few months passed before she began taking his boastful claims seriously. He liked to tease that his incredibly lucrative pay for a few days' work probably equaled her hard-earned two-week salary. He admitted he had dedicated his life to satisfying women, and his sole livelihood came from servicing any female who was legal and able to pay.

She had to admit he was a decent lover, but she couldn't fathom anyone willing to pay him the kind of money he bragged about—certainly not her. After a while, she noted the numerous calls he received on his cell phone when they were together. This convinced her there was more truth than lies to what he said, and the calls got on her nerves, so they said their goodbyes. Within a few months, she was back in the social saddle again.

Then there was Carl. Things just became too strange with him. He was a personal trainer at the fitness center she had frequented at the time. He was always very watchful of her, complimenting her and making small but flirtatious talk, offering tips on her exercise technique and wanting to spot on her certain pieces of equipment. After a few dates, she had the weird feeling that he was interested in 'turning her out,' using the age-old phrase from the world of prostitution. Yet, she told herself that it could not possibly be true. The man constantly hinted at how his buddies would love to have a good whack at a fine piece of white a** like hers. One with some meat on her bones in all the right places, and they were willing to pay big bucks. And he'd all but for sure guarantee her good tips. The first time, she was drinking and had brushed it off playfully. But when the uncomfortable subject came up once too often, she was forced to confront him and let him know she didn't appreciate his remarks. He simply laughed it off and said she needed to lighten up, that he was just kidding. Soon after, he called to say for both their sakes that it was better that he moved on—probably to his next target. Whew, that had been a relief.

She had cooled her dating for a quick minute, then met Dorsey just before Braxton was killed. She'd been of little comfort to Erika and stood by helplessly, watching her grief grow until her own desperate need for distraction surfaced and she started hanging out at the bar where Dorsey worked. Tamarra knew she was of little use to Erika during the early days of Braxton's death. Her own search for some unknown need had gotten in the way. She didn't want to use that as an excuse; it was simply the fact of what happened, and she seemed helpless to do anything else. *What a group of losers,* she thought momentarily to herself. She had buzzard's luck at love.

She heard the distant ringing and strained to listen to what sounded like the phone downstairs. The upstairs ringer was off—a little trick she picked up from Erika. She waited for the voicemail to catch it.

The ringing stopped, only to start a few minutes later. She wrapped herself in a towel and raced to the phone, trying to reach it before it stopped ringing.

"Hello," she said, out of breath and dripping wet. She could tell someone was still there.

"Hello!" she snapped louder. She heard a distinct click.

"Hello," she repeated, though she knew the line was dead now, and she felt terribly annoyed. She replaced the receiver and returned to the bathtub only to find the water too cold to get back in and the bubbles gone flat. She tried recapturing the mood with more hot water and fresh suds, but for what it was worth, it wasn't the same.

The phone started ringing again. After several rings, it stopped, and she was sure the voicemail had picked up. This constant calling was bordering on harassment. She wondered how much longer he would continue with this. Was she really that good?

7

Lydia answered the phone, certain that it must be Ashton checking if his gift had worked its magic and earned him back into her good graces. Instead, she was surprised to hear her sister's usual way of identifying herself.

"Lydia, it's me. You busy?"

"Hey, Me," Lydia teased, mocking Erika's habit of referring to herself whenever she called lately. "No, just trying to get something to eat. What's up with you?" Lydia wondered whether she was up to hearing the answer.

"It sounds like you're feeling better today. Can I come over? I need to talk with you about something."

"Yeah, sure. Did something happen?"

"I'm on my way. We'll talk then." She hung up before Lydia could ask more questions.

By the time Erika and the twins arrived, Lydia had started on her Stouffer's microwavable stuffed peppers and iced tea. Brea and Brandon quietly watched *Wheel of Fortune* while she and Erika slipped into the kitchen.

"I'm almost numb with worry," Erika started abruptly. "I've been getting myself all psyched up over the latest bombshell from Silvia, I guess."

"What in the world happened now? And take your time." Lydia frowned, not liking the sound of the conversation.

"Oh, there's nothing new…at least not like what you mean…about the marriage. Just some things I should have told you when we talked yesterday. I wanted to, only you sounded so out of it… I didn't." Erika's voice was breaking.

"Arwh." Sadness filled Lydia's voice as she pulled her sister into a quick hug, suspecting that it was more bad news from the counselor. "I told you I'd go with you. Why didn't you—"

"No, that wouldn't have changed things." Erika was clearly frustrated. "I know you would've gone. I got that, alright. And believe me, I appreciate the thought." She wrung her hands and walked back and forth as she talked, like Lydia often did when she was upset. "You've always been there for me, but believe me, your being there with me today wouldn't have changed this mess. And I mean it's a bunch of pure you-know-what. I didn't want to burden you with this, hoping it would all work itself out, I guess, because of the type of man I knew Braxton was. I wanted to handle things myself. But, Lydia, this just won't go away… instead it's getting worse."

"Okay, okay. You're making me super nervous here." Lydia didn't want to break Erika's flow but wanted to calm her while she talked. "Take a deep breath and tell me slowly. What happened?"

Erika took a deep breath and exhaled loudly. "Hell, I don't even know where to start," she began, then took another pause. "It seems that Braxton was married before… more than twenty years ago. That's who this Silvia is."

"He was what?!" Lydia cried out with her mouth full of food, as Erika paced nervously around the room, then in front of the refrigerator before opening it, only to stare inside blankly without fully realizing her actions, then quickly shutting it—an indication of her muddled state of mind. "Get out of here! And you didn't know!"

"Of course I didn't know. It wouldn't have been such a blow if I had a clue. And I guess Braxton didn't consider it important enough to mention, since it was so many years ago and there were no children. Who knows? But get this: she was waiting for Ms. Z after I left Friday.

"Waiting for her where?"

"She didn't say, but I think she was in the waiting room while I was there, and I got a look at her," Erika pointed out in amazement. "She claims she's still married to Braxton and that our marriage is illegal. She's trying to get all his benefits immediately, but Ms. Z promised to check the marriage out carefully first."

Lydia had stopped eating altogether. "Oh, my goodness! And once they do this checking, then what?"

"Who the hell knows. I guess we'll just have to wait and see what they come up with. But I do know that if I keep allowing negative thoughts to take over, I'll be stirred crazy."

"Okay, so Braxton's been married before and for some reason never breathed a word," Lydia said slowly, trying to reason it through. "But if they divorced, it doesn't matter that her name is still on his papers."

"Lydia, I never said they were divorced. That's part of

what this whole mess is about."

"Wait! No, please don't tell me that. Are you telling me that my man Braxton married you without getting a freaking divorce?"

"No, I'm not, because I don't believe that. I'm saying that it *looks* that way because that's Silvia's story," Erika answered more quietly now without much emotion.

Lydia cursed under her breath. This supposed routine situation she had hoped that Erika had under control was certainly getting worse as they talked.

"So, it *appears*—with emphasis on *appears*…as if Braxton was a bigamist?" Lydia concluded with a look at Erika that made clear there wasn't an ounce of judgment in it.

"All I know is that woman just shows up out of nowhere and, even though she sees what a mess things are, she's in a hurry to process benefits she's calling hers. She even produced a marriage certificate that carries more weight than mine. They were together barely a year, way back when, yet she claims they were still married when Braxton died all these years later. Under the circumstances, that sounds a little convenient to me."

"Why did she wait so long to claim the benefits? It's been a good minute."

"Those are my questions exactly. She claims she got the word from an old friend just recently. Of course, she didn't say who the friend was, and I can't imagine who that could have been."

"I see what you mean. That wench is gambling with nothing to lose and everything to gain."

"And the devil must've whispered that Braxton's papers weren't in order. Besides, armed with a marriage certificate, that's a chance she's willing to take."

"I don't mean any disrespect, Rikki, but you know this crazy situation sounds like a storyline straight out of the soaps. I tell you, after the week I've had, I don't know if I can stand to know any more."

"You and me both… but Lydia, there *is* more. Ms. Z says that because of the certificate, they'll check with the Office of Vital Statistics before making a final decision. That when Silvia found out I was the beneficiary of the insurance, that didn't faze her a bit. I guess she felt the kids and I deserve something from Braxton for being in his life. She asked if there were other assets, as in other property." Erika's voice became more dramatic. "She referred to my marriage to Braxton as common law. When I heard that, I almost blew my top. I didn't mention anything about the house to Ms. Z, but Silvia probably guessed that we have a home. And Lydia, I'm afraid she'll come after it."

Now Lydia better understands the full magnitude of Silvia's ruthlessness. "Sounds like she's going for broke—all or nothing. She probably knows if she walks away with anything at all, it's a coup for her regardless. Did you two have wills?"

Erika frowned regretfully and breathed heavily. "We meant to but never got around to it. You don't know how many times over the past few days I've wished we had. That might've simplified my life, and I wouldn't be playing truth-or-consequences with that lying conniver," she spat sarcastically.

"There's no 'might have' about it. It would simplify things… period! D**n!" Lydia exclaimed in exasperation at this unfortunate turn of events on top of everything else. "That should be at the top of your to-do list. Rikki, I declare, this saga must be one of those character-building tests they say the Good Lord lays on us sometimes to get us ready for bigger and better things. This is a doozie. It wasn't enough to lose your husband so tragically; now you've got to suffer through all this agony," Lydia summarized. I feel so bad for you. I guess we'll just have to play this one out," she concluded.

"Yeah, well, while the insurance is more than enough to replace our totaled SUV, I just might end up homeless with character to spare at this rate…because you know she's going to come after everything she can get her grubby hands on."

"We just have to stay in prayer that everything works out like it should. But in the meanwhile, we need to do something…at least our part. Alright," Lydia announced as much to get herself on board as for her sister. "Do me a favor. Get your settlement papers together and I'll look at them."

"Okay. But one more thing and then I'll leave. It's getting late. I remembered the woman in the waiting room. She was a fair-skinned Black woman. That was probably her…had to be."

"Get a grip. Just because you saw a Black woman in the room with you…"

"No, honestly," she insisted. "I'm telling you it was her because Ms. Z said she was waiting after I left. It was after three when I left, and they close at four. That doesn't leave much time for other appointments or walk-ins, you know. She probably saw me and knew who I was when my name was called." The inflection of her voice indicated she was convinced she was right.

"Hmm…I see your point. That's a big coincidence…or not," Lydia finished thoughtfully.

Erika was silent, and Lydia sighed loudly. "You know I always thought a lot of Braxton; he was one of the few good guys around. And I know he loved you and the twins dearly, but I swear I am really peeved with him right now for leaving you in this…" Lydia's eyes darted around, and she sputtered, searching for the right word.

"Yeah, tell me about it! Sugar, honey, ice, tea!" Erika spit out the words in exasperation.

"Exactly," Lydia accepted. "Just like some reality nightmare from TV. For such a loving man—" Frustration seeped through her words as she made her head shiver in disbelief and her sentence trailed off. "Sorry 'bout that, kiddo."

"It's okay, I understand. I've been having some of those same feelings myself, but I still miss him like crazy. Frankly, it's pretty embarrassing how conflicting my feelings have been. I mean, I've felt pretty upset at him for leaving me alone without any warning at all, with all this mess in my face. But in all fairness to the good and loving man that I remember, how could he possibly know Ms Craziness would materialize out of the woodwork to wreak havoc on his family? And that woman's marriage certificate being like a secret password for her that gives her the upper hand," Erika spoke in wonderment. "Anyway," she announced soberly, "I'll get those papers together and have them ready for whenever you get by. And now, we're out of here."

"Okay. I have a date with Sondra tomorrow, so I'll swing by afterwards, okay? The sooner we check on this, the better."

"I know. Thanks for listening?" Erika stared intently into her sister's face through eyes that shone with an admiration she had not given much thought for a long time, and her voice trembled with emotion. "I know I need to do things on my own, but it's just been so… hard…and I feel…so lost and alone right now. And half the time, I'm not feeling well."

"Hey, you don't have to tell me. When you need someone, all you have to do is call." Lydia slipped an arm of comfort around Erika and held her close. "I still remember how things were when Mama died. I felt as scared and lost as a body could back then, and I still get that lost feeling sometimes even now. I had to do a lot of praying—still do."

Erika stiffened in surprise and looked compassionately at Lydia. "You never told me that. You always seemed so strong and in charge to me."

"Did I really have a choice? No one had a clue about Daddy, so it was just us. But I also had some divine intervention," she said, referring to the surprising amount of her mother's insurance and her getting guardianship of Erika over the objections of the few relatives who came forward but offered no real help at all. "I just tried to do what I knew Mama would've wanted and what I had to do, to keep us together. Now, as you're learning, life has a lot of surprises and we've got to be strong and keep the faith. God only knows how often Mama's been on my mind and how much I've needed her over the years. But I'm not trying to get into all that. So, Rikki, please hear me on this. I understand that you've got a mind-blowing situation on your hands, but with determination and prayer, we'll get through it together—because we're sisters, and that's how we roll." She smiled. "And always remember, as long as I'm around, you're never alone. Understood?"

Erika studied her for a full moment, mildly amused at her comfortable use of the slang 'how we roll'. "I'm sorry, Lydia—understood. I never give you enough credit for all you've done for me," she said, embracing her tightly. "I didn't realize—" *As soon as this madness was over, maybe she and Lydia could get away together for a few days so she could find out more about Lydia's feelings.*

"No problem. That wasn't a complaint. Besides, we're in this together, remember? It's Ms. Silvia we need to be concerned about."

For the past few days, Tamarra had been getting calls from Dorsey morning, noon, and night. At work, it was easier to avoid him because calls were usually screened. But at home, she relied on her voicemail to intercede. And when she played the messages, he'd sound angrier and uglier with each call. He would start out sad and apologetic, pleading for another chance, pouring out his heart about how good they were together. By the end of the last message, he would be close to calling her names. The other night, she had seen him waiting in front of her house, and it sent shivers down her spine. But as frightening as that was, it was his constant barrage of strange calls that unnerved her more. They gave new meaning to that visit, making her considerably more uncomfortable than anything else he had pulled so far.

That evening, she distracted herself by taking advantage of the big sale at a Macy's that was closing down, so she got home later than usual. She made herself comfortable in the kitchen and braced herself to hear Dorsey's latest declarations of love, then his veiled threats. The familiar chill went through her at hearing his cold, angry words. *Why can't he just leave me alone?* she wondered. Did he have to be hit with a two-by- four to get her message? Did he really think this type of behavior was the way back into her life? She turned on the radio feeling depressed with his message implanted in her mind. Except for the music, the house was unusually still. Most of the time, the neighborhood quiet was welcomed, but not tonight. It felt just a little unnerving.

She desperately needed a friendly voice to help drive some of the crazy creepiness away, she thought, turning the radio off to dial her friend's number.

"Hi, Erika. How are you?" she asked, feeling a little awkward.

"Hey, Tamarra." Erika answered, suppressing her surprise at hearing from her again so soon. They hadn't talked since the ride from SITER, and before that, weeks had passed between their phone contacts. "I'm here—for whatever that's worth."

"I didn't disturb you with the kids, did I?" Tamarra wanted to know, offering her a quick out, but glad she didn't take it.

"No. I just put my munchkins to bed." Erika knew her friend well and detected an odd flatness in her voice. "Are things good with you?" You sound strange," she quizzed out of maternal habit. These days she wasn't sure if Tamarra would tell her even if she wasn't alright. Things between them had been strained over the past few months, yet she felt hopeful–whatever the reason for the call.

"Yeah, fine. I just need someone to talk to and want it to be you. I'm feeling a little spooked tonight." She tried to laugh the comment off. "I hope you don't mind. I know you've got your own problems and all, but I've been getting these weird phone calls from Dorsey."

Erika wasn't really up for this, but what could she say? "Sounds serious," she acknowledged.

"Yeah, a little, I guess. Though I tried to tell myself otherwise, that I'm overreacting. It's not working anymore. It's a long story, but Dorsey and I fell out. I thought I saw his car parked outside my house the other night when I came home. And he's been calling every chance he gets, leaving loving and nasty messages on my voicemail. Tonight, he called me everything but a child of God. To say that I'm a little rattled at this point would be an understatement." She laughed nervously.

"That must have been quite a falling out. I mean, what is he so upset about?"

Tamarra knew that for Erika to get a true appreciation for the situation she had created for herself, she would need to come clean with her whole humiliating story. Their conversations and visits since Dorsey came into her life were less frequent and had become more superficial than ever before, except when she picked Erika up from SITER. That was the closest Erika had felt to her in weeks. Every conversation since Braxton's death had seemed strained and had left them more distant than before. Erika's behavior and attitude were understandably sullen, and she always seemed preoccupied and busier than ever with the twins. Tamarra didn't know how to handle that or what she could do to help. She was not good at just being there and doing nothing. They quickly got into the irritating habit of giving each other those quick, one-word answers that didn't take much effort—responses so short, they felt more like a brush-off. Tamarra never fully understood how the loss of Braxton had affected Erika. After all, she, herself, had never lost anyone to death that meant as much to her. She wondered how someone as smart and sensitive as Erika could be so blind to what was happening to their relationship. She felt that Erika's self-indulgent behavior had put more distance between them than all the time she spent with Dorsey ever could. They had not shared real feelings or anything meaningful in weeks, and picking Erika up from SITER that day was the closest they

had managed to get lately. And it had felt good. She could not really say they had yet shared the loss of Erika's husband and her friend, Braxton, but hopefully, they would be able to do better. Yet however reluctant Tamarra felt now, her latest sob story poured forth.

"I ended things and refused his calls," she said after giving Erika her account of what happened. "I gave him every chance to tell me the truth on his own," she began to softly sob. Erika, he just didn't seem to get, that on top of the lying, he had made me feel like a fool. Now, he's not letting up. Girl, he's been wearing my numbers out, both at work and home, day and night, for the past few days that feel like forever. He's the one that lied and screwed things up, not that they were that great anyway, but now, I'm the b-word and everything else he can think of because I found him out," she finished bitterly. "How messed up is that?"

"Um…yeah." Erika would interject quietly to let Tamarra know that she was still listening. *Welcome to my world,* she thought.

"I guess between all the screened calls at work and being forced to leave messages, he worked himself into a real frenzy. But I just don't feel like all the hassle, you know what I mean?" she asked, knowing Erika would understand.

"Fortunately, I can not speak from first-hand experience on your particular situation, but I have an opinion from observing people playing the dating game, including my dear sister. And I do know that some men don't take rejection and being caught in lies very well, regardless of the size. Must be some automatic defense mechanism," she related lightheartedly "…part of what's known as the male ego, I guess."

"Yeah, he's got plenty of that. Every message he leaves sounds more macho and hateful than the one before. Now, is that supposed to be my incentive to take him back?" she questioned rhetorically. "I'm beginning to think the man has a real problem. And, if I chance talking to him—which I don't plan on doing—how do I make someone who behaves like that understand, and go away quietly? He wants to be back together. I don't. Not after that stunt he pulled. So, now he's on the warpath."

"I hear you. I'm not trying to frighten you, but this situation does not sound good at all. Do you think calling might calm him down?" she asked suggestively.

"Call him! Have you heard what I've been telling you? I can't believe you think I should call him. Remember, that's how this whole mess started in the first place. I tried to call him. But you must mean beep him, don't you?" she corrected tersely. "…if that's not a bum number too.

That's the only way I can reach him unless I go over to the dealership, and right now, I'm just not feeling that brave."

"If you paged him, he should recognize the number."

"Yeah, that's for sure," she agreed, feeling as if this was the old Erika talking instead of the stranger who had briefly stolen her away. She had become totally at ease telling her everything and was relieved for a chance to let it all out. "But I think it's already too late for that. You should've heard him. He's really beginning to sound sick. And I must admit, when I got home and saw that dark car parked down the street from my door, looking like a big, black attack dog waiting in the rain… I tried to be cool and play it off, but I almost s**t myself. Excuse my French."

"I can only imagine," Erika said almost to herself.

"Of course he didn't say a word to me. He didn't have to, but being there like that just spooked the red balls of fury out of me. Girl, I was no good…you hear me? Now I'm fidgeting around like a paranoid idiot, jumping at every little sound I hear and some I don't. I don't know what I've gotten myself into this time."

Tiny shivers prickled over Erika's body at the reaction Tamarra described. Unsure how strong the relationship with this guy had become, she was more than a little shaken by what she heard. She knew less about this man than any of Tamarra's previous men-friends and had been thankful that she had the good grace to keep this one under wraps while she worked the kinks out of their relationship. But now that things had turned ugly, she wished she knew more and could offer better insight.

No matter how much Tamarra's male friends sparkled in the beginning, it seemed the dark side always materialized, to overshadow all good that ever existed about them, and the tarnish was always revealed in pretty short order. Only her husband Avory had lasted longer, but not by much.

"Oh yes you do," Erika corrected. "You know exactly why your alarm has been triggered, because you are really a lot smarter than you've been acting or least I hope you are." She rattled on rapidly in a voice edged with built-up unacknowledged and unvented frustration toward Tamarra over their strained relationship over the past several months. "You think you know all about Black men because you've been fooling with them for so long. But I've told you more than once that they don't turn loose as easily as a White guy might. Now, don't quote me on that one because I've never dated a White guy. But don't you listen to the news? These men out here today can be a little crazy depending on how you allow the relationship to develop. Considering what some of the guys you've come across have been into, you've been extremely lucky so far."

"D**n, Erika. I thought you weren't trying to frighten me! My problem with Dorsey is not because he's Black—it's because he's crazy." The conversation had taken a wrong turn and suddenly was not giving Tamarra the warm, reassuring fuzzies she had hoped for.

"Look...sorry, I'm not. Really, I'm not. It's just that this guy sounds scary to me, and I don't think you fully realize how stupid some of them are when they are not ready to let go. And once they know you've wimped out, they often seem to get emboldened, like a shark smelling human blood. Don't you listen to the news? Remember that young girl whose boyfriend shot her while she was sleeping on the sofa...and they were just teenagers!" Amazement filled her voice. "They have to do something awfully bad to let you cut them off with no problem, and getting caught in a lie doesn't usually count because that's no big deal to them, even if they don't really want you anymore."

Wow, Tamarra thought. The turn in their conversation had taken both her breath and energy away. "For one thing, I haven't been seeing the guy long enough to justify him acting like a lunatic with me, even if he is one. And two, let's just change the subject because you're not helping the situation or making me feel better at all, Erika."

A few silent seconds passed while Erika wondered if she had said too much. *What the hell,* she reasoned. It wasn't pretty, but those words had needed saying for a long time, and since they were supposed to be friends, she was the one who had to say it. Tamarra had called her and wanted desperately to share. She didn't ask to hear all her business. "Yeah, okay, but that won't solve your problem," she reminded gently.

Neither will scaring me to death, Tamarra thought silently. *And batting it back and forth between us like this doesn't help.* The sympathetic ear and moral support she had always counted on so readily and unconditionally from Erika was turning into something closer to a good, old-fashioned scolding tonight. Their friendship had always had the privilege of expressing their feelings and opinions straight and upfront. And though Tamarra knew Erika had openly admired her comfort and *ease-osey* with people of color, even hinting she might be cutting herself short by dating only Black men— the type she seemed attracted to—Erika had never shared such strong feelings about Tamarra's choice in men.

"Okay. I know we haven't been as close lately, and I'm sorry about that. I should've done better. So, thanks for the ear." Her words strained under disappointment. "Before I go, how are the twins? Are they doing alright?"

Erika immediately thought about Brandon. And she didn't need to mention that they missed their Daddy. There was no question about that. She took the abrupt switch for what it was—a change in subject. "They're managing, for the most part." She kept to herself what she ordinarily would have shared about Brandon. "But they still ask about their Daddy sometimes when we do something that Braxton used to do with them. But all in all, they seem to be hanging tough," she offered.

"I'm glad to hear that. I kind of miss the little buggers," she said softly. "But it's getting late. Maybe I'll talk with you sometime over the weekend."

"Tamarra, wait. I'm sorry. I hope you know that I don't mean to scare you. I'm just worried about you. You're still my best girl," she volunteered, sensing immediately that Tamarra was stunned to hear her say that. *And, I don't want to read 'bout you in the Post's Metro section one day,* she finished to herself. "Please don't be mad at me for caring. How about having dinner with me and the twins tomorrow? I won't tell them you're coming so they'll be surprised. Maybe you'll help my appetite," she offered, sincere in her apology.

Tamarra managed a chuckle, but the letdown was still detectable when she spoke. "Girl, you sure make that offer hard to pass on. I'll have to call you tomorrow and let you know for sure."

The quiet returned the instant Tamarra hung up the phone, challenged only by the louder-than-usual dragging grind from the wall clock. Her friend's words had left Tamarra even more unnerved than she was before, and now she really heard the silence. In a few swift moves, both the radio and TV were playing while she opened a wine cooler, wishing she had something stronger, like rum or vodka.

A song by a new female group boomed over the radio and the voice on the TV promised 'details at eleven' of the day's dose of unprovoked violence and more senseless deaths of innocent bystanders in yet another drive-by shooting of inner-city Black youths. She muted the TV, leaving the picture on, and blasted the radio while she anxiously gulped from the bottle she held. She listened and got caught up in the rhythmic beat of the song and even nervously sang along, out of tune. The buzz she hoped would dull her senses was not there yet. The phone rang, and she froze in-step. The thought of Dorsey popped instantly into her head. She snatched up her phone with the intention of talking with him this time, like Erika had suggested, before she lost her nerve.

"Hello?"

"Tamarra. Uhh, it's Jaite." He sounded surprised that she picked up. "I was prepared to leave a message."

"Now you don't have to, unless you want me to hang up so you can call back and leave one," she teased, and he seemed to get the humor.

"No, this is good. Did I interrupt something?"

"Not really, just unwinding a little. Sometimes it's harder than others." She eased onto the stool facing the silent TV and sipped her drink. This is a surprise, trying to recall when he could have gotten her number. "What's up?"

"Look, I know we don't really know each other that well, and I hope I'm not being too forward and all that other stuff…but a buddy of mine is having a small thing Saturday. He suggested that I bring someone, and I thought about you."

"Oh, I see," she answered haltingly. "Are you asking me out?" she asked, surprised. "Like on a date?"

"No. I wouldn't call it that. I mean…we're neighbors, both single, on friendly terms, so—" He left the statement hanging but waited expectantly.

"And this wouldn't be a date?" she countered.

"No, not unless you want it to be. It's just a little gathering. And I thought it might be a fun thing to do for a few hours if you're not busy. Can you make it?"

"I don't know. Sounds like the same thing to me."

"It doesn't have to be, but we can call it whatever you're more comfortable with. Listen, you just came to mind when I thought about asking someone." His tone turned slow and emphatic now. "And yes, I also thought this could be a chance for us to get better acquainted." He was yelling over the noise from the radio in the background. "As friends, of course, because I don't want my asking to become a problem," he concluded with a slight hesitation. "Sounds like you're having a party of your own."

"I guess the radio is a little loud," she said aloud, pushing the volume way down. Her gut reaction was to say no quick, fast, and in a hurry—just nip whatever this was in the proverbial bud.

"So, tell me more about this small thing," she found herself saying.

"As I said, it'll be small and casual with some friends and their guests…a few of them from work. If you're worried about the people, don't. I'll be right there with you the whole time. My friend does a thing at his place a few times a year." He neglected to mention that he always went alone, and his friend had noticed and insisted that he bring a date this time. "There's dancing, drinking, munchies, and card games. And if you become the least bit uncomfortable, we leave right away."

It definitely sounded like a date to her, but she let it go and played along. "So, what time does this small, casual thing start?"

"Around eight. So, what do you think?"

That's an odd time to start partying, kind of early, she thought. "Do you need an answer right away?" She sipped more from her drink, feeling a bit sexy now leaning against the counter. "Maybe we can talk in a day or two."

Jaite laughed, feeling encouraged. "Okay, I see. You want to sleep on it or consult your busy calendar. I can understand that." He was sounding more upbeat now. "Sounds good, and thanks for not blowing me off." His voice softened with gratitude.

"Well, thanks for the invitation," she replied graciously, yet feeling skeptical about the date. "If it's okay, I'll let you know by Friday," she offered, knowing she was purposely putting him off. "I need to check something first." She could just as easily have given him an answer then and mentally chastised herself for even giving him any sort of explanation. She mainly wanted to see how this whole Dorsey situation played out first over the next few days.

"Great. I'll wait to hear something soon—or I'll be in touch with you myself."

"That works for me." She chuckled at the use of an expression she picked up from Lydia. "Goodnight."

What was she doing! Her mind screamed when she hung up. She told herself that Jaite seemed sane enough, but didn't they all at first? She had to admit that he certainly passed the test in the looks department, but she didn't want him getting any ideas. His timing couldn't be any worse, and she would make a note to find out how he had even gotten her phone number. Yet, his interest surprised her, especially since he must have seen Dorsey all over her the other night. Unless he hadn't noticed the guy sitting in the double-parked car, whom she had almost fallen over him getting to, was Black. But then, why should she care anyway. Besides, being Black wasn't the problem she had with Dorsey. She shuddered at the apprehension that crept over her, warning that it would be wiser to decline an invitation from any man for a while.

She did not know if the drink was affecting her at last or what, but she began to reminisce about Dorsey in happier days. Like the nights she perched on a barstool at the Tijuana Room, or the Club, as he called it, enjoying the music while he plied her with complimentary cocktails and finger food. She had even struck up an acquaintance with other female regulars, and they had some great girl-talk sessions. On more than one occasion, the effects of the drinks and rich conversation had left her so uninhibited and sexually stimulated that she had waited for his shift to end and invited him home with her, where one thing had raunchily led to another.

Though Tamarra craved the closeness and felt the occasional need for intimacy, she readily admitted that after the first ho-hum encounter, the wild thing with him was less about pleasure and more about scratching an itch—what she commonly called getting the monkey off her back. She had hoped it might get better with time, but so far only marginal because of either rushed or flat-out poor repeat performances each time. Tamarra was convinced that too much alcohol must be a major factor, but Dorsey swore that he did not drink while working. And while she had never saw him drinking while working, he seemed always on a high, or a bit hyper.

Other than appearing completely taken with her, his only saving grace was how he would work on her breast as if that was his favorite sport. She felt the man was a bona fide pro at that. His mouth would open enough to cover a small portion of her ample breast, so she could feel the heat inside, just before his tongue darted circles and teased repeatedly in an even, rhythmic motion. Then his front teeth would bite ever so gently at her taut, wet nipple, and that monkey that was undoubtedly already there would start its slow and steady climb. The first hot, moist touch of his tongue always sent shivers clear to the middle of her intimate area. Yes, he was a master at that. She sighed aloud at the thought. Then she quickly put that out of her mind and drained the last drops from the cooler bottle.

That's where Dorsey's talents had sadly ended, and that was a major strike against him. She had learned that his power was packed in that single wallop. While he was a strong starter, working well outside with the breaststrokes, he had a weak finish and crucial deficiency on follow-through. He also had a tendency toward premature equipment failure while working with the ball on the inside, forcing her to the finish line, barely so much so, that she was surprised to even get there. But, being an understanding woman, she had not held that against him, then.

Now, the thought of him evoked fear. Between the unnecessary lying, his stalking, and nasty phone calls, she felt like she had entered a twisted version of a horror movie. She headed toward the stairs but, unable to resist, peeked out the window. The saliva caught in her throat, and she gasped immediately at the sight of that black car parked back on the street, and she was pissed.

She released her tight grip on the curtain, wondering who she could call. She didn't want it to be Erika this time, but then, who else? She rushed through the kitchen to check the rear door and bumped her shoulder hard enough to bruise it. Was she overreacting and just being paranoid again? Secure in her safety for the moment, she sat on the first step of the stairs. Maybe Erika was right. After all she had been through with all these men, she still didn't know anything. Everything was badly out of hand. Several months ago, she thought she was living a good life. There was no man, but Braxton was alive and well, and she and Erika were as thick as thieves. Now he was gone, her friend was a mess, their friendship was strained, and one flirt too many had landed her a possible psychopath. After so much rehashing about how the past weeks with Dorsey had led her to that moment, it was depressing to pull her burdened body from the step for the short climb up, but she made it and two decisions came with her. She needed to take some "alone time" and, going forward, a new way to do things differently. It was long overdue. For starters, she would accept Dorsey's next call so they could talk, and he could get whatever he wanted so badly to say over with. The dinner date with Erika and the twins would be a good idea for them all.

8

Erika lay sprawled spread-eagle on her back sideways across the king-size bed, the cover kicked away—an unusual sleeping position for her. Even in deep slumber, expressions of fear and sadness claimed her soft, youthful features, causing frowning, flexing of her nostrils, and a twitching mouth. Creases flickered across her forehead as her head moved fretfully from side to side, as if avoiding some unseen annoyance. A slight tremble in her cheek stirred just beyond the corner of her slack, sagging mouth. Her mind grappled within the delicate confines of the semiconscious dream state, while something stronger tugged at her less than conscious mind. Whatever it was, it gently but firmly urged her awake.

Her eyes popped open like a jack-in-the-box, and in the midst of the silent darkness came one clear, sobering thought: something had to be done about Silvia. A matter as sensitive and important as this certainly could not be trusted entirely to SITER. So far, where had that gotten her? She rolled to Braxton's side of the bed, hugging his pillow tightly against her stomach, wishing with all of her being that it was him. Thoughts of him filled her mind. Indeed, picturing him with someone other than herself was a stretch, to say the least, but with this Silvia person, it was impossible. The woman she remembered, while attractive, hardly seemed his type. With a marriage certificate as proof, she supposed it was reasonable to accept their marriage as likely, but believing her own marriage invalid and Braxton a bigamist was a step she just was not willing to take.

The woman in the SITER waiting room had certainly seemed older than Braxton. Even beyond that, as hard as she tried to imagine them together in her mind, they didn't fit—it was no surprise to her that their union was so short. At mournful times like this, she could not suppress memories of their happy marriage, and the caring mate Braxton had been. He was a quiet sort of guy with a great sense of humor, always finding ways to have her laughing at something. Erika remembered his profound joy at becoming a father for the first time after passing forty, and how he had gloated over their twins. Herein was her most treasured loss—a devoted and loving father for her children.

Her stomach flipped and churned, and she groaned deeply, clutching the pillow as tight as she could. The pain persisted with a pressure that extended to her bowels, quickly forcing her to the bathroom. A captive on the commode, Erika vacillated between uncontrollable spurts of diarrhea and strong waves of nausea until she was spent. Somewhat relieved, she visited the kid's bathroom and drained the remains of the *Pepto Bismol* she hated and checked on the twins as she always did on nights like this. Then, she dragged her drained body back into her room and flopped onto the bed. She tried to lull her body into relaxation by stretching, flexing, and allowing her thoughts to drift freely. Slowly, her mind rolled back until pictures formed, resurfacing an almost forgotten time in her life.

More than twenty years before, the sunny afternoon held the bitter essence of a January freeze that forced Erika to run the few blocks from her junior high school to the waiting warmth of their small, well-kept row house. Their Linc-Kenn Dwelling neighborhood was part of what was known as the Anacostia City-Vest Development Program that provided decent, subsidized housing for struggling single, working heads of households, like her mama.

She was surprised to see her mother's old car parked haphazardly outside. It was angled crookedly with the front passengers' tires pressed against the curb and the rear driver's side jutting out too far. Mildly panicked, Erika could not get into the house fast enough since her mother, as a head clerk at the main post office, never got off early. In fact, she worked overtime nearly every evening to keep the household flowing smoothly.

Inside, her mother's coat was tossed carelessly on the floor and her purse rested a few feet away. Now Erika felt something must be terribly wrong. Her long, lanky thirteen-year-old legs took the squeaky wooden stairs two at a time, and she yelled out frantically for her mother. A muffled cry from the bathroom stopped her, fright rising at what she might find. Trembling, Erika stepped into the doorway and caught sight of the disheveled woman nearly unconscious. There was blood, but she couldn't tell where it came from. "Oh, Mama, what happened? Where are you hurt?" she screamed, scrambling to her mother's side and attempting to lift her.

"No, baby, no," her mother whispered, pushing Erika away and clutching her stomach. "Call an ambulance… quick," she stammered in a cracked whisper between tears before the pain cut her off. She whimpered, pleading for her child to hurry. Erika hesitated for only a moment, staring into her mother's tear-stained face, before something prompted her into action like a shot from a cannon.

The emergency call was made, but Erika remembered being scared silly as she pulled a small blanket from her mother's bed, draped it over her, and pulled her limp body into her trembling arms. Fear gripped at her heart, unable to take her eyes away from the semi-conscious figure sprawled on the cold tile floor in a bloody mess.

She sobbed, calling out repeatedly. "Mama, can you hear me? It's me, Erika. The ambulance is on the way. Can you open your eyes, Mama? Please be alright!" The ambulance seemed to take forever, and Erika wanted to believe that if she just kept rocking her mother gently and talking to her, everything might somehow be alright. And, of course, praying never hurt either.

When the paramedics finally reached upstairs, they carefully lifted her mother with care. There had been more blood on the floor than a body could afford to lose, and even young Erika knew that was not good. *Oh God*, she cried silently. *What could be wrong with Mama*, she asked herself. She longed for Lydia to be there to tell her what to do, shaken to the core and worried out of her mind, but she knew Lydia wouldn't be home from the city college until much later. The responsibility to stay with their unconscious mother fell to her. She held her mother's cold hand as the ambulance sped toward the nearest hospital, likely the one in Southern Maryland. Erika remembered watching her mother's closed eyes and her peaceful, still expression as they wheeled the stretcher away, never realizing that someone as dark as her mom could turn chalky.

Lydia arrived at the hospital hours later in their mother's car, tears unshed in her eyes, and pulled Erika tightly into her arms. Erika couldn't shed much light on what happened to their mother, only how she had found her. They waited together for what was eventually the bad news. Emergency surgery had been necessary, but they lost her anyway. Alicia Riley was forty-one years old and had for many years since Erika's birth, suffered severely with fibroid tumors. Several large tumors had suddenly ruptured, causing a fatal hemorrhage. And they had no idea how long she was probably lying there unattended. If they had reached her a little sooner, she might have had a fighting chance. But she had lost consciousness and a massive amount of blood and slipped deeply into shock.

The sisters were alone now, and Lydia was all Erika had. Her mother's occasional male friend came to the hospital and acted appropriately surprised and hurt. He offered his condolences and what little assistance he could and hung around until the funeral was over. For several more weeks he showed up on the pretense of supporting the girls, but once it was clear that Lydia had no interest in his unwanted, not-so-subtle advances—and would not pick up with him where their mother had left off…he vanished.

Erika and Lydia prayed that their estranged father might somehow hear the news and show up, though they had moved since he left. No one knew his whereabouts, and no one had heard from him in more than eight years. They waited and hoped as the months turned into years that he might surprise them, wondering if he might already be dead himself.

Though a few maternal relatives strewn throughout the city, all unwilling to offer any assistance themselves, recommended turning to the child welfare agency. Lydia refused to lose Erika to the District's foster care system. She was legally an adult, and so it would be her and Erika.

Lydia dropped her evening classes and, because she had always been attracted to fashion, took a part-time job at the Hollingsworth department store, in addition to her full-time clerk-typist job with the Federal government. She became everything for Erika—guardian, sister, and friend—teaching, supporting, and shielding her younger sister as best as she could from life's hurt and pain. She even tried to somehow make up for their parents' absence. It was an enormous responsibility for a young woman just a few years out of high school, but she was determined to make it work. Besides, what choice did she really have? Her sister was all she had.

Their mother's life insurance wasn't a fortune, but it was more than adequate to pay off all the funeral and personal bills. Then, there was enough left—thank God—for a decent car, to finance a move to a deluxe apartment complex in the Jaxson-Mason area in time for Erika to start high school and put a little in an emergency fund. All of this had made the sisters' transition into their new life a little easier.

As a teen, Erika was studious and slow to take interest in boys. She seemed content with her solitary pursuits and simply happy to be included in most of Lydia's outings with her friends. In those days, Lydia had lots of girlfriends and little interest in having a steady boyfriend. She'd occasionally accept a movie date with the understanding that Erika would accompany them—that is, until Aaron entered her life the year Erika was a senior in high school. He was different than the other guys and made a favorable impression on them both.

At some point, Erika drifted off. Several hours later seemed only minutes ago when the noisy buzz of the alarm clock yanked her awake. She still lay clutching the pillow when she crawled to her side of the bed and, out of habit, blindly slapped at the clock before flopping wearily back onto the bed. She dozed some more. Only when the alarm blasted again did she lift herself enough to see the dim early morning light, groaning the whole time. The time was quite blurred in her eyes, but she knew it was time to rise.

To Erika, working a full day after yet another sleepless night and feeling completely wiped out like she'd been running instead of resting was hardly the wisest choice. Still, she knew she'd have to force herself into action today. The stomach pains had lessened considerably, which helped, though not enough to drag herself to the office. She sat quietly on the bed, and as if out of nowhere, a plan began to take shape.

She would call Tamarra to make sure she was coming to dinner. Erika missed their friendship, especially now with Braxton gone. She needed some girl talk about silly, mundane things instead of all this heavy seriousness that had weighed them down lately. She had been more upset than she realized. Although she wanted to be understanding and supportive, Tamarra's poorly timed abandonment had left Erika an unrealized disappointment.

Spending some quality time together would do them both a world of good—to reconnect and reaffirm their bond. Feeling inspired, she forced her eyes open and saw that it was already six o'clock. Tamarra should be awake now.

Tamarra was still in bed like she had nowhere to go. She even thought about letting the phone ring through to voicemail. With her luck, it might be Dorsey. Still, she had decided to talk with him the next time he called, despite not feeling ready for that this early. He had been her last thought last night and her first this morning. She chastised the caller under her breath before picking up the phone. Who in their right mind would be calling at this hour anyway? She could believe it was Dorsey calling because she was convinced, he wasn't quite rational, at least not lately.

"Whoever it is, it had better be good," she grumbled, grabbing the phone before voicemail took over. Her husky tone was sharp when she answered. "Hey!" she said simply.

"Good morning. You awake?" Erika questioned, surprised, it sounded like she wasn't. "You're not up yet?"

"Yeah, morning. Not quite. What's up so early?"

Now Erika second-guessed herself if calling so early had been a mistake. After the way she'd spoken to Tamarra last night, she probably felt this was awfully nervy of her.

"I was sure you'd be up by now. I wanted to catch you before you left," she explained. "Sorry to wake you. I know you were spooked last night."

Tamarra grunted softly. "You certainly did wake me. So, you *do* know what time it is?" she asked, propping herself on one elbow to check the clock.

"I do. And I hope you're not still upset with me about last night? In my own tactless way, I meant well, really."

"No. Enough about last night. It's okay, really," Tamarra lied, and after allowing a few awkward seconds of silence, she conceded, "Well, maybe I do feel a little beat up on, but I'll get over it." *But, it's better from you than anybody else I know,* she thought. "Is that why you're up and calling me with the chickens?"

"Well, yes and no. I called to get a firm commitment about dinner today because we're looking forward to seeing you. But while I have you on the phone, I wanted to check that everything is still good between us, too. And I feel like it is, right? You *are* coming to dinner? Erika hoped she wasn't being too pushy.

"I am—as long as we don't talk about Dorsey. I'd like to enjoy the evening, thank you very much," she admonished, her tone lower to take the sting out of her words.

"Message received. Can you come over a little early and hang out with me before I pick the twins up from Nana's?"

"I can't leave work early today, so girlfriend, you'll have to see me after you get the kids."

Erika was thrilled at her acceptance. "Since you get off so early, I'll just wait until you get here and we'll go together. Don't dilly-dally."

"Fine, but now I need to get ready. I'll be late as hell as it is, laying here like it's the weekend."

Erika suppressed a squeal. "Thanks, Tamarra. The kids will love it." She felt excited about something for the first time since her world fell apart.

The official happy hour at the Palisades Socio Dinner Club was already in full swing when Lydia and Sondra walked in. The popular new nightspot sat in the redeveloped downtown Federal Southwest district of Washington, D.C. The patrons were mostly career-oriented thirty-, forty-, and fifty-something working class employees and 'hot shots', from the nearby agencies and private contractors. The scuttlebutt on the Palisade was that they had just about anything on the menu, from delectable Southern cooking to reasonably priced, excellent seafood and other delicious selections in between. From six to eight, drinks were half price while the deejay spun one of the best mix of oldies and hip-hop to a crowd impatiently waiting for the dance floor to open. Tonight, the kind of music that most patrons appreciated— hand-dancing and swinging—was the specialty.

Sondra started with a Perrier then switched to Moscato, a tastier drink with more zip. Lydia was on her second Asti-Spumante, her mind already contemplating a third. As soon as they finished their seafood dinner, Sondra slid a large department store box onto Lydia's lap. She suppressed a scream of surprised delight when she opened the gift. She loved the deep fuchsia color and tested the softness of the cashmere garment against her check. The tunic length was perfect for her height. She peaked at the label and smiled with pleasure when she saw *Ellen Tracy,* size L, meaning it would fit a little oversized just the way she liked.

She looked directly at Sondra. "Thank you so much. It's beautiful. I love it. I don't see much ET around anymore. I absolutely love it and you too. You've got such wonderful taste. I almost want to pay you for this, give you a kiss, or something."

Sondra sipped her wine, amused at Lydia as she waved off her remarks. "No, you don't. And close your mouth. You should see your face right now. That's good stuff, but sometimes the staff makes out like bandits between the employee discounts and the sales," she reminded.

"You think," Lydia teased, leaning in for a thank-you hug, although she knew that her reaction and obvious pleasure was all the reward Sondra needed. She carefully repackaged the gift. "Simply gorgeous," she marveled. "Just find me some black suede slim pants and I'm good to go," she added playfully, thinking about her birthday gift and hoping her words didn't sound too much like the hint that it was meant to be.

"Now, how was your birthday? I know something happened." Her tone was tinged with curiosity. "I get the impression there was some drama."

In her relaxed, rather lightheaded state, Lydia seemed to take great pleasure in replaying her exhilarating encounter with Ashton and how she'd left things. "Didn't happen is more like it. But in retrospect, Friday was more like a mental health day for me. I got a chance to blow off a little steam and get a few things off my chest. I'm trying to get my head on straight." She made it fairly clear she wasn't up to going into every detail.

"So, definitely trouble in paradise, huh?" Sondra smiled, hoping Lydia wouldn't take her sarcasm too seriously. "So, does this mean he's really out of the picture?"

"I'm not completely sure what it means. What I can say is that I'm so tired of wasting myself on someone else's man. Then again, I kind of miss him, if you get what I mean. I probably need a good shrink to really explain why. I just don't know for sure, Sondra," she said in mild anguish, as if she really didn't know.

Sondra recognized it so soulfully, and she recounted her experience some years back. She'd been there once, when she was involved with a married man, but she concluded proudly that her sole pleasure in life now was as Miss Style Personified. At forty-five, she was considered by her few friends and many colleagues a woman of unadulterated class with her astonishingly fashionable wardrobe and astute manner. In recent years, she had avidly practiced abstinence and vowed to continue as long as she had other means of gratification. That was a subject that was never up for discussion. If she at some point was blessed with that special someone, great; if not, she did not feel pressed. Working hard and dressing exquisitely had become a central point of her lifestyle. And of course, she enjoyed friends like Lydia. Men were welcomed to admire and look but not touch, unless someone amazing came along.

She was flattered that Lydia would confide so openly about her personal life, though she didn't have much to share about hers. It saddened her to see her friend struggle with the merits of a married man's affection. She was happy to share her experiences, give advice, make suggestions, or give whatever information she could offer to give a different perspective of Lydia's situation.

"Sometimes, it isn't the man himself that we get attached to but the thrill, or habit, of having a mate. And we have trouble turning that ideal loose," Sondra offered knowingly, sounding like the voice of hard-earned experience. "Lydia, I have to mention this, and it may sound odd, but I could swear I saw him in my store a few weeks ago when I happened into the women's department."

Lydia's eyes urged Sondra on.

"He caught me looking at him, and subtlety put some distance between us. When he moved the other way, I wondered if he might recognize me, because most men usually start flirting when they catch me watching them," she added looking coy. "I've only seen him briefly a few times, but he does leave an impression, so I'm pretty sure it was him. He seemed aware of my looking his way and I kept my eye on him too, but he acted like he didn't recognize me. He was hoping I would disappear, I guess. I could give him the benefit of the doubt and say that maybe he felt like I looked familiar and couldn't figure out why."

"Not as strange as you think," Lydia looked thoughtful. "In the women's department…that means he wasn't alone, right?"

Sondra smiled coyly, looking glad she had asked. "Right, I don't think so," she answered, remembering that he held a young woman's coat while she browsed. "He hovered around this woman, more like a young girl the entire time, like as much as he wanted to, he didn't dare move too far away. You know…walking around with his hands in his pockets, checking things out, like he was trying to keep a safe distance away."

"Yeah…sounds just like him. That description fits perfectly. He was probably with his wife—Miss Benette," Lydia enlightened her for the first time.

"I don't know about that. I didn't get the body language of a married couple. I think a wife would come across much different than this woman. I'm surprised the man still has a wife with all his catting around. She's probably one of those faithful-to-the-bone women. No offense to you." Sondra smiled ruefully. "And, she still doesn't have a clue?"

"Well, he thinks he's pretty smooth with it, but I really don't get into all that with him. But it's just as well because things aren't right between us and my thrill is about gone. I don't think what I go through with him is worth what I get. After all this time, he still hasn't changed a bit. I don't know if he's just spoiled or plain selfish."

"Probably both and see…those are the operative words you just spoke," Sondra explained. "Is the thrill about gone or is it definitely gone? Because you can't change them, honey, so the thrill will need to be plain gone. And hopefully you'll realize that sooner rather than later."

"But am I wrong to think he might grow just a little somewhere down the line, even if by accident? He's still doing that same old tired, juvenile stuff."

"Please, nothing personal, but the man is still with someone else after all. He sounds like your typical married slob to me. Like I said, I had one of those once. He was inconsiderate most of the time too. What can you do? It's the classic issue of like it or lump it. After getting tired of being kicked around, let's just say, I decided on the latter." She finished with an undeniable note of pride.

"I'm working on it. So, what was the girl like?" Lydia switched the subject back. "I mean– well…you get my meaning."

"Was she good-looking?" Sondra finished.

"Well, not exactly. I mean, did she seem his type, you know? But you can tell me that too. I can't imagine that she wasn't. I mean, look at me," she added humorously striking a cutesy pose. "I have never wanted to admit it, but deep down, there were times when I wondered what Benette had, other than that legal leash, that kept him so close, but not at home."

"I didn't pay her much attention. I was too busy keeping up with his movements and trying to figure him out. From what I saw—no I wouldn't say she was. I mean, there was nothing striking about her like there is about you. Look at you sitting over there, dressed like a model, looking great as usual. The sister's hair was in a young-ish marcelled style, and her leather dress was too short and too tight. More hooker like if you ask me—which you did. Take my word for it: she'd need a complete makeover to be as fly as you. Then again, I guess it depends on what tickles your fancy and there's no accounting for bad taste."

"So, you didn't pay much attention, huh?" Lydia shook her head and gave Sondra the wryest of smiles.

When their date was over, Lydia wasn't sure if the drinks made her feel better or hearing about Ashton made her feel worse, but she did not mistake the light buzz she had. Even driving carefully, it took her all of twenty minutes to reach her sister's house. When Lydia arrived, Erika and Tamarra had finished the dinner dishes, the twins were in bed, and the two friends were deep in conversation.

Lydia came in carrying the box Sondra gave her, fully intending to show off her gift. She and Erika went into the large kitchen, where music played softly. "Hey, girl," she spoke happily, surprised to see Tamarra. "I haven't seen much of you lately. How are you?"

"I'm surviving." Tamarra embraced her, casually returning the affectionate greeting. Lydia found the response strange since Erika was the one with the mess going on. She checked out the open coolers. This whole scene told her that something was up, knowing Erika was not much of a drinker at all, especially during the week.

"Excuse my timing, but I've had a few, and I'm going down slow. I can't stay long," she announced, feeling a bit mellow and spurred on by the music. She faced Erika. "So, let's rock and roll, get this show on the road." She clapped her hands and snapped her fingers to what sounded like the upbeat Cee-Lo tune, "Crazy" that Erika liked so much. "So, I can get my behind home."

"Did we have a good time this evening or what?" Erika joked, observing Lydia's behavior.

"Yeah, it was nice. Sondra's a real blast. I needed that."

The papers she wanted lay on the island counter. Lydia excused herself and imposed her own solitude and became engrossed in the legal jargon. She couldn't help but hear a hushed conversation about some guy, and glancing to see Erika staring with genuine concern into Tamarra's bright blue eyes. Her sister was speaking in her no nonsense voice.

"Like I said, you can stay with us if you want to get away for a few days. You know there's enough room, and you're more than welcome."

"I know. Thanks."

A fearful part of Tamarra wanted to accept Erika's kind-hearted generosity on the spot, but the guilty part resisted and won out. She had deep buyer's remorse about the time she'd given Dorsey—time that she could've spent supporting Erika and the kids, simply being present like Erika was now for her. From the look of things, Erika was clearly still distraught, still struggling to deal with her grief. Tammara hated that she'd been of so little comfort. She didn't know the full details on the Silvia situation—Erika didn't talk much about it—but she intended to be there whenever she was ready.

"So, what do you plan to do about this new admirer?" Erika asked, referring to Tamarra's neighbor. "Because it doesn't matter which door he comes through, he's still asking for a date from where I sit. You see that, right?"

Tamarra had second-guessed telling Erika about Jaite, but she seriously needed some advice because she was still not sure of what she was doing. "Unless we call it something else…because I don't even want to go there right now," she offered playfully, using Jaite's words, while she watched Erika's eyes glaze over in a mocked exasperation. "So, should I? What's your take on this? I promised him an answer." She wondered if she were to give him an inch, would he take try to take a mile—and keep going?

"I know you're not asking me," Erika said, disbelief in her tone. "Since when do you need anyone to tell you what to do when it comes to a White guy?" she feigned a laugh. "You usually don't give them the time of day."

"But this is my neighbor we're talking about. He seems like a nice guy, polite and cute, I should add. He's got that rugged facial-hair-that's-not-quite-a-beard thing going on. Besides, for some reason, I just don't want to hurt his feelings, okay? So…?"

Erika shrugged her shoulders. "I don't know. If you're that worried about your nice, polite, cute neighbor's feelings, then go for it. Just set him straight up front. Tell him, it's a one-time, no hanky-panky date, as friends. Yes, I said date. But you didn't hear that from me." She grinned.

Lydia held up her hand and stuck her forefinger to get Erika's attention. "Excuse me, please," she cut in, pointing to a clause on the paperwork. "Rikki, check this out. It says right here: 'Braxton Marselle and Erika A. Marselle, tenants in entirety,' which means the two of you own the property jointly, and if one owner passes—like Braxton, the surviving partner inherits. In this case, Erika A. Marselle. You. She can't touch it." Lydia' words came out emphatically. "She cannot legally touch it!"

Lydia moved her knee from the seat of the stool and allowed her behind to drop onto it for emphasis. "You and Braxton purchased in both names, basically as partners, which means when one dies, their share automatically reverts fully to the remaining partner. There. Settled!"

Erika squeezed Lydia's arm in relieved gratitude. It was the best news she'd heard since before Braxton passed. Today felt good, starting with her call to Tamarra. She smiled warmly at her sister, remembering how Lydia always stood by her since their mother's death. And she felt a pang of sadness thinking of Lydia's longing for a mother's comforting love so often herself.

"Thanks, Sis. Can I get you anything?" Erika finally offered.

"Nope. I'm out of here," Lydia answered. "I don't need another thing except maybe a chauffeur and my bed," she said, gathering her stuff. "Oh, look at this, from Sondra." She pulled the beauty from its box, posing with the garment held against her body for full appreciation in all its splendor. "She's a buyer for Saks," she explained for Tamarra's sake.

"Does she give gifts like that to all of her friends?" Tamarra asked, stroking the sweater's softness. "This is drop-dead gorgeous. I sure could use a friend like this."

Ignoring her remark, Erika faintly gasped as her fingers brushed the fabric. "Lydia, this is so soft. It feels like cashmere."

"Correction—it is cashmere," she whispered back happily, reclaiming her treasure. As she prepared to leave, she turned to Tamarra. "Is everything okay with you? I couldn't help but overhear you talking."

"I'm fine. Just trying to decide about something. Little Mother's keeping me straight though." Tamarra smiled weakly in Erika's direction. "Hey, but isn't that the story of my life? One of these days, I'm going to learn, I swear," she advised, gathering up her things too. "Look, girlfriend," she said, hugging Erika, "thanks for everything. I loved every minute of it, but I need to leave with your sister. I don't know about you, but I'll be working tomorrow."

They exchanged parting embraces all around. Then, Lydia rushed out the door, leaving Tamarra to linger a few seconds longer.

"If I go out with Jaite, is your offer good for Saturday night?"

"You know it is. So, you've decided to go?"

"I think so." Her mind flitted briefly to Dorsey but pushed him out. "You talked me into it," she joked, moving toward the door.

Erika smiled. "Well, see you Saturday night then. Be careful."

When Lydia stepped into her apartment, a white envelope lay conspicuously on the carpet just inside the door, slid under with the address facing down. Her first thought: it must be Ash's handiwork. She picked up the envelope and tossed it on the table and checked the voicemail. There was a message from her credit union asking that she contact a representative. Something about her credit card, which she erased and dismissed. She went about settling in, but the envelope nagged her thoughts, until she finally gave in to her mounting curiosity. *Why couldn't he just leave a message on the machine,* she fussed, drawing a blank stare at the handwriting on the envelope.

This wasn't Ash's scrawl, she thought, finally opening the envelope. The note inside read: *Hi Lydia. You may not know me, but my name is Benette. I am leaving this note because of Ashton.*

I would be grateful for a few minutes of your time. If you are as curious about this contact as I hope, please call any evening— the sooner the better. I can be reached any evening after six.

Lydia noticed the phone number had a 703-area code. It was signed simply: *Benette*.

Lydia walked thoughtfully into the living room and sank onto the couch, rereading the short letter. She recognized the name—Ashton's wife—but the Virginia area code puzzled her. Had they moved from Maryland, and he forgot to mention it? Panic momentarily rose as she considered the possibilities for Benette's visit. *How did she know where I live? What if her note is tied to something that has happened to him? Or could it somehow be related to that bizarre business with the ring?* Either way, she decided it was probably better to find out what was really going on. Ashton was such a mystery man.

The note urged her to call, but it was certainly too late to call a stranger's house. Perhaps, it would be smarter to disregard the note altogether. After all, hadn't she promised herself that she and Ash were at the end of their road? Of course, she knew that they weren't through yet from Ashton's perspective. That night-call he had made bearing a gift was his desperate way of smoothing the road for his return into her good graces. There was no question in her mind that it would be good let him know about Benette's visit before contacting her—but that meant waiting for him to call, and she wasn't sure she was willing to do that.

She marveled at the strength and willpower she had to exercise sometimes to restrain from calling him for fear of alerting Benette. The urges seemed so strong at times she could almost taste it. But now his wife comes to her asking for a call. This was just too much. And if she called and Ash picked up, she would be too rattled to speak and hang up. These thoughts plagued her as she prepared for bed, dogging her until she couldn't keep her eyes open any longer. She was more than a little grateful that tomorrow was Friday.

All the close parking spaces were taken again, forcing her to park farther away than she wanted. *Here I go again,* she chastised herself for staying too late at Erika's, surveying the unnervingly still street. Though this was not unusual, something felt disconcerting about tonight.

As she neared the cement steps leading to her unit, she turned around and caught sight of a black car lurking several car lengths away. Her first instinct was to run, but she thought better of it and instead began to walk briskly. She climbed the stairs quickly and aimed for her door when the slam of a car door froze her mid-stride. She willed herself to keep going and not turn around. If he knew she'd seen him, it would be impossible to ignore him. She decided to risk the extra distance to Jaite's door.

Relief flooded when she spotted the dim lighting from his kitchen, and she silently thanked God. *He's there,* she thought, pushing on the doorbell for several long seconds and dropping the heavy doorknocker repeatedly as the panic mounted.

Except for the parked cars, the street was empty, but she dared not check. *Please hurry,* she begged softly, bouncing anxiously in anticipation, as if she had to go to the bathroom.

One side of the decorative double door swung open and Jaite stood in jeans, tee shirt, and socks. He squinted against the soft halo of his outer light, and he moved his fingers through mussed brown hair, smoothing it down.

She allowed herself a quick glance at the empty spot where the black car was parked only seconds earlier and breathed easier since Jaite didn't seem to notice her nervousness.

"Hi, Tamarra," he smiled sleepily. "You got my message, huh? I wasn't trying to rush you."

She shook her head in protest. "No. I'm just getting in, so I decided to stop by and give you an answer in person."

"Oh, I see." His smile wavered, as if expecting the worst.

Tamarra smiled back nervously. "Saturday sounds like fun, *as friends*." Her voice rose for emphasis, her expression telling him that she wanted confirmation.

"That's great! An answer worth waiting for—*as friends*," he agreed, taking her cue and smiling with open glee despite the grogginess.

"Well, I like to keep my word," she concluded, backing away. "Just knock on my door around eight. I'll be ready. Goodnight."

He lingered in the doorway and watched her cross the few doors down to her place and disappear inside.

9

The following morning Erika was, again, not dressed for work. She wore a sporty jog set, white sneakers, and a leather cap. It didn't matter so much to her that the clothes fit oversized today, since it was well-coordinated and sharp enough, she thought.

Energized by orange juice and toast with strawberry preserves that she managed to get down, she stared thoughtfully into space. Here it was another Friday. A week since the sugar-honey-ice-tea about Silvia hit the fan. Things were so far off course now. Work would just have to wait, because her intuition told her a break had to come her way. So, today she felt especially hopeful, though she was not sure why. But as strong as her intuition seemed now, she had no idea what her next step should be—only that good vibes pressed her to act, and she wanted to go with it, wherever it led. And she was ready to make a move now.

So, going with her feeling, she dialed the number she had called enough times to know by heart now, and familiar voice answered. Ms. Z and Erika talked briefly. The counselor understood that Erika felt taking action felt essential, and that for lack of anything else to do, calling to check on things was her best option for now. In fact, she was glad Erika had called; she could keep her apprised of the latest as she had promised.

"Mrs. Marselle," she responded warmly, "we did receive a fax late yesterday afternoon from the Vital Stats Office, which, I'm sorry to confirm Silvia Marselle's marriage to your husband. They have no record of a divorce."

Erika politely interrupted before the woman continued, "Mrs. Zimmermann, please don't get me wrong. While I appreciate the confirmation, at this point, Silvia's marriage isn't my concern. My focus is on what my kids and I might lose because there's considerably more at stake here. What I could use from you is a little more help with this. So, tell me—what happens if her claim is processed but later found to be invalid or illegal?"

"That would be highly irregular."

"Indulge me. What happens?"

"Well, I believe it's safe to say that any mistakes made can and will be rectified immediately if we catch it before too long. Otherwise it really muddies the water, as they say, and just takes longer to straighten out…but it will be resolved."

"Any idea how long her claim will take?"

"It depends. Maybe two weeks to thirty days, if everything goes smoothly. I don't know what else I can tell you. We've no valid reason to delay things any further, but if you come across additional information relevant to this case, I'll personally see to it that it's considered before her claim is finalized."

"I needed to hear that. Because you must admit—this whole situation seems somewhat peculiar. Between all the things that have gone wrong since I first tried to file my claim and her popping up just as I thought I had it settled, I don't mind telling you I've wondered if there was some sort of conspiracy against me."

"I can assure you that SITER has nothing against you or to do with any conspiracy."

"Mrs. Zimmermann, I don't really think that" Erika spoke softly for a change. "I apologize for the remark. I could try to blame it on my frustration, but I can't because I know better. It's just—it would do my heart good to see Silvia get a dose of that slow processing for her claim that I got a few months ago. By accident or on purpose, I don't care. I just want her slowed down." Her voice was slightly tinged with frustrated sarcasm as she talked on. "It's been two months already; a little while longer shouldn't bother her. Anyway, any little thing that can be done along those lines would be most appreciated. I'll be talking with you soon." She placed the phone down softly without waiting to hear another word from the counselor.

Erika's eyes misted and her face flushed as if someone had slapped her hard across the face. She felt she had to do something, but what? She stared around, paced the room, and then moved from one room to another, from the living room through to the dining room and to the den that was Braxton's sanctum, desperately seeking a hint that might be helpful.

A messy pile of papers she had pulled out the other night and forgotten caught her eye. Braxton's old personal items lay on top—his birth certificate and DD214, some old photos, and his yearbook with an aged, discolored driver's license tucked between the middle pages like a bookmark. They were just as she had left them, only this time the driver's license drew her attention. As she studied his young face and the information on the license, an idea popped into her head, shooting twinges of excitement through her with just the adrenaline rush needed to guide her next steps.

A short time later, her sneakers glided along the tile floor of the Foxmaine County courthouse in Virginia. It was 9:45 when she entered the light-colored block of stone known as the municipal building and approached one of the guards.

"That's all the way down the hall. Make the first right and hang a left to the court corridor. The fourth floor, ma'am," the guard directed.

She could only hope that this visit would lead her to where she really needed to go. The inquiry SITER made in D.C. and Maryland had turned up nothing.

Braxton's old driver's license had been issued in Virginia, leading her across Wilson Bridge, though she couldn't say why she chose Foxmaine County. It just came to her. The license, long expired, showed a youthful, unsmiling convict-like image of her late husband. The address on the license might have been from during his marriage to Silvia, though he had never mentioned living in Virginia in the past. But then, he had never spoken of Silvia either—not even a hint.

She pushed the elevator button and felt so keyed up that she bounced as if Mother Nature were calling. It crossed her mind to walk the four flights up—both elevators were taking too long for her—but the court building didn't have a lot of floors, so she forced herself to wait.

When she opened the door, she saw that only a handful of people were waiting ahead of her, which bolstered her. At the counter, a young man and an older woman waited on two customers. Somewhere the piped-in sounds of western country music played softly as she approached the counter. The guy drew his gaze from what he was doing to acknowledge her presence but said nothing. He motioned to the side of the counter with his free hand but continued writing while his head bobbed in time with the music. She picked up a number and sat in the first row to wait for her turn. When her turn came, she wasn't clear what to ask for. "I would like to look up records or information on marriages and divorces," she explained.

Without moving his body, the clerk reached across the counter to pull a form from the piles, undoubtedly out of habit, and he slid one toward her.

"Fill this out with as much information as possible. There's a ten-dollar charge, cash or check, no charge," he relayed flatly.

She provided what little she had. There was too much she didn't know about Silvia Marselle, but she knew the approximate year of marriage and hoped that would help.

After a brief wait, she was escorted to a short hallway, where a computer workstation awaited. For all Erika got from the clerk's quick demonstration and instructions, he might as well have spoken in another language.

"My name is Beastrom. If you have a question, just holler and I'll be right with you." Then, he left her alone to struggle with the machine.

Erika wasn't at a loss on what to do with the machine, only on how to use it. It was a dinosaur of a computer, not the latest. Where were all the laptops that all of civilization was so into? She examined the machine from top to bottom. She was not sure whether it was on or not. Still doubtful, she clicked its buttons a few times and jostled it slightly until the machine came to life, startling her.

For more than an hour, Erika searched, then flicked through files, scanning for names similar to either Silvia's or Braxton's, randomly at first, then chronologically. Finally, in frustration, she turned her attention to marriages licenses, scrolling and scanning repeatedly. As luck would have it when she felt at the end of her rope, her husband's name appeared. Then a date, twenty years back, leaped out. The names listed were Braxton Marselle and Silvia Antwonnette Rollins. Erika had tried to prepare herself for finding something, so she was unscathed at seeing this; instead, she was pushed into a state of renewed motivation.

Since she couldn't confirm a divorce between Braxton and Silvia as she had hoped, she instead searched for names following yet another idea that came to mind. That what she was thinking could be a possibility made her heady. The time passed quickly, and Erika could tell it was lunchtime, well after twelve. Her light breakfast had worn off, and she knew that she could ill afford to miss a meal, but she felt that the exhilaration left little room for anything else, except her continued search. She wouldn't get a thing down at this point even if she tried.

She returned to the waiting area for more information and caught Beastrom on his way out. A broad smile covered her face as he directed her to access additional information.

10

That intriguing note from Benette lingered in Lydia's mind most of the workday. She kept reminding herself that calling might be an even bigger mistake than her too-long entanglement with Ashton. In the meanwhile, she became increasingly inquisitive about what this woman could possibly want to say to her, except for something to do with Ashton? Not a word from him yet, but that wasn't so surprising; he'd never phoned her at work again since that ill-fated real estate incident when they first met. She understood that the ring had seemed a big deal to him, though at the core of things she felt it was just another phase of his game—a power play on his part. He probably wanted her to drool and puzzle over it before he made his climactic move at some point of his choosing. That was more the way of the mystery man that was Ash.

That evening, she lounged in lightweight sweats and loafers, questioning more if delaying the call to Benette—and waiting for Ash to call—was wise. She opened a fresh bottle of wine and pondered between listening to a popular CD through earphones on her small player and an old album onto her equally old Fisher Hi-Fi turntable. Tonight, the album won out. She was in the mood for something special while she thumbed through the Post's Metro section, then flipped through Style, and stopped at the Horoscopes. She glanced at hers—Pisces—and it read:

You have a tendency to discount yourself and build up the abilities of another person. Put a stop to that today. Give yourself credit because it's due. If you don't, who will?

My goodness! She was floored. She did check the horoscopes occasionally out of curiosity, but she had seldom felt it was as relevant to her life's happenings as it seemed today. 1Emboldened, she read on the check for her Gemini sister, Erika.

Brave people deal with problems head-on. You should count yourself among the bravest because you rush after the thing that bothers you— virtually chasing an irritant down instead of running away from it.

Wow! Lydia marveled. Again, she felt the horoscope was dead on for Rikki right now. She made sure to keep the paper so her sister could see it for herself.

In the meanwhile, the sound of Nina Simone's slow, sexy drawl on the song *I Want Some Sugar in My Bowl* penetrated her consciousness, and she closed the paper. Music like this helped her to relax on most days. CDs might rule the day, but she still appreciated her old albums and 45s that brought her those old-school, down-home lyrics like the ones her mother had loved so much. In fact, many of these records had belonged to her mother, and she could always imagine her either singing along or prancing around happily as they played. How she enjoyed the music she was hearing. The gritty clarity of Nina's voice spoke to her heart.

'I want some sugar in my bowl, I ain't foolin', I want some sug— ga—aaar… inn my bowl.'

She found herself staring at the sparkly gemstone Ashton had insisted on leaving behind, trying to appraise its value, his next move, and his sincerity. *It's a small beauty,* she thought, wondering what had possessed him to buy a ring, of all things. She knew, though, that in his mind, leaving it with her meant they were back together. Without stopping to overthink things anymore, she positioned herself at the edge of the bed to consider her next move.

It was after seven when she dialed the number on the note, lest she lose her nerve. The phone rang, her stomach knotted. What would she do if Ash answered? By the second ring, she was tempted to hang up.

Maybe no one was home, she thought—and part of her wished just that. For sure, if there was voicemail or an answering machine, she would take that as her cue to hang up. She knew that if she didn't make contact with Benette today, she might never try again, regardless of what her note said. And she would have a few choice things she saved for Ash the next time she spoke with him, too.

"Hello. Hello?" The voice on the other end sounded pleasant.

Lydia's heart raced and she hesitated, suddenly unsure what to say. "Benette…" she faltered, shocked by her own nerves. But she need not have been.

"This is Benette." The woman's voice held a hint of caution and expectation. Her voice sounded young, sophisticated, and pleasant—to Lydia it was sensual with a slightly noticeable accent.

"Hello, Benette." Lydia psyched herself up to sound more confident than she felt. She reminded herself it was Benette who had started this, yet she wasn't feeling this call, not one little bit. "This is Lydia Matthews," she managed, certain that Benette knew exactly who she was even before she opened her mouth. "You left a note." Lydia spoke matter-of-factly.

Benette spoke with an open, friendly tone. "Yes, yes. Hello Lydia," she responded eagerly with an enunciation that made the name sound more like 'Leed-yah.' "I am glad to hear from you. Thank you for calling so quickly. How are you?"

Lydia was surprised by the pleasantry and how exotically polished this young woman sounded. She made her think of the former model Iman. It was difficult for her to determine the influence of the woman's inflection of certain words, and it was not important. It was just another point of curiosity. Was it African? Jamaican? French? Lydia didn't know which, only that it was beautiful.

"Lydia, I know you must be wondering who I am and why I left that note. I certainly wouldn't presume you to know of me, but we have a mutual friend. Ashton—Ashton Still. When I learned for sure of your acquaintance, I felt it would be good for us to talk. You do know Ashton?" Benette's tone was more a statement than a question that indicated she already knew the answer.

"I do. But talk about what?" Lydia asked quietly. "Did something happen? I mean, is there a problem?" What a dumb question to ask. Of course there was a problem. She'd been seeing the woman's husband for the past five years behind her back.

"There could be. Oh boy, I don't know how to start this," Benette admitted awkwardly. "A few things have happened and I'm not sure what Ashton is trying to pull these days, but I don't believe he is being truthful with either of us."

"What does that mean?" she asked, confused, wondering why Benette cared that Ash was lying to her. "And how specifically should I be concerned?"

"Look," Benette started. She was beginning to doubt how effective a phone call would be for speaking with a stranger under the circumstances. "Can we meet and talk in person? It's not good we should get into this over the phone." Her accent seemed to vary with her level of excitement.

"Get into what?" Lydia questioned. "I don't know what Ashton's told you, but there's nothing to worry about from me. And I'd prefer to stay out of your business," she replied strongly. She had no desire to meet with Ash's wife. Though Lydia could understand Benette wanting to be discreet, this notion of meeting alone did not strike her as such a good idea. She did not know what this woman had in mind. "I admit Ashton and I are friends, but I only called to find out why you left that note." Lydia was getting more nervous and uncomfortable. "So, what's on your mind?"

"Your relationship with Ashton," she responded very calmly. "And mine."

"I don't mean to sound rude, but I didn't call you to talk about Ashton. I am more curious about how you know where I live. Why did you come to my house and leave this note under my door? Besides, why can't you just say whatever is on your mind over the phone?" She was nervous that Ash might walk in while they were on the phone. "Because, I don't mind talking now."

Benette remained calm and pleasant, but Lydia was sure she already knew about them. Why else were they talking? What could she possibly say to the woman?

"I understand your curiosity, and I intend to explain. I just feel it's better if we meet in person. But I can tell you this now, and perhaps it will help. I saw your name on a business card some years ago, but I was surprised when I saw it again a few months ago. That's how I knew you and Ashton must be close friends—and I suspect, more than friends, because I see he has used your credit card."

There was an uncomfortable silence on Lydia's end. "Sorry," she blurted, confused about how she should respond and just how much she should say. "I don't usually—" she started, about to trap herself.

"No. No," Benette interjected emphatically. "This is not about accusing you of anything or putting you on the spot. It is over between me and Ashton, and has been for a while now. We're more of a formality than anything now, because of our daughter. He just hasn't accepted that yet."

There was silence again from Lydia, who was truly speechless with still so many unanswered questions.

"Look, I really don't want to go into any more of this over the phone, Benette concluded. "I know how mysterious all this must sound, but I believe it will be worth your while to hear me out. We can meet anywhere that makes you comfortable, even at your place if you want. Privacy is the important thing. Lydia, I mean you no harm, I assure you."

She had to admit that Benette sounded pleasant and understanding. She seemed genuinely concerned about sharing something with Lydia. All of this only heightened her curiosity. That strong pull was not easy to resist or dismiss, and it was the reason Lydia gave herself for reluctantly agreeing to the meeting.

"I'm not sure why I'm doing this." She spoke with skepticism, biting her lip thoughtfully. She was even tempted to try convincing Benette that she and Ash were merely casual acquaintances and somehow put an innocent spin on the credit card thing she had mentioned. But a little voice inside asked: Hadn't she been living a lie long enough? Unsure of how much Benette really knew or what she wanted to say, Lydia decided that it was clear that she had a clue about what Ash was all about.

"We just need a little time to talk, so you can hear me out. There are a few things I think may be of interest to you," Benette reassured. How about seven thirty at, maybe the National Harbor? Pick a place. There's good lighting there and we can stay in one of the cars. Will that work for you?" she asked, probably guessing that it was close to where Lydia lived.

"No," Lydia answered flatly. She most certainly did not want to meet with the wife of the man she had a five-year affair with, in some isolated parking space, even if offered all the privacy in the world. Though it was a popular place and relatively close by, she still was not familiar with the places at the Harbor. She rarely had the opportunity to go there. "Let's make it someplace busier like Rivermarks Plaza, where the movie theater is. There's a carryout called Sutton's a few doors down," she announced, as if by naming the meeting place, she had taken control. "There's enough parking and open activity, I suppose. I can see you there."

Benette chuckled lightly. "Fine…see you around seven-thirty," she confirmed. "By the way, I'll be wearing jeans and a denim jacket."

"Well, I'll be in black fleece-wear and a red leather jacket," Lydia replied.

A short while later, a young Jamaican woman showed up—good-looking and shapely, with smooth brown skin that would be the envy of most women. In addition to the jeans and jacket, she wore a pair of stylish eyeglasses, and a cute denim cap. Lydia was already seated at a small table when Benette entered. She looked around the small shop filled with younger people and smiled knowingly when her eyes found Lydia's.

Lydia couldn't help but notice how attractive she was—and she seemed exactly Ash's type. Benette approached, still smiling.

"Hello…Lydia. I'm Benette." She extended her hand.

"Beautiful name," Lydia greeted—*for a beautiful woman,* she couldn't help thinking—as she accepted the small, slender hand, hoping her nerves didn't give her away. "Nice to meet you," she forced herself to add.

The two women took note of the young people, both waiting for their orders and just hanging out, socializing at the tables. They both decided to order tea-lemonade drinks while they talked.

"Thanks for meeting me," Benette whispered sincerely, her lips still formed into that sweet, reassuring smile of hers. "I didn't know what to think about you, so I knew I was taking a chance leaving that note. But you're not what I expected at all…in a pleasant way. I mean, you are a lot more sophisticated than I imagined."

"Thank you." *I could say the same about you,* Lydia thought as she considered Benette's comment. Was it a compliment, or maybe a nod to the age difference between her and Ash? A condescending smile crossed Lydia's face briefly as she acknowledged that truth to herself before she spoke, "Well, now that we're both here in person—what's this all about?"

"How long have you and Ashton been friends?" Benette asked inquisitively, obviously attempting to jump right in by making some basic point.

Lydia exhaled and answered honestly, "It's been a few years."

"Yeah, I would say at least that," Benette nodded knowingly. "You know, Ashton and I go back over seven years. Things happened fast with us." The reassuring smile had disappeared, and her speech became more emphatic as her accent thickened. While her English was great, her dialect made the word 'things' sound more like 'tings. "Too fast, he charmed his way into my heart and my efficiency apartment… like within three months after we met." She held up three fingers, then continued on for a few minutes almost as if she were talking to herself.

"I got pregnant the following year. We have a beautiful little girl. Her name is Sydney," she was saying. "And after that, our relationship was never the same, no matter what I did. I guess he just wasn't ready for a family or to be a father. I took his mess for three more long years before I got sense enough to call it a day. I cannot imagine for the life of me why I didn't see the light sooner because I always had these tell-tale signs that he had other relationships all along. Still do. We've been off and on lately—more off to be honest," she reiterated, looking casually into Lydia's eyes.

"But, getting to you." Her gaze sharpened. "The first time I saw your name was several years ago on a realtor card. He said you were recommended by a friend for whenever we were ready for a house. That sounded reasonable at the time, though that time obviously never came for us. I got a hold of the card and kept it all this time. No special reason—just kept it. I forgot all about it, or so I thought, until I came across it recently."

Benette pulled a small white card from her pocket and held it up before setting it on the table. Lydia recognized it right away and could almost remember the exact moment she had handed it to Ashton after touring the house he claimed interest in. She was sure that Benette would reveal more about her suspicions regarding the affair, yet her interest was growing nonetheless to whatever this attractive young woman had to say.

"A few weeks ago," Benette continued, "I took Sydney to see her father, and we really had a good time. Long story short, I ended up staying overnight at the apartment with him, which I later regretted. I came across a credit receipt from American Express, VISA, or some credit card…ok, with your name on it," she described as calmly as someone reading a well-known report. Except what she was saying was so riveting that Lydia was hanging on her every word. "And he doesn't know that I saw it."

Lydia knew the receipt must be for the jewelry Ashton charged and still owed her for. The very same gold he had so thoughtlessly worn when he had shown up on her birthday without even bringing a card. But for the moment, she focused on Benette's words about staying with Ash. What did she mean she stayed overnight at the apartment? Didn't they live together? Were they separated and Ash hadn't told her? Is that why she had a 703-area code, while Ash's was in Maryland? Part of her wanted to interrupt this interesting report and bombard Benette with questions right then and there, while a wiser part bade her to just listen.

From what she had already said, Lydia couldn't believe this was the same person Ash had always referred to as his wife. That this was the same person he routinely cut short their time together to get home to. Something was terribly wrong with this picture. Benette's account contradicted everything he had led her to believe all this time.

Benette continued her story. "I don't recall the name of the store, but I remember your name from the card. It's a nice name also…Lydia. Anyway, at that point, I was sure you were involved with Ashton or, in any case, more than just a name on a card."

Lydia was inside her own head with gnawing questions rather than listening to what her informant said. And as she talked on, a strange uneasiness crept inside, not so much over what was said but what was implied.

"So, excuse me," Lydia reluctantly interjected. "You and Ashton *never* married after you had your daughter?" she asked, afraid of the answer.

"Heavens no! Thank God," Benette whispered with relief. "We would no doubt be divorced by now if we had. Never," she confirmed. "Is that what he told you?"

A bomb of sorts went off in Lydia's head. An explosion so expansive, her whole expression and demeanor changed. A bitter scowl crossed her placid face, and she did an unconscious double take, screaming inwardly. Catching the expression on Benette's face, she tuned out the rest of the conversation from that point on with a combination of disbelief and embarrassment. She had been deceived, manipulated, lied to, and literally screwed by this single rat of a man masquerading as a devoted marriage partner. And she had fallen for it. This was just a little much for her to absorb.

She pulled herself together as best she could, more to save face than anything. "Well, let's just say Ashton made it clear he had an obligation to you. I guess he was referring to your daughter," Lydia covered, too ashamed to tell her the truth of what she was learning.

Benette went on to share more about her time with Ashton than Lydia had ever imagined she would hear.

11

Tamarra checked her messages and tensed when she heard the second one.

"Hello, Tamarra. How have you been? Yes, this is Tenni. I know it's been a while and I'm sorry to call under these circumstances, but Mother is in hospital pretty sick. Will you please call me? Please," she pleaded.

Tennille was Tamarra's younger sister and only sibling. Thirty years old come September, and to her knowledge, still living in their parents' house. Tamarra had not called or seen her family for nearly five years now. She had kept them out of her life—an extreme difference of opinion about her personal lifestyle had alienated her from both her parents and sister. Her mom had never understood or accepted her attraction to people of color—especially the men. Neither did she for that matter, but she didn't question it either. By twenty-one, she refused to tolerate her mother's feelings and meddling in her choice of friends, relationships, socializing, and whatever. From then on, their narrow-mindedness gradually drove a boat-sized wedge between all of them.

According to Mother, they had put up with her risqué behavior and sneaking around with Black men long enough. They chose to turn their backs on her several years later, after she eloped with Avory Wilson, calling her out of her mind. And now, her sister Tenni wanted her to call.

She still loved her parents deeply, despite all their flaws and meddling, and she missed them more than she

157

ever thought she would. To say that she was upset by her mom's illness would be putting it mildly, yet a residual disappointment, resentment, and even anger lingered closer to the surface than she had realized. She couldn't forget how stubborn and unrelenting they had been about her marriage—unforgivable and unacceptable. Her parents weren't even willing to give them a chance. She could think of far more forbidden or questionable relationships. It was not as if she was violating one of Mother's most sacred codes of morality: being a lesbian or wanting to marry her gay lover.

The hurt from her parents was not quite gone. She couldn't see it back then, but she was willing to admit now that the wounds have gone both ways. Tenni, adding insult to her parents' injury, had sided with them by chastising her on more than one occasion. 'You know, Mother is right,' she would say. 'Why can't you ever find a nice White guy? There are plenty of them around, you know, if you'd just give them half a chance,' she nagged. They all acted as if she was snuggling with a close relative or having an affair with the pastor of the church or something as equally sinister. She didn't understand them any more than they understood her, except she could not see for the life of her what all the fuss was about.

Hearing from Tenni stirred ambivalent feelings to the surface about seeing her family again. Her last contact was years ago. She'd called to share her new phone number after her last move. It was a number they'd never bothered to use until now. Back then, she'd have died before giving them the satisfaction of knowing that her marriage had failed or why it did—but they never bothered to call, so she was saved.

How could she tell them that her life with her beloved Avory went to pot—both figuratively and literally speaking?

She had come across stashes of marijuana hidden in out-of-the-way places throughout the apartment, and he reasonably explained it as along the lines of "evidence" since he was a police officer. The truth came out one day when she came home earlier than expected and she caught him and a fellow officer in a compromising position. He confessed that the weed she had discovered was his, that he smoked regularly, and thought it helped spark his homosexual relationship with his fellow officer, who was his former partner. Things between them ended rather badly.

She knew the reasons her marriage ended had nothing to do with her parents' antiquated thinking, but regardless, she was sure they would do Hail Marys had they heard the news and pray extra thanks that there were no children.

Within a few hours, she had spoken with her sister and visited her mom briefly. That was where Tamarra's mind lingered when she returned home and unlocked her unit door. She nursed the feeling of satisfaction in her heart that she had not been too stubborn to answer Tenni's plea. They met at the hospital, which turned into a tearful reunion. Now she was exhausted from the adrenaline rush of Tenni's call and the emotional rollercoaster stirred up by the hospital visit. She was completely preoccupied—definitely not paying attention to her surroundings.

Tamarra stepped through the doorway when she felt a push against her back that made her stumble. She grabbed the knob to balance herself while turning just enough to find out from where the sudden pressure had come. The kitchen light had been left on, and it spilled enough for her to glimpse into the otherwise dark foyer. It was Dorsey.

She let out an involuntary angry scream.

"Stop, Dorsey! What are you doing here? Get out. Get out of my house!" she screamed at him, trying to fend him off.

The dark, bulky figure seemed to take up all the space in the doorway, shoving as he moved her from the entrance area and kicking the door shut behind him. He muttered something as he moved closer to her, while she backed into the lighted kitchen, tripping over herself.

She tensed with fear and trembled, but she held back her tears and tried to calm him. He brushed her attempts aside. She backed against the counter, glaring at him with moistened eyes. She wanted to stand up to him like she was not afraid, but she was, and her voice betrayed her.

"Dorsey, what do you want? What are you doing?" She moved away from him with nowhere to go. "I know you're upset because you want to talk," she sputtered when his hate-filled eyes flashed at her.

She had meant to talk with him the next time he called, but not like this. "What do you want me to say?" she begged in frustration. The smell of alcohol hit her like a slap in the face. It was stronger than she could ever remember. She looked into his watery, dead eyes and shrank, knowing she didn't want him to answer. He looked like a madman and smelled like stale still.

"I need you to leave." Her voice shook noticeably. "I want you to leave right now," she managed to yell in a stronger voice.

"I heard you, b**ch! You need, you want. It's all about you. And what about what I want?" he drooled viciously, grabbing her by both arms. "A man makes one little mistake, and you make a big f***ing deal out of it. Had me fooled for a minute there. I thought you were different, but you're just like all the rest," he ranted.

In one swift movement, he pinned her arms to her side and lifted her onto the nearby stool, pushing her into the seat with brute force. Then, he snatched her eyeglasses off her face. Her vulnerability instantly doubled—without them, the room blurred. She guessed that was the intent.

"Please…no! What are you doing? I need my glasses!" she cried out in panic, close to tears. She held her face in her hands and released the dam that had held back her tears.

Dorsey paced the kitchen, spewing a bunch of dirty names and not making much sense as he had sufficiently worked himself into a maniacal frenzy.

"Yeah, feeling frustrated and helpless?" he asked with bitter satisfaction. "Yeah…just the way I want you. Helpless," he screamed at her. "B**ch, what are you sniveling for? I'm the one that got dumped. You've got some motherf***ing nerve, you know that?" he yelled bitterly, stepping closer to her. "You keep dodging my calls. I've been trying and trying to talk with you, to tell you how sorry I am. Who do you think you are anyway?" he spat out.

She never saw the first blow coming but screamed bloody murder the instant she felt it. And he hollered right along with her as if he was getting off on hearing her pain.

"I've been trying and trying to talk to your b**ch a** all week." His eyes bulged. "And just who the f**k do you think you are, anyway? You just White trash…is all. Yeah, you just like all the rest. But all you need is a good a**kicking to straighten you right out, that's all. And I'm just the man for the job," he hissed with a sinister level of glee that was new to her. He continued to curse on and on as if pumping himself up.

She could feel him moving back and forth and picking up steam, but she couldn't tell for sure since she shielded her face and braced herself. Another kick that was harder than the first struck the side of her face, and she fell off of the stool trying to fend it off. She begged him again to leave but found herself on the floor tasting blood.

Tamarra sobbed openly now, begging him repeatedly to stop. To leave her alone. But that wasn't enough to stop the next crashing blow to the other side of her face. She felt his hands pulling at her, trying to lift her from the floor and ready to strike once again, no doubt, when suddenly his grip fell away. She dropped to the floor like a sack of old potatoes.

"What the hell's going on here?" A strong voice bellowed angrily above her as she felt Dorsey being ripped away from her.

At the realization that someone else was in the room, she stayed slumped where she'd fallen, sobbing. Merciful Jesus was all she could think. The man had his hands full holding Dorsey off at first, then, he forcefully wrestled him through the foyer and out the door.

Tamarra huddled in the corner against a kitchen cabinet. She could hear them banging, scuffling, and arguing back and forth. She moved a little ways toward the men, listening, when she realized one of them was a familiar voice—Jaite. She instantly feared for him and cried harder. What a mess she had made; now he was being drawn into it. She feared that Dorsey might have a weapon on him or in his car. She remained in a crumpled heap on the floor until Jaite returned and helped her into the kitchen chair—the same one that Dorsey had slam-dunked her into.

The soreness and swelling felt like it was starting immediately. She remembered the feeling of his fists on her face. He obviously meant to hurt her and could not image what might have happened if her neighbor had not intervened, she thought between sniffles.

Jaite grabbed paper towels, soaked them in cold water, and pressed them into her hand. "Mercy! Are you okay? Maybe, I should get you ice." He moved toward the freezer, not really waiting for an answer. "What the hell happened?" he asked. "Do you want to me call the police so you can file a complaint?" Again, not waiting for a response. "Who was that guy anyway?" He peppered her with questions before she could say much of anything. "You okay?" he repeated more gently now, pulling another chair very close to hers so he could inspect her face.

She managed to shake her head.

"Gosh...look at you! What's the hell's wrong with that creep? Man!" he exclaimed, clearly ticked off.

She sat staring, dazed through red, swollen, and bleary eyes, struggling to collect herself. Dorsey's assault had taken only a few minutes, but in her mind, it had played out much longer.

It was amazing to her that Jaite knew she needed help, but she had the presence of mind to appear thankful that he came to her rescue. Although she was grateful to him—he had ended the 'punishment'— shame pressed heavier. She knew her face was tear-streaked, probably swelling black and blue and bloody, her hair and clothes a rumpled mess. She didn't know what Dorsey had done with her glasses, and she couldn't see anything clearly. She just wanted to be left alone right now. She looked into Jaite's blurred face, sensing more than seeing his deep and sincere concern.

"I can't thank you enough for getting that a**hole, creep-dog out of here," she rambled weakly in frustrated anger. "Thanks so much for being here." She almost broke down again as she slowly slid off the stool, shrugged off her raincoat with minimal movement, and let it fall into the seat. She stepped carefully toward the counter on unsteady legs, blinking from the sting of salty tears, squinting to see. "Where are my glasses? Do you see them anywhere?"

"Yeah." Jaite glanced around to the spot where the glasses had been tossed and quickly scooped them up. "I got them." He tried to put them on her at first. "Here you go."

"Thanks. I'm okay," she insisted, taking them with a slight tremble. She realized that she really was not okay by a long shot. "If you don't mind, can we talk later?" She was guiding him toward the door as she headed for the stairs. "I just need some time." She faced him with sad, tired eyes pleading for understanding.

The gentle look and hint of a smile that Jaite returned before he let himself out the door told her he only wanted to help, and Heaven knows he had done well. "I hope it's okay if I call you tomorrow to check on you, because I will," he said with quiet firmness, not leaving room for debate.

Tamarra's response was reactive, like a plea of a frightened young woman who had just been assaulted in her own home. "Jaite, please make sure he's not out there before you open that door. And you will be very careful, too."

12

Benette Benard, with her pleasant boldness, revealed long, thick, dark wavy hair neatly pulled into a ponytail, a thick braid wrapped around it, when she took off her cap. She had done Lydia a big favor, whether she realized it or not. She certainly looked nothing like the woman Sondra had described.

She briefly described her beginning with Ashton. They had met at the BWI airport. She was way too early for an outgoing flight, and he was waiting for his mother's delayed arrival. They got into a pretty lengthy conversation to kill the time and felt a strong attraction to each other. They ended up exchanging numbers. He started calling her right away, and soon, the connection was made.

At the time, Ashton lived in a Maryland apartment in the area, or so he said. He claimed he was staying with his sister, whom neither Benette nor Lydia, for that matter, ever got to meet. But almost as soon as their dating became steady, his sister supposedly suggested he might be better off staying with her, according to Ashton. That unexpected bit of news had been just fine with Benette at the time. So, within a few short months, they were living together. Months later when she became pregnant, Ashton promised both marriage and a larger place in time for the baby. But after the birth, he never delivered on anything.

He stopped talking of marriage at all and became defensive if he even thought she was bringing up the subject.

When she found Lydia's card, he had misled her, and in time it was clear that he had no plans to move. Finally, she and Sydney moved to nearby Foxmaine County. Ashton had stayed at the tiny apartment that she was foolish enough to renew the lease for each year as long as he paid rent, which she had to frequently remind him about.

She made a point of telling Lydia that Ashton had initially seemed content to let her leave without any resistance. She did not hear anything from him for months—not even seeing their daughter. There seemed to be little interest in her at all if the two of them had nothing going. Months later, she began dating again. Then, as if he were a fly on her wall, he began calling and coming around just when she became interested in one particular guy. He told her that all he wanted was to be a real father to his daughter, a child who had seldom entered his thoughts. When she was out of his sight, she was also out of his mind as well. Against her better judgment and for her daughter's sake, she gave him the chance he so desperately begged for. She put her new relationship on pause—at least for a while. Luckily, the man didn't give up on her and never went very far away.

Benette admitted she often took Sydney to visit Ashton, sometimes spending the night at her old apartment with him. Yet she had the sense not to let him move in with her again, and her voice was filled with unmistakable pride when she had thanked God for it.

They continued seeing each other on occasion, although he often socialized mostly without her, forever making whispered phone calls and always picking her up late for the few dates they had. Benette was very attractive and had plenty of chances to meet other guys, but she discreetly renewed her relationship with her former friend. Dissatisfaction with Ashton only allowed her increased time—and more reason—to lean on her new man-friend. Now she had grown quite fond of him, and he doted on her daughter.

The week before, Ashton surprised her with a proposal and even produced a ring. This convinced her that he must be suspicious of the other man in her life—someone who was nothing like him and was on her mind all the time these days. This was his game to throw her into an emotional tailspin. He left the ring even though she refused to give him an answer. She knew her answer would be no but wanted to turn the tables on him for once.

"That snake doesn't know I came across that first receipt," she reported. "Anyway, that made me want to get in touch with you—but I needed his unwitting help with that."

Lydia looked on with renewed interest as the woman she had always considered her rival filled her in. She described Ashton had been distraught and preoccupied lately—surely it must be related to his other women, maybe her. Just last week, he'd been pacing like a caged animal when she visited.

At long last, Benette got into how she discovered where Lydia lived. She had followed Ashton the first chance she got— the same night he gave her the ring—and trailed him straight to where she was certain Lydia lived. She noted the building and returned one evening to check the names on the mailboxes until she came across Lydia's name on one of them. That evening she came over, she'd barely missed being caught. He had seemed in no special hurry to leave his car, so she waited quietly until she saw him walk toward Lydia's building. When his back was turned, she drove away in the opposite direction. Distance and darkness were her camouflage.

Lydia stared at nothing for a long time, letting the meaning of what Benette had said fully sink in. Tears slipped quietly from her eyes. She felt like a class-A, number one total and utter fool, and she wanted to believe that Benette was a fraud and all that she said were vicious lies. But she knew it was true without even that deep-down-inside search one sometimes felt the need for. Ashton Still had conned her good all this time, and she felt sucker punched.

Lydia's conversation with Benette left her stunned and devastated. The woman had talked almost non-stop for over an hour. The place was ready to close when they left. The shell-shocking truth that stuck in her mind, was that the bastard was not married and never had been. Once she returned home, drained from thinking of all that Benette had said, Lydia acknowledged it had been risky for Benette to reach out and meet her so to personally tell her the type of man that Ashton was—the man who even reached the point of possibly misusing her credit card. Yet it was almost as risky, too, for her to accept. There was no way for this *sister* to know the true value of what she had shared with Lydia. The meeting turned out to be more than worth her time than she ever could have imagined. And she had openly expressed her appreciation for the enlightenment as best she could. Lydia stared into space in amazement, wondering what she'd say the next time she talked to him, and there was no doubt she would. She closed her eyes and anger burned inside her bosom like smoldering charcoals.

Erika slowly sipped her java drink and daydreamed. It was four thirty and she had only a few minutes to replay the fascinating scenario through her mind before picking up the twins. She reminded herself that it was just a matter of time before Silvia's claim would be processed; the counselor had at least agreed to take her time, but time was of the essence. After all, the bureaucracy usually moved at its own pace, the more in a rush, the slower it seemed to move. If things got too far, it would probably spiral into another mess, and lead to another wait to straighten it out.

Rush hour was in full gear as Erika approached Wilson Bridge, yet she was making surprisingly good time. The lane extensions had made traffic light years more tolerable. She had worried that she'd get home too late to call SITER, but with minutes to spare, she knew the tide was turning her way when she caught Mrs. Zimmermann before she left.

Erika was delighted to share her findings in Foxmaine County with the counselor. Her sixth sense and strong intuition affirmed what she had learned about Silvia, creating a level of positive energy, a magnitude she hadn't experienced since her children's birth. She fought the overwhelming urge to share her incredible news with someone—Lydia, Tamarra, even Nana—lest she risk jinxing things by talking too much, too soon. Besides, she was exercising her faith in the good Lord by trusting that she would work it through. Mrs. Z promised to personally pursue every reasonable possibility Erika presented, despite Silvia's hell-bent insistence that her claim be processed immediately. And that is exactly what she had provided, another possibility that seemed more the likelihood.

She leaned back on the stool with her arms folded across her chest in mild satisfaction, finally feeling as if she had done something. As her mind raced on, the numbers on the clock blurred, and her mind's eye saw the names in the files as clearly as they had a few hours before. She was rejuvenated as she stared in disbelief at the names her eyes fell upon. She prayed aloud that her instinct was on target and somehow knew it was. "Yes, thank you, Jesus," she whispered. Someone named Silvia A. Marselle had applied for a marriage license—but it was not with Braxton, the voice inside her head echoed. The sense of relief that she smothered earlier now rose freely again. "Yes!" she screamed aloud to no one.

Only now did Erika dare admit to herself the full ramification of what she suspected—only now did she chance voicing what she prayed the counselor would officially uncover and confirm on her own. She knew she was onto something. The ideas in her head seemed so much more plausible now. She hugged herself with deep gratitude to a higher power for giving her hope. She was becoming increasingly convinced that she had hit the nail's head beyond a shadow of a doubt.

If Silvia Marselle had applied for a marriage license with someone else in Virginia years before Erika and Braxton were wed, what did that mean? What if she just continued to use the name Marselle after that marriage had ended, as many women did after multiple divorces?

Oh, what a difference it would make for Erika's claim. But if Silvia married someone else even before Braxton married her, who was likely the bigamist now? Yes, the more she thought about it now, the more plausible a divorce seemed. There it was, the whole scenario completely laid out for her to study. She realized she had stretched the idea a bit around the bend and back, but stranger things had happened. Plus, it could account for this mess and clear it up at the same time.

She was completely enthralled in her thoughts, soaking up the comfort they offered, until she sipped and got nothing. So caught up in the strong possibility, she did not realize her coffee was finished. The fact that today, she knew exactly where her head had been made her smile. The time had passed quickly, and it was now almost five. She had just enough time to start a real dinner before picking up the twins. Her appetite was growing, and she felt more hopeful than she had in weeks.

An hour later, she kneeled to help Brea change her clothes during the twin's competition to talk about the day's events at school and their afternoon with Nana.

"Momma, why does she have to tell everything? It's my turn," Brandon implored. Instead of shushing their back and forth like she often did, she looked off in that distracting way she had these days. Only today, the reason was different. She was cognizant of every thought. A smile lifted the corners of her mouth as she pictured the file again so clearly that she started to hum.

A burning twinge pressed momentarily into the left of her abdomen. Could it be excitement? She allowed it to pass while she helped Brea into a sweater, still half listening to their banter. But as she prepared to hustle them toward the bathroom to wash their hands, a sharp burning sensation followed the pain and took her breath away. Still on her knees, she pressed a hand to the spot and slid to the floor, causing the twins to stop chattering.

"What's the matter, Momma?" they cried almost in unison.

"Does your tummy hurt?" Brea asked, and the two almost tripped over each other trying to help their mother.

Erika kept moaning and clutching herself, while fear and confusion spread across the twins' faces. She couldn't answer at first and remained motionless as she waited for the pain to subside. Finally, she cautiously let out all the caught-up breath. "I'm okay," she managed. "Can you two help Mommie up?" she whispered reassuringly. "Can you do that for me?"

What just happened? she wondered. She let them clumsily assist her to the kitchen, making them feel they were helping more than they really were—just to ease their minds and wipe those frightened looks off their faces.

Her heart grew heavy at the sight of the unshed tears that glistened in Brea's round brown eyes and Brandon's wide hypnotic stare. She wanted so badly to give them the security they needed and chase away the nightmarish thought of something happening to her. Her own tears mixed haltingly with laughter when Brandon muttered hesitantly through trembling lips, "Momma, want me to get the *Pepto Bismol*?" His head cocked inquisitively to the side.

"Mommie, do you want some *Tylenol*?" Brea added. "We can get it for you, can't we Bran?" She elbowed her dazed brother.

Through teary laughter, Erika whispered words of calm to them, promising she'd feel better once they all had eaten the wonderful meal she had fixed—their favorites: meatloaf, green beans, and mashed potatoes with gravy. Hopefully, it would help. She was painfully aware of how badly she needed to eat better; her clothing probably looked better on a mannequin these days than on her. Only her foot size seemed to remain the same, and between the headaches and the body aches, she popped *Tylenol* like she was being paid.

The twins were more alerted to Erika's mood than usual and had ceased their idle chatter altogether. They watched her intently with questionable stares, glancing at each other repeatedly with solemn expressions as if to confirm with each other what they saw. They ate in troubled silence that they both seemed afraid to break. *They were so attuned to be so young,* she thought. *Had Braxton's sudden death played a part in that?*

Erika ate along with them, not quite as hungry as she had originally thought. She noticed they seemed afraid to be their usual selves. "Hey guys, come on. I'm fine now. Aren't you enjoying this good dinner I fixed for us?"

Then, as Brandon dared to speak, Bre rudely interrupted. "Be quiet, Bran," she spoke matter-of-factly. "Can't you see something's wrong with Mommie?" Then they both chewed their food slowly and stared quietly at their mother.

"I am fine." Erika smiled reassuringly at them in return.

Erika was forced to finish her dinner together with them—they had been eagle-eyeing her. The kids no longer looked worried, but she knew they would remember her little episode. She noticed how expressive Brea was and how intently Brandon sometimes looked at her, as if they were readying for the next time something happened.

While the twins were in the bathtub, Erika medicated herself with a few *Tylenol.* Once she helped them wash up and get into their pajamas, she reluctantly allowed a short time to play in their rooms before bed. She usually kept the kids up later on weekends so they would sleep later the next morning, until around ten depending on the amount of activity the day before. But tonight, they were so quiet she thought they'd be ready for bed very soon. She didn't know if her total exhaustion was more physical or mental. Her thoughts drifted to Tamarra, so she reached for the phone.

Tamarra's voicemail picked up, but Erika wasn't inclined to leave a message tonight. What she needed was a live voice. She was disappointed. Despite feeling tired and totally wasted, she yearned to talk to her friend. She called out to the twins, and seconds later the pair rushed in, stumbling over each other and sounding out of breath as if they had run five flights of stairs nonstop. Brea was in front of the bed, rubbing her eyes with the back of her hand, while Brandon stood next to her bedside. When Erika mentioned bedtime, she was met with the usual resistance parents know too well.

"No," they both chimed in unison. Brea's eyelids drooped so much that Erika thought she might pass out right where she stood any second, while Brandon looked sleepy too. "We still playing the word game." He sounded bored.

"I want a snack," the little girl announced too loudly, as if it were some sort of emergency.

Her brother chimed in calmly as if he got her cue. "Yeah, Momma, can we have some potato chips?"

"Bran, I asked first!" Brea cried out with tears in her voice. And Erika knew it was time. It would not be long now. This was one of their most common ploys: asking for water, cookies, ice cream. Anything they could do that might prolong their late night for fear of missing something. Usually, she didn't give in once it got this late. But what happened tonight probably made their fear more real for them. So, as a way of appeasing the fear that she felt must still be with them, she gave in. She rationalized that forcing them to go to bed under the circumstances might be more harmful for them than good.

The kids hurried through their small snack as Erika rested patiently at the counter, watching them eat, reminding them they only had a few minutes. While she waited, she dialed Lydia's number. Her voicemail answered too. Maybe she was out for a change instead of wasting her weekend waiting for a few precious hours with the Ash Man. Then the horrible thought came in that maybe they were busy making up.

A short while later, the twins were down and Erika stood before the medicine cabinet, studying medication labels while the shower water warmed. She still felt dull twinges around her midsection and knew she needed help resting tonight. She found an old 400 mg bottle of *Motrin* prescribed for Braxton's back pain and hurriedly took one. The phone rang, but it was late—surely it must be a wrong number.

"Hello," her voice sounded weary.

"Erika, this is Tamarra. I hope I didn't wake you." She was apologetic with an unmistakable strain in every word.

Erika struggled to hear her over the TV and running shower but was instantly alert to the need in her voice.

"No-no, I'm just getting ready for a shower. What's going on? You don't sound right. Are you okay?"

"No, I'm not." Tamarra barely managed, sniffling back tears and becoming momentarily silent.

Alarm now crept into Erika's voice. "What happened?"

"Uh…um." She braced herself in an effort to get her next words out. "Dorsey forced his way—" Her voice broke halfway through the sentence, and she cleared her throat. "He attacked me." Her attempt to hold back the tears gave way and she sobbed uncontrollably into the phone.

Erika could not believe her ears. "No, he didn't!" she repeated, knowing she had heard correctly the first time.

Tamarra blew her nose, hard. "The dirty bastard caught me off guard and forced his way in."

"No…oh my *God!* Oh, merciful *Jesus*," she exclaimed. "Where are you?" she groaned regretfully. "Are you hurt? Do you need me to come over?" Erika offered without thinking.

"I don't know," she yelled, "I don't know, but I'm still at home."

"Okay. First, try to calm down," Erika encouraged. "You're sure he's gone? Did you call the police?"

"Yeah, we're sure. And no I haven't called the police. My nerves are shot to hell."

"Who is *we?*" Erika asked.

"Jaite. I hate to think of what would have happened if he hadn't come by." Her voice cracked with emotion.

"Well, what about the police? You *are* going to call them, right?" Erika questioned emphatically and was disheartened at her answer.

"Not right now. My head is spinning, my mouth is bleeding and swollen, and my face hurts like hell. It'll probably be black and blue before morning. But thank God Jaite happened to be nearby before the jerk could do any real damage. I don't know what got into that monster," she rambled on tearfully.

"Oh Lord. I had a feeling he might try something, but I didn't want to think it would be this, and I certainly didn't want to scare you anymore than I already had." Erika felt awful about what happened to Tamarra and that she was probably alone. Her heartbeat rapidly and her own tension grew steadily as she listened to her friend painfully describe her ordeal.

"He was acting so mean and crazy—like the son-of-a-b**ch he really is," she sobbed brokenly. "I think he really wanted to hurt me and he had been drinking and who knows what else. The alcohol was so strong. I should have smelled it before he got to my door."

"So, is Jaite still there?"

"No. I asked him to leave," she answered sadly.

"Tamarra, why did you do that?" Erika chastised. "You need someone there with you right now to make sure that creep doesn't come back."

"I am so embarrassed I can't stand to know he's looking at me right now," she had placed a hard emphasis on the word *so*.

"Tamarra. This is no time for embarrassment. This is scary…sounds like Jaite's your hero. He knows firsthand what you've been through. I just hate that you're alone right now."

"I know. You're right, but I can't help how I feel." Her voice was barely audible. "That's why I called." She broke down completely. "I'm so scared."

Erika spoke soothingly to her. "Tamarra…Tamarra, come on, girlfriend, it's going to be okay," she comforted.

"You know you don't even have to stay there if you don't want. I'm glad you called." She tried to calm her as best she could over the phone. "Now, grab some things and come over here. I would come to you, but I can't leave the twins. Are you alright to drive?" she finished firmly.

"Oh, of course you can't leave the kids. Yeah, I think so. I just need to get away from here," she said, feeling better already.

Tamarra was more afraid than anything that Dorsey might come back or, worse, linger outside for an opportunity to jump her as soon as she stepped out her door. She also hoped that he wouldn't come back later to hunt down Jaite.

13

Lydia wasn't sure how long she had sat digesting the reality of her situation. Feeling humiliated and stupid, she wondered how she could get even, even though she knew the blame was as much hers as his, maybe more. She had given him too much space in her world, ignoring the significant shortcomings of their relationship, knowing there was no love lost between him and the people she cared most about—her son and her sister.

The dam broke and the tears flowed. Not over him—he was not worth it, and he was going to pay, she vowed, though she had not a clue as to how yet. She was crying for herself. The whole situation seemed ironic. Just when she thought she could take off her blinders and enjoy her dream world, Benette had come along and shaken her awake. Her milestone 40th birthday had certainly turned into a lesson.

She wished there was some objective friend she could confide in. The few there were had drifted away after Ashton, and she regretted not keeping in closer touch now. Now there was no one really close except Sondra. Her relationship with Ashton had cost her friendship. Oh, there were a few co-workers and acquaintances, yet no one close enough to share this devastating mess with and feel her pain. Lydia thought of one other person.

Erika heard the phone on the third ring and rushed from the bathroom shower wrapping a towel around herself. She picked up the phone. "Tamarra, I hope this isn't you, girl. You're supposed to be on your way."

She was caught by surprise to hear Lydia's voice. There was a stark difference in her tone and choice of words, as if she were trying to speak without saying anything. Erika's earlier enthusiasm about the day's events had ebbed considerably. Lydia's voice was barren, and her dialogue was strangely cryptic.

"Rikki, I tell you, I was given an unexpected, much-needed shake-up look at my life from an unlikely ally today," she had related flatly.

Goodness, what does that mean, Erika wondered. "No fun, huh?" she prompted.

"Well, as it turned out, this homegirl got schooled instead of screwed for a change. Another year older and a few hard lessons smarter, but that's okay, because you can bet your sweet behind I'm wised up now." An artificial lilt came into Lydia's voice.

Erika had no idea what her sister was getting at, but if she was not hurt, she was perfectly willing to hear her out. She got no particular meaning from what she spouted off, but Lydia seldom rang her phone this late unless something was wrong. Tonight, Tamarra had called about trouble, and now Lydia was talking strangely, not sounding like herself at all. Her intuitive senses twitched, warning her that something was up with her sister.

"Well, it's been quite a day," Erika advised in a rather flat tone, considering what she had learned. "I thought about calling you earlier, but time got away. So, I'm glad you called me. If you are feeling up to it, I could sure use your company for a while. Are you alright to come over? Please don't say no." She made it sound as if Lydia was doing her a favor.

It was well after midnight when Erika's unexpected guests made their entrance within minutes of each other, creating the makings of an impromptu slumber party of sorts. She set up the den that had once been Braxton's man-space for them. Lydia's mood was sallow, and her attempt to be her usual self was not working. Tamarra was in far worse shape, favoring one side as she moved. One eye partially swollen shut, her top lip was puffy and her jaw sitting out as if she had dental work—looking greenish purple, but she insisted she was fine. Erika could tell she was still scared and wondered how she had even managed to drive in that condition. She took off her shoes and sat quietly on the carpet in her socks, leaning against a large ottoman, hugging herself with an accent pillow. Erika turned on the electric fireplace to take the chill out of the room, and no one objected.

Lydia looked around the room and thought about her brother-in-law for the first time since shortly after he had been killed. The room looked and felt like him and reminded her what a good guy he had been. She popped the cork on a five-liter bottle of *Asti* that she brought with her. She had been saving it for something special for months, but that time had never come. She looked through the record collection and claimed the turntable. Just as Braxton had, she also preferred the older records over the newer sounds on CDs. They had very much in common.

Tamarra jerked as her eyes lit up at the sound of *Millie Jackson's* sultry voice. This music was a little before her time, but she knew who Millie was and had always enjoyed hearing her soulful, raunchy style. She was singing a song called '*Keep the Home Fires Burnin,*' and even as bad as she felt, it sounded pretty good.

Lydia went to fill glasses all around. With the music filling the air, the room came sensuously alive. She enjoyed hearing Millie masterfully break her lovers down to size and was sorry she had never gotten the chance to see her perform live. Tamarra leaned in and listened intently to the lyrics while Erika went for snacks.

The three women settled where they pleased—the floor, the hassock, and a chair—wine in hand and the last of the potato chips within reach. One bluesy and tantalizing ballad rolled after another. The bottle sat on the coffee table, ready for quick refills. Each of them had their own concerns to drown.

"Well, I don't know much about her," Tamarra spoke up, referring to Millie, "but is there any other woman who can sing quite as dirty as she can and get away with it? Whatever happened to her anyway? Did she pass away? You don't hear anything about or from her these days. I hear her daughter was a lot calmer and was quite an entertainer too, at one time. Probably no ladylike match for Mama Millie, though," she added jokingly.

"I really don't know…probably retired," Lydia answered. "She is considerably older than we are because these records are as old as dirt." Tamarra's mention of Millie's daughter made her think of her own son, so she changed the subject, "Guess who called the other day?"

"My baby Jackson, and no relations to Millie." Lydia looked pointedly at Tamarra.

Tamarra smiled at the mention of Jackson, knowing the difficult dilemma Lydia had encountered that made her decide to send him down South.

Erika walked in, crunching a potato chip. "So, my favorite nephew is hitting it off with his father? I am not surprised. Aaron was always an interested father and a good guy."

"Yeah, he seems to like it down there. He says his grades are better, but then, they couldn't get any worse and he passed on to the next grade. He asked about you and the twins, and said to tell y'all, 'hey.'"

"Well, that's sure good to hear. Sounds like Jackson just needed some quality time with his dad," Erika said thoughtfully as her twins came to mind. They were so young, but how terribly they must miss their dad. It gave her a chill to think about how their father's absence would affect the children, especially Brandon, in the future. The change in him was so noticeable. Over the past weeks, Brandon seemed to recede more into his sister's shadow. They had always been competitive, but somehow, lately, the field was no longer level. He had become somewhat withdrawn, as if he was not sure what his place in life was anymore. She wondered what she could do for him and knew that she had to come up with something. "And how is Aaron faring? Is he enjoying being in the trenches of fatherhood?"

"I think he loves every minute of it. They will be visiting over the Memorial weekend. He asked about staying in Jackson's room instead of a hotel," Lydia volunteered, expecting to get a reaction from Erika.

"And?" Erika eyes widened.

"He thinks that would give Jackson a chance to spend time with us together," she concluded decisively. "And nothing. I agreed."

"That's just wonderful!" Tamarra exclaimed sentimentally.

Erika was ecstatic at the thought of seeing her nephew and ex brother-in-law. "So, Aaron's coming back to Maryland. That sounds very interesting," she noted aloud and then mumbled something about how kindhearted men often slid quietly off the radar into the wild blue yonder and women were left trying to peel away the real nutcases from the wreckage of their lives.

"I just had a reunion with my family, too," Tamarra spoke up. Erika and Lydia tuned in with surprise at the same time and gave their undivided attention. Lydia had never heard her mention any family, though she presumed they were local.

If anyone knew the details of Tamarra's family dysfunctions, it was Erika, so hearing a mention of a reunion of any type was big news. She stared at Tamarra intently for several seconds, wondering if their relationship had deteriorated so badly that she would be hearing this for the first time.

"For goodness' sake, when did all this happen?" Erika asked, dumbfounded.

"This evening…a little while ago," she answered quietly, wincing in pain, looking into space. "If my parents could just see me now, I would never live it down. Tenni called to tell me Mother was hospitalized, and I rushed right over. That's where I came from when Dorsey blindsided me and muscled his way in. Things were so emotional between all of us…nothing bad, though. I just wasn't paying my usual attention to things when I got home, so that dog got the drop on me." She faced Erika with sad, watery eyes. "You know it's been five years, and my parents look so much older now than when I last saw them. And I didn't know I missed them so much. We were so happy to see each other…and Mother kept crying, while Daddy wouldn't take his arms from around me. I sure wouldn't want them to see me like this. I am relieved they don't know about this latest mess I've got myself into," she finished, almost in tears.

"Oh, I'm so sorry your mother is sick. How's she doing?" Erika asked.

"Actually better, she says, once she saw me." Tamarra managed a weak smile.

"And, what about your dad? How's he doing with all of this?"

"He's good. He seemed glad just to have everyone in the same space again, even if it was in Mother's hospital room."

"Oh, that's just so special," Lydia added with a momentary flashback to her own mother.

Erika gave Tamarra a congratulatory hug of support. "I'm so glad you got to see your parents. I sure wish mine were still around." She smiled, then added, "Look, I want to check on the kids. Be right back." She left the room quickly.

Lydia didn't acknowledge Erika's comments as she quietly began refreshing their drinks. Alone with Lydia, Tamarra sipped quietly at first, taking in the words of the music, which must have hit a nerve. Suddenly, the words poured out like someone had pulled a string. She recounted the entire gruesome ordeal with a blow-by-descriptive-blow dramatization of her wretched experience with the lunatic Dorsey. Lydia's unspoken curiosity about her bruised face was quickly satisfied without even having to ask. The indignity that Tamarra suffered only deepened Lydia's irritation toward men in general. She shook her head in disbelief. The insightful, wise, and often stinging lyrics that Millie spilled out penetrated their conversation and thoughts. Lydia felt if Millie couldn't break a man down, nobody could. She would've had a field day with the likes of Dorsey and Ash; they would get their feelings hurt royally.

"Yeah, she can talk more hullabaloo than anybody I know," Erika laughed, walking into the room. When she headed for the wine again, Lydia and Tamarra both noticed. Erika rarely drank anything alcoholic, though she had tasted and had always liked this particular wine. Sharing a drink under these circumstances was understandable to both Lydia and Tamarra, but Erika's second and third glasses got their attention.

"Rikki, have you eaten this evening?" Lydia asked, trying not to sound too motherly. "You need something on your stomach to drink. I should have asked you that before I poured the first one."

Erika held her glass high, nodding her head in the negative that she was not drinking on an empty stomach. "Nope, I had dinner with the kids and ate all my veggies, she added lightly. And I see that look. Just finish what you were saying about what's-his-name," she egged on, referring to the observation Lydia was making regarding Ashton and Dorsey.

"Tamarra, I think you should slap his a** with an assault charge," Lydia added contemptuously, stepping back into the conversation without missing a beat. "Let him know you mean business." She slurred just a little now. "The whippings these men lay on women might do better on some of their kids."

"Yeah, then get the hell out of Dodge, right?" Tamarra replied helplessly. "Because I know that would be like declaring war. He's upset enough as it is."

"And you're not! She's right, you need to do something," Erika agreed. "You can't let that slimeball get away with this. He's probably done this before. I don't mean to sound nasty but check the mirror. Your face is swollen like a rainbow… and you're moving like you've been in an accident," she reminded.

Lydia stepped in, cutting her eyes at Erika as if to say, ease up on her… all that isn't necessary. "Don't feel bad Tamarra, get even," Lydia reassured.

"Hold up a minute," Erika interjected with a look that indicated she had an idea as she proceeded from the room. "…Be right back." She left the room again.

"Like the words from that old *Sparkle* song," Lydia began softly, singing a few memorable lines.

Everybody's got a story—yes, they do—about love and the good things. But, for the spices of your life, you have got to pay the price—if you know what I mean.

"Remember that one?" she questioned, looking affected by the wine. "A lot of women are having their share of men problems right now. But they are probably more in the Mary J. Blige or Mariah Carey mind frame these days, maybe even a little Beyonce—you know, like they know what they want and can take care of themselves. And I got a jerk I need to do something about myself," she declared as Erika reappeared carrying a digital camera with a knowing expression on her face.

"I thought you and the Ash-man had broken up. So, what's there to do?" Erika commented, casually aiming the camera at Tamarra. "You're not back together already, are you?"

"No way," Lydia insisted with annoyance at the mere suggestion. "But what if we were?" She shot Erika another aggravating cut of her eyes as if it were her fault that she felt like an idiot every time she was reminded of him. "Let me share a little something with you—something I would rather keep to myself." She knew the wine was about to start talking, and she felt helpless to stop it. "But it will certainly let you know that you are not alone. Who knows, it may even in some strange way make you feel better," she added mysteriously enough to get their attention immediately. "Now, mind you, this is some…" She hesitated and thought about Erika's previous substitution. "…sugar honey iced tea, that, before tonight, I didn't know myself," she felt compelled to add in her own defense.

As she finished her saga about Ashton, a strange silence hung in the air, and you know the saying about the "pin dropping". Erika's jaws tightened visibly as she flopped back into the huge leather sofa, looking stunned. She had never thought much of the Ash Man, as she had not-so-fondly renamed him. For all his good looks and dapper clothes, she had always seen him as a first-class creep. And he must have sensed her feelings because he steered clear of her as well. In fact, as close as the sisters were, he seldom came around Erika in all these years, which had suited her just fine. Lydia's pain and humiliation came through loud and clear as she sat quietly for a minute, reflecting again on her painful lesson. Tamarra didn't know how to respond to a story like that. Most men lie that they weren't married; she hadn't come across a situation in all her young years yet where the opposite happened. How ingenious had his game been in just the right type of situation—at Lydia's expense?

"Lydia…" Erika started.

Lydia put up her hand to silence her sister. In her mind, she could not handle anything even remotely resembling the proverbial 'I-told-you-so.' She really didn't want to hear any sympathy either, for that matter. She had just wanted to get it all out. "Rikki, save it. Don't, please. Not right now. I'm not ready to hear anything on this." Her voice pleaded softly.

"All I want to say is that I would like to get that dog in a dark alley with a blind person behind the wheel of the car headed straight for him. A nice, neat little *incident*. Lord, forgive me please for such a thought!" Erika whispered slowly. "I'm just sooo angry."

"As much animosity as I feel toward that man right now, I know that he is not totally to blame. I was there too," Lydia offered sadly. "You can't crucify someone for lying… people do it every day. But this was so wrong on every level that I feel like doing something. But look, I'm not trying to get into all that negativity…at least not right now. Anyway, I got it out, so now we can just drop it."

"But you weren't the one who lied with malicious intent to take advantage of someone," Tamarra interjected unnessarily. "I realize that we live in a lying society and that people lie for different reasons. By omission, like Braxton did to maybe spare somebody's feelings, or you can substitute the truth with your own made-up version like Ashton and that no good Dorsey to get what you want at someone else's expense," she finished sadly. She chuckled lightly through her painful mouth at the irony of her own realization. "I don't think anyone gets themselves into worse messes than I do. Do I have a sign stuck on me somewhere inviting the idiot men of the world to have a free piece of me?" she asked in disappointed resignation. "In order for me to find a decent man, someone would probably have to bring him to me because I'm sure not doing worth spit on my own." She seemed close to tears again.

"There you go again…" Lydia scolded sympathetically. "…being too hard on yourself. You know that unfortunately the a**-holes of the world seem to far outnumber the sweethearts. Now that may be the fault of women in general, but you can't blame yourself."

"But there are a few sweethearts out there," Erika assured Tamarra. "Lying by omission aside, my Braxton was one," she added with teary pride as she closed in for another close shot with the camera.

"We all find ourselves caught between the lies. Dorsey's behaving like some psychopath, Ashton's been playing you for years, which stinks to high heaven, but going with someone else's husband wasn't such a wise choice anyway." Tamarra offered up innocently. She was sorry the moment the words were fully out of her mouth. Somehow that statement had not come out as she had intended. One look at Lydia's face confirmed that before she even finished her point. "And Braxton didn't tell you about his marriage," she concluded, looking in puzzled disdain at Erika. "And he was one of the good guys in my book too. Wow, this is all messed up."

Lydia bristled at Tamarra's words and caught Erika's eye. Erika understood the naked truth of her intent, but her sister was evidently uncomfortable and agitated by such a profound assessment of her situation coming from this forlorn, bruised creature. Not to mention the poor timing of it all. She could also admit that Lydia's experience with Ashton hadn't reflected well on her common sense or family values. That she had gotten so badly burned had shown a lack of judgment, especially for a woman her age.

But Erika knew Lydia didn't need to be reminded of her shortcomings, with the wounds still fresh and raw. Punctuating that the whole contentious relationship was a bad idea from the start was the last thing her sister needed to hear right now.

Lydia had already made it clear that she was not ready to hear a commentary on her situation. *Had this woman not been paying attention?* she wondered. Misguided as Lydia's own actions had been, Tamarra had dared to go there—and so bluntly. Lydia gave her a withering look, deciding she liked her better when she was quiet.

"Look!" she snapped, perturbed and unable to hold her tongue. "Clearly, things are pretty messed up right now for all of us. But *Sistah*…you are in no position to advise anyone, much less me regarding choices in my life. It sure doesn't take a damn 'Rhodes Scholar' to know I should've and could've done things differently, especially five years after the damn fact. We're all seeing some major twenty-twenty hindsight here, but I suggest you keep your thoughts about my situation to yourself. It's none of your business what I do or who I'm doing it with. I was trying to help you feel you're not alone tonight in your troubles when I shared that with you—not for you to use it as some Freudian lecture for me. Get your own business under control before negatively respond about someone else's."

Tamarra's eyes, already puffy and bloodshot from all the crying, clouded over, and she stared at Lydia as defenseless as a wounded child. Wow, had she hit Lydia's button? She had probably smashed it. "That wasn't meant as a personal attack on you. I was simply making a general statement," she whined honestly, feeling totally outdone by how insensitive her remark had sounded.

The mood had shifted sharply, so Erika came to her friend's defense. "Lydia, you know that's not what she meant," she coaxed. "She didn't mean any harm. We're all just talking girl-talk here. I thought we were having a good time…trying to make each other feel better, right?" She attempted to get confirmation.

"Well, it sounded pretty d**n personal from where I'm sitting," Lydia shot back. "What she meant or whether she meant harm is beside the point, as far as I'm concerned. We could've flapped our lips all night without her going there. What part of 'I did not want to hear anything on that' did she not understand?" Her voice was stern as if Tamarra was no longer in the room. Feelings stung that Erika failed to understand her sensitivity over how foolish Ashton had made her look did not help. "Haven't you learned yet? A person doesn't have to mean harm to do harm," she chastised.

"I know that you're hurting right now and I hurt for you. I just don't understand why you are so sensitive about what Tamarra said," Erika stated with mixed emotions? Look at her. We're just blowing off a little steam here. That's all. You can tell she's sorry, but I suppose your last remark was directed at Braxton, right? Well, I refuse to get into that with you tonight," Erika asserted.

"Come on, you two. This is getting out of hand," Tamarra dared to intervene. "Lydia, I am so very sorry. I hope that you will forgive my insensitivity," she apologized directly, as if she were afraid to speak.

Lydia waved her off impatiently and stood. "I'm feeling really tired all of a sudden. I guess it's time for me to go home."

Erika picked up the near-empty bottle and held it toward her so she could get a good look at it. "Do you know we drank this whole thing and it's after three o'clock in the morning? So, I guess we should all be tired. But it's a little late all the way around to think about leaving. Tamarra's spending the night, and I think you should do the same," she said with finality, hoping it wouldn't come to her having to put her foot down.

Lydia was too drained to argue, and she really did not want to drive home anyway. Perhaps she was overreacting, but right now, she didn't care. When she stood, she felt the wine but had not completely taken loss of her senses. She knew Erika was right, and from the way Tamarra looked at her, it was obvious she agreed but was hesitant to say so. Drinking and driving were definitely a publicized 'no-no' these days, but add some emotions to it and that's almost a guaranteed instant disaster. It was an easy sell to convince her to share the spare bedroom with Tamarra. Fortunately, the relatively large room had twin beds and they would not have to be in the same space. That was probably the main reason that Lydia had agreed without resistance.

Erika felt that the past week had taken a toll on all of them for different reasons, so maybe it wasn't the worst thing that they got a chance to blow off a little steam. But she was glad this evening was ending. The last thought on each of their minds before sleep came was how to claim some measure of justice—or revenge, depending on your perspective—against the person responsible for their respective situations: for Erika…Silvia Marselle; for Lydia…Ashton Still; and last but surely not least…Dorsey Kimball with Tamarra.

14

The following morning, Erika awoke early only because of the twins. She forced herself into the kitchen to fix their favorite cereal, holding her head as she sat at the table, silently vowing she would never drink wine again anytime soon. She was still so sleepy that if she had sat on her usual stool at the island, she would have probably fallen off. Anything more complicated than cereal and milk would not work out well for her at all this morning.

Brea and Brandon knew instinctively that visitors were in the house. They sat amazingly quiet, fiddling at the table as they watched their mom. They had already made several trips to the spare bedroom, peeking in on a sleeping Tamarra. With each trip, they closed the door harder than before until she got up and came downstairs.

The wine the women had so aptly divided to conquer the night before obviously had them under its spell this morning, except maybe Lydia. Erika dragged around the kitchen to fix cereal, then pondered over coffee, tea, or juice, before finally settling on waiting for the coffee to brew. She did not have a stomach for food.

Tamarra entered the kitchen in time to find the twins slurping the milk from their cereal bowl while Erika looked as if getting up from her chair was a struggle.

She walked over and touched Erika on the shoulder. "No. Stay put," she urged, pointing toward the coffee. "I'll get it. Good morning," she said cheerfully to the kids

195

through her still swollen lips. "Hey, I could go for some of those." Tamarra's eyes lit up at the sight of the *Bisquick* box on the counter, while she tried to distract them from staring at her face. "What about you, munchkins, want some pancakes?" She was already washing her hands when they screamed, "Yeah," in unison and acted as if they hadn't noticed a thing.

"Thanks. How are you feeling?" Erika asked, trying not to bring any special attention to Tamarra's bruised face in front of the twins.

"Better. Where's Lydia?" she said, hoping she hadn't left already.

"She's been in the bathroom for a while. I hope she's okay. She didn't say anything when she got up."

"I'm sure she'll be fine after her tonic wears off. After all, we were on her turf last night." Erika gave an eye signal referring to the wine being Lydia's personal choice.

By the time Tamarra finished making bacon and pancakes for everyone, the coffee had long been ready. Erika tried to get down a single pancake with her brew, which was better than nothing. Lydia was fully dressed when she walked into the room, feeling as dragged out as Erika and looking far more subdued than Tamarra. She whispered 'good morning' under the curious stares from the children and sat down at the table with the kids. Tamarra quickly fixed her plate and sat down. The kids exchanged looks between them that clearly indicated that they had picked up on something even if they didn't know what it was. Now with everyone seated, Erika held out her hands and bowed her head in prayer, signaling the others to follow.

Everyone, including the twins, mumbled together, "Amen." Lydia had nothing much to say as she finished only the pancakes and coffee. Erika was trying to decide whether to tell them about her visit to the court, thinking it might ease the leftover tension between Lydia and Tamarra. But she really didn't want to talk about it in front of the kids. Their antennas had been up enough lately. Besides, she felt nausea coming on that made her feel that all she really wanted to do was crawl into a tight ball in her bed and forget everyone. She held her head in her hands, this time hoping she wouldn't get sick right then and there.

The longer she sat the worse she felt, and she foolishly tried to cover her feelings so that the twins wouldn't get upset again. Her stomach didn't feel right, and the pounding had started in her head again. She had doubts about whether she could make it upstairs.

Erika looked up to see Lydia watching her intently. "Are you feeling sick?" she asked.

Erika burped loudly and swallowed the thick saliva that had built up in her mouth noticeably, unsure if the urge she had to burp was a warning that she would soon throw up. "I think so," she said, doing all she could to suppress it.

Both Tamarra and Lydia were at her side in an instant, taking her arms. "Do you want us to help you back upstairs?" They moved to assist her in getting up, but Erika waved them off with her eyes riveted to her quiet twins. "No, I think I can make it." Their large eyes were taking it all in. They quickly left the table and went to their mother's side as well. "What can I do, Momma?" Brandon asked, sounding so grown up and serious. "We can help, too, can't we, Mommie?" Brea wanted to know.

"Okay, Brea…Brandon, your mom is going to get help back upstairs, whether she wants it or not," Lydia instructed, and they both hovered nearby.

"It was probably all that tonic," Lydia whispered into Erika's ear, wondering if she had indeed drunk it on an empty stomach. "You know that's not you." She looked directly at her sister.

"Yeah, but who bought it over?" Erika managed as she left the room, partially assisted by the children, with Tamarra following closely behind.

Fifteen minutes later, Tamarra and the kids returned to the kitchen to find Lydia had gone and the place returned to its usual spotless condition. After downing more *Tylenol,* Erika lay in bed willing herself not to be sick. Pain settled in her lower abdomen and extended around her waist to her lower back. She tried to sleep, hoping the *Tylenol* would kick in soon, but the discomfort continued. Pains, both sharp and dull, persisted, that she considered if she should go to the hospital.

Her soft moans slowly turned into loud groans as she curled into the fetal position. Suddenly, her inner thighs felt sticky and the thin material of her cotton pajamas moist. She slid a hand between her legs to touch the warm, wet spot and felt a heavy gush between her legs. She yanked back the covers. All she saw was red.

Her piercing scream sent Tamarra running upstairs with the twins scrambling behind. The three found her doubled over in pain, clutching her midsection in the blood-filled bed. The kids held each other and began to cry at the sight and yelled for their mother. Tamarra tried to quickly remove them from the room, promising that she would take care of

Erika, but they resisted. Tamarra desperately wished that Lydia was still there.

Erika's mind flashed back to that long-ago bathroom scene with her mother—the first time in many years. It almost brought her to the point of hysteria, yelling out between groans. Fear and wrenching pain were written all over her drawn, contorted face.

Tamarra was not sure what was happening, feeling scared as well. "My gosh, Erika, what's all this?" Her eyes froze at the scarlet-painted sheet. "I'm calling an ambulance," she whispered, dialing 911. "Is this supposed to be your period looking like this?" she asked, working to make her more comfortable while they waited for help.

Erika could only moan, cry out, and rock back and forth, shaking her head as the pain tore through her body. The bleeding was far heavier than normal, and that she had made a big mess. Her thoughts focused on what had happened to her mother, for the first time in years, and remembered the terrible outcome. She couldn't bear for her children to see her like this. Their lives were already gripped with enough fear after losing their dad.

"You need to go to the bathroom?" Tamarra asked, not sure at all if she should move.

"No, don't think so. Where are they?" she mumbled too softly.

Tamarra was not sure of what she was referring to. "Oh, Erika," she said tearfully, examining the amount of blood. "What do you want me to do?"

"Where are the twins?" she whispered frantically. Her period had been just a few weeks ago, hadn't it, she tried to think, but the pain made it almost impossible to concentrate on that.

"In their room," Tamarra dialed Lydia's number. She got voicemail and left a message. "I will check on the kids and the door for that ambulance. They are real hawk-eyes, Erika. I told them that I needed to take care of you and asked them to play a game." She added on her way out the door, "but I'm not sure they bought it."

"I know. They're scared…hell, I'm scared," Erika answered, squeezing her legs together as hard as she dared to slow the bleeding.

Tamarra stared at her for a long moment before leaving the room to check on the kids. "Stay calm," she pleaded on her way out of the bedroom.

Erika was so tired of having her children filled with fear, but she was scared too. Finally, she heard the faint blaring of a siren approaching and noticed that Tamarra had left the room. *Why are they always so noisy, letting the whole world know they're coming before they even arrive,* she wondered sadly.

The paramedics took longer examining Erika on site than Tamarra felt was necessary. Considering the sheer amount of blood, she thought it was a clear sign to just rush her straight to the hospital. She tried to shield the children from the messy scene, but there was only so much she could do. They were inconsolable and didn't want to be controlled. They just wanted their mother as she was carried away.

Relief filled Tamarra once Erika was safely loaded into the ambulance, but Brea and Brandon were distraught. She wanted so badly to be in the ambulance with Erika, but she had no choice—she instead followed in her car with her beaten face and the twins in tow. She desperately reassured them, telling them they were going to the hospital to make sure the doctor took care of their mom. Keeping her nerves together was a real chore with the twins crying most of the ride, despite her attempts to soothe them.

And as hard as she tried, it was nearly impossible for her to keep up with the speeding ambulance in the busy Saturday afternoon traffic. Cars poured out of church parking lots. It was a good thing she knew where the hospital was. At last, Tamarra pulled into the lot and entered the crowded waiting room, leading the sullen kids to seats in the corner while she checked in at the information desk. She brought Erika's cell phone to call Lydia again, praying that she would finally pick up.

15

Back at the apartment complex, Florita's door flew open just as Lydia slipped her key in her door. The older woman frantically summoned her inside with a hushed tone, looking as if she might be caught at an indiscretion. Lydia didn't know what she was so up-in-arms about, but she went quickly across the hall. The older woman had difficulty containing herself as she described Ashton's peculiar behavior over the past week.

"Chile, that young man of yours been wearin' himself out tryin' to keep track of your comin's and goin's," she snickered with obvious amusement. "Tryin' to hide that little bug of a car. But he don't know me. I don't miss much that goes on 'round heah."

Lydia smiled at her neighbor's sassy commentary. Ash's "little bug" was, in fact, a relatively expensive BMW, which was more of a sports car. *He definitely doesn't know her,* she thought. "I know he came by the other night," she admitted reluctantly.

"Did he tell you or you seen him for yourself? Because my man…I mean, your man camped out there for more than two hours this mornin'," she chuckled with open excitement. "But I know you wasn't home when he came. And that was good. That was real good," she grinned with pleasure. "He must be pressed, if you ask me."

Lydia smiled wanly. Is that why she was so tickled? She was often surprised by how Miss Flo expressed the things

202

she noticed and was always intrigued by her turn of phrase. It was interesting to listen to her talk sometimes. She had a rather hip and unconventional way about her. But she didn't want to continue a conversation with her about Ashton. The tea kettle whistled, and Miss Flo rushed to the kitchen.

"It ain't a good sign when a man camps around your place signifyin'," she yelled from the kitchen. "Looks suspicious, like he ain't got nothin' good on his mind…but you probably know that already."

Lydia waited awkwardly in the living room, studying a small mural of black and white pictures, some old Polaroids hung with tacks and others in antique-looking frames on the wall, where they had aged to a faded taupe gray. "Yeah, we're on the outs, so to speak," she felt obligated to offer, but that was all she was willing to share.

"If you and that fella ain't gettin' along, you need to be even more careful of him hangin' around like that. You listen to me good now, because he sat out there in that lot several evenin's for a good while, like he was waitin' on somethin'. He got somethin' pressing his mind. Let him know that what he puttin' down won't change things if your mind made up."

Miss Flo was obviously preparing her afternoon tea while waiting for Lydia to get home. She reappeared carrying a round aluminum sheet pan that held two ceramic mugs filled with hot water, sugar, and herbal tea bags. Of all teas, this was Lydia's least favorite, but she wouldn't risk hurting her neighbor's feelings after she'd gone to the trouble. She accepted her gesture graciously, telling herself she would hear her out and stay long enough to finish one cup.

"Yes, Ma'am. If I hear from him again, I'll ask him about that unless you would rather that I didn't say anything."

"Nawh, go right ahead. If he says different, tell him," she snickered at the thought. "Tell him he was out there so long, I felt like I should go down and speak," she snickered again. "… just so he wouldn't feel like he was wastin' his time. Let him know that he may think he foolin' you, but ain't nobody actin' a fool around heah, but him. Yeah, chile, that man got somethin' pressin' his mind."

Lydia knew this woman did not miss much. She had no intention of confronting Ash. She just hoped Miss Flo wouldn't go on and on about him and what he had and hadn't done because frankly, she didn't give a d**n. She doctored her tea with lemon and sweetener as much as she could to make it tolerable and returned her attention to the faded black and white photos on the wall. She boldly inquired for the first time about the pictures and who the teenage girl was in several of them, more to steer the conversation toward something other than her personal life. The cute and chubby girl stood frowning with her arms folded defiantly. There was another attractive headshot of the same young girl.

"Who's this cute girl here?" She pointed at the photo.

Miss Flo hesitated and her face paled with painful regret. So much so that Lydia was sure the woman would burst into tears any second. She wondered if she had said the wrong thing or struck a raw nerve. An apology was on the tip of her tongue.

"That's my daughter, Sil," she answered after a labored silence. "Yeah, she's it. All I had. Was always sorry I didn't have more," she added so softly Lydia almost didn't hear.

Lydia felt so bad now, thinking something awful must have happened to Sil for her to react so strongly to such a simple question. She had only mentioned her daughter once when she said that Lydia was a reminder of her.

Miss Flo sank into her chenille-covered armchair and began to quietly tell Lydia the sad details of how her only child had walked out of her life so long ago. It must be about twenty years now since she had heard anything from Sil, except for the inklings she got through a few old friends and relatives. It seemed like a lifetime for her. She was heartbroken that her only child had carried a grudge for so many years.

Fascination replaced Lydia's initial nonchalance as she listened with a sympathetic interest and cautious probing, and soon it became compassionate curiosity. "Is Sil short for Silvia, by any chance?" she asked.

"Yeah. Her name is Silvia…Silvia Antwonette." Miss Flo seemed eager to talk. She explained that Sil had always been a little spoiled and used to having her way. She was twenty-five when she fell for some boy several years younger she'd met through a friend. Then, she became hell-bent on marrying him. Exactly how many years ago that was Lydia didn't know, and she didn't ask. She just let Ms. Flo talk on. Sil had some medical problems when she was young, so was unable to have children of her own. Miss Flo got wind of her plan to fake a pregnancy to trap the boy, so she gave her daughter a preachy lecture—which only made her angry. She warned Sil that "God didn't like ugly and wasn't too fond of cute," and threatened to find out who the boy was and tell him the truth. They had an intense back and forth. Sil became resentful as hell and left.

"Back then, lots of people married if the gal got in the family way. Chile, you know what 'family way' mean—expectin' a baby," she explained as if Lydia might not know. "Never mind, I didn't even know the boy, threatenin' to tell was enough, and that scheming hussy shot out of there quicker than a field mouse. Didn't bother to come back or call. She sent a message by a relative that she was getting married and I wasn't invited. That same relative told me that she and her husband moved to Virginia, but she had special instructions not to give her business out to me—not even a phone number."

Miss Flo's voice dropped. "Later, when a baby never came, the young fellow figured it out and left. I don't understand for the life of me how she ever expected to git away with that one. They were together for less than a year. Not long at all. Sil's young man wanted a divorce. Lord, when I think back on the mistakes I made with that gal…" She shook her head, taking such a deep shuddering breath as if it might be her last. "I just wish I had another chance and could do it all over again. I just wish I had another chance."

Lydia frowned. Something gnawed at her mind that she pushed away. A ring of familiarity in something she said. A long-shot notion began crystallizing in her head as Miss Flo's daughter's name fixed firmly in her mind. Slowly, a few details of her brief marriage settled in. She continued sipping her tea, now grown cold from not wanting to break Miss Flo's momentum or risk she might stop talking.

But she need not worry. There had not been anyone around in a while that Flo felt comfortable enough to talk with about her only child. It was her shame about why she never came around or even called to see about her. Lydia wondered if what she was thinking was possible. The half-filled cup of tepid tea almost fell from Lydia's hand at the mere prospect.

Lydia's hand trembled slightly as she eased the cup onto the bare wooden floor. She was feeling a little excited, and it was difficult to refrain from giving Miss Flo the third degree. She finally asked—casually, as though a mere point of curiosity—about the young husband's name, even suggesting if it might have been Braxton. But after a few subtle questions, it was clear that it had been so long ago and the Miss Flo never had the pleasure of meeting him. She didn't know his last name. Still, Lydia felt more certain for her own reasons.

Miss Flo, puzzled by Lydia's interest about her daughter's husband and why she had questions about Sil. For a fleeting moment, she even looked hopeful—that Lydia might have some information about her daughter.

So, Lydia explained. She shared all that had transpired with Erika and her problem claiming her benefits. She confessed to her long-shot conclusion that this long-lost daughter might actually be the same Silvia Marselle. The timeline lined up as well as some of the missing details. Lydia laid out her entire line of reasoning for her older friend.

Miss Flo slumped back in her chair, as if shot, holding her chest and shaking her head in shameful condemnation of what she was hearing. Tears filled her eyes, and she looked so dismayed that Lydia feared she might have an attack altogether—until at last she found strength to speak again.

"I ain't heard nothin' or seen hide nor hair of that gal in *God* knows when. And, I know my Sil was spoiled and had her faults, but I don't want to believe this woman you talkin' about is my daughter."

"Miss Flo, I'm sorry to get you all worked up. You're not getting sick on me, are you?" Lydia stared quietly at her for a few seconds. "If this is your Silvia, what she's doing is not your fault and has nothing to do with you. And she probably wanted to get in touch many times over the years but, from what you say, was just too stubborn with misplaced pride to do it."

"Well, I never knew the man's last name," Flo repeated.

"The woman is Silvia A.," Lydia whispered, thinking what a hell of a coincidence that would be if her hunch was true. "We don't know her maiden name."

"Well, if this woman is Silvia Antwonnette, she's a Rollins and probably should get a closer look. And you say that if this is my Sil, then she and your sister are married to the same man, Braxton Marselle?" She looked Lydia straight in the eyes.

Lydia nodded her head in the affirmative, wondering if she was wrong and whether she may need to apologize to Miss Flo, but convinced she was likely right. As painful as remembering was for Miss Flo, she knew that delving into the details with her would not be a mistake.

"When he died, his company found that her name was still on his papers. This woman, named Silvia A. Marselle, came in with proof she married the man first," Miss Flo was recounting, "so your sister can't get his benefits. Am I gettin' this, right?"

Lydia remained silent but again nodded affirmatively. It was close enough. That was the essence of it in a nutshell.

"But, if the woman's name's on the papers, I don't understand why that's a problem," she wondered aloud.

Lydia softened her voice as much as possible and still could be heard. "Miss Flo, Braxton married my sister almost six years ago, and as you know, they have twins. He was a good husband and dedicated father who loved his family very much. Although his first marriage comes as a shock, I would hope he bothered with a divorce first. I can't believe he didn't because he was not that type of man. It just doesn't fit him. If he didn't, that's one thing. On the other hand, if he did," she left the words unsaid but could almost see the wheels turning in Miss Flo's head.

An image of Erika and her good-looking, innocent children—who visited Lydia in the summers—flashed across Miss Flo's mind's eye. "But this other woman says there wasn't a divorce?"

Lydia bobbed her head in the affirmative.

"My Lord. You think she's lyin'?" Miss Flo searched Lydia's eyes. As much as she hated to admit it, lying was not beyond the daughter she remembered. Although she desperately hoped that this woman was her Sil, she didn't want to think she was still causing people pain.

"We don't know much about her. She is rushing the company to process death benefit claims for her, and we need to get any information we can to delay that."

Now it was Miss Flo's turn to get worked up. "Lydia, I apologize a thousand times if this is my daughter, but how can we find out for sure if this is my Sil?"

"If you can give me some personal information, Rikki can have the counselor do a more thorough check. I don't know how much they can confirm, but she can at least ask them. Birth date, birthplace, Social Security number, maiden name…anything like that," Lydia prompted.

Flo was regretful beyond words about what Lydia had told her that she would willingly provide whatever details she could. Lydia felt strongly that her instincts were on the right track and promised to let Miss Flo know how things worked out.

Lydia had ignored the first call—she'd been stuck in traffic. Now, it rang again and she saw that it was Erika. It had been more than an hour since she left, and she was surprised when she answered to find herself talking with Tamarra.

Almost thirty minutes later, a worried Lydia stormed into the emergency room, anxious for news on Erika's condition. Of course, there was none yet. Tamarra shared the details of what had happened after she'd left. And although Tamarra would never know it, Lydia was reliving her own hell about the similar incident that happened in her life long ago and how it had ended. Lydia did all she could to calm her upset niece and nephew, who broke down again the moment they saw her.

Hours later, a receptionist called out for Tamarra and they all ran to the desk, where a tall, brown-skinned man dressed in surgical greens waited. Dr. Morrison explained Erika's condition. Lydia braced herself for the worst, even though he offered as much assurance as she could hope for.

"Mrs. Marselle is fine. She's recovering. We did perform emergency surgery," he said with words that smacked Lydia to attention. Those same words echoed from the past about her mother.

He went on to say that Erika had suffered a miscarriage and tubal pregnancy. She appeared to be between twelve and sixteen weeks. Her condition was complicated by the existence of small tumors in her uterine wall and trauma to the body caused by vitamin deficiencies and dehydration. Lydia answered a few questions about her medical background and told him about Erika's recent loss. Dr. Eli explained that she had a rough time of it and would be in recovery for a while.

"Does she know what happened yet?"

"No, I have not spoken with her yet. She hasn't been fully conscious since she arrived and will most likely be out until sometime in the morning. I will see her then and go over everything."

"Well, I know she hasn't been herself lately, but she never mentioned being pregnant. She's had a lot of personal matters on her mind. Is it possible that she didn't know?" Lydia hoped her question didn't sound silly, but she herself was shocked to hear all this.

"That's always a possibility under the circumstances you describe. I mean, if she's grieving, she may not have paid much attention to what's going on with her body. But women usually have some idea about these things, as you know, well before the end of the first trimester. But I'll keep that in mind when we talk. I appreciate your telling me that," he said, looking up from the pad on which he was writing, unable to ignore the intensity of the exotic but serious brown eyes staring into his own light brown ones. He gave her a relaxed smile. "Listen, you two should go on home and visit tomorrow. And I assure you: she's in good hands." Then he did something extra special—the doctor acknowledged the kids who were quiet but looked afraid. He knelt down in front of them and asked their names. He introduced himself and looked them squarely in their teary faces to tell them that their mother was going to be fine…assuring them that she was now getting some much-needed rest. "She is going to be just fine," he repeated and gave them both a big smile.

Lydia stared after the doctor a few seconds longer than normal thinking how much she agreed that his hands did look pretty good to her. *I know that's right,* she was so tempted to say aloud but refrained. She, Tamarra and the twins all returned to Erika's house.

Early the next morning, Erika was awake and positioned in time for the usual nurse prodding that included blood work, blood pressure, and temperature. She peeked groggily through heavy eyelids at the shadowy silhouette of the nurse. She felt the prick of a needle before the nurse disappeared. The hall lighting reflected some faded luminance through the open door of Erika's room, enough for her to see the IV hooked to her arm. It didn't take long for her to figure out where she was. Within seconds, she drifted off again.

Several hours later, a hand rested softly on her arm. "Mrs. Marselle? Mrs. Marselle? Can you hear me?"

Her eyes remained closed at first, but she could hear him. Yet her first attempt to respond failed, and she put out her hand so he would know that she was awake. When she opened her eyes seconds later, she tried to lift her head to speak but felt a hand lightly restrain her.

"Please, don't try to move. Let's try this," the man said, leaning to the side of the bed.

The upper portion of the bed glided upward until she was in the perfect position to get a better view of the man who spoke to her.

"Good morning, Mrs. Marselle. I am Dr. Morrison. How are you feeling today? Better than when you came in, I hope, but still not so good, huh?" He read her expression as he pulled a nearby chair close to the bedside. "Well, that's understandable. You've been through a lot. Are you comfortable? Any pain?"

"No, fine." She was surprised by his youthful appearance and watched him closely the whole time he talked, nodding her head until her voice allowed her to answer clearly.

He scanned her chart and made notes. "You came in by ambulance to the emergency room with severe abdominal pains and heavy bleeding. You were a little out of it, so if you don't remember, it's okay." He paused for confirmation that he did not really need, and that never came. "I'm glad your family got you here before anything more serious happened. Do you have any idea what your problem was?"

"Well, not really. Things haven't been right with me since my husband died several months ago. My appetite has been the pits, and I've been working on very little rest. She thought about mentioning that she had twins who could be a handful too but didn't. I've been having some stomach pains and headaches. You know, stuff like that." She decided that was enough. "I guess I haven't been taking very good care of myself." She gave him a resigned look, preparing for whatever blow he would deliver.

He leaned in closer and spoke gently. "Mrs. Marselle—"

"Can you just call me Erika, please," she insisted for some reason that she didn't know of and was not in the frame of mind to analyze. He seemed so calm and down-to-earth, yet he sounded so formal and serious.

"Okay, Erika. I am very sorry about your husband, and the change in your eating and sleeping habits is understandable and quite common. I am sure we can help you with that. But there were a few things going on with you that became quite serious." He paused and studied her worried expression. "I don't know if you were aware, but you were pregnant with twins, carrying one in your fallopian tube, which created a tubal pregnancy that you were running out of time on. The other fetus in the womb was aborted… probably the result of stress and other factors."

A low groan escaped Erika's lips at the thought, and her body went limp in the raised bed. All sound was momentarily suspended as the magnitude of his words was absorbed. How long since her last period, she asked herself. This was mid-May. Was it in February? She tried to think back but got nothing. Had there been one since Braxton's death? She couldn't recall because she had not missed the lack of a period at all. Somewhere in her depth came a strong sense of relief for reasons she either was not sure of, would not admit to herself, or was embarrassed to say. "I guess I'm supposed to ask how far, right?"

Dr. Morrison had no reaction, and his expression told her that he had no expectations and made no judgments. He was here to treat her and gladly provided answers to the few questions she had. "I will say this. An aborted fetus is usually painful enough, but the tubal pregnancy was the source of your most excruciating pain."

Erika wasn't sure how she ought to feel or whether her reaction fit the weight of such shattering news. What she did know was that the Lord was good and merciful. She was in the frame of mind to consider what happened and the way it happened as a blessing in disguise. It was this thought, more than grief itself, that brought tears to her eyes.

"Am I alright?"

"Mrs. Mar—," he stopped himself and had to smile at that because he prided himself on doing all he could to make his patients feel better. "…Erika. Fortunately, the unviable fetus was removed before any real damage was done. If that tube had burst…well, we don't want to talk about that, since it didn't, do we?" He shook his own head in answer. "You will be just fine. And there should be no problems with having more children…even twins again, someday." A big smile revealed beautifully shaped white teeth that lit his face as his hand covered hers briefly in reassurance and confirmation. "A doctor's assistant will be by sometime today to talk with you some more so that we can better tailor your treatment to you. "Any more questions?" He ended with a broad smile.

She was pleased that his bedside manner was as nice as his smile. It did not escape Erika, even in her condition, that his teeth were some of the straightest and whitest she had ever seen. "So, when can I go home? My kids are probably freaking out with fear," she croaked.

"Now, why did I know that was coming?" he kidded, then softened into a gentle scolding. "Let me remind you that the work we did on you is considered major surgery, and though you're doing fine, we have to make sure everything is working properly and that infection doesn't settle in. I must be doing something wrong," he mused almost to himself. "All my patients ask that same questions."

A weak smile flashed on Erika's face at his comment, and she looked into the friendly eyes of the man who had saved her life. *I'm sure it's probably the hospital and not you, doctor,* she thought about adding, but didn't.

"So, let's not rush things. In a few days we'll see how it goes, okay? Now, Erika, unless there's something else, I will see you tomorrow. How's that?" he concluded politely.

By the time visiting hours rolled around that afternoon, her eyes were closed again, but she wasn't really sleeping. Her mind was so preoccupied that Lydia and Tamarra's entry went unnoticed.

"She looks pretty good to me," Tamarra said quietly. She and Lydia tiptoed closer to the bed.

Erika opened her eyes and smiled at them. "Hey," she greeted and could not believe the two of them had come together.

"Hey yourself," Lydia kissed her forehead, and Tamarra patted her hand.

"You gave us a real scare—you know that. Are you feeling any better?" Lydia looked for telltale signs that the doctor had talked with her but detected none.

"Sore, but a lot better. Are you two behaving yourselves?"

"Look at you, worrying about us," Tamarra said with a half-smile.

"We are behaving just fine, Little Miss. You just focus

on yourself," Lydia added.

"My babies…how are they? I know they must have had a fit when the ambulance took me away."

Tamarra expressed mock shock at Erika's understatement. "Fit? They were only almost out of their little minds, but we did our best to talk them down. Including the nice doctor, I might add."

"We took very good care of them. Brandon was quiet—I get the feeling he's thinking about his dad. And Brea was so scared. She's a smart cookie and so sensitive. We didn't know what to say to her. You can't tell that one just anything, you know."

"Yeah, I have to do something about Bran. He's changed a lot over the past few months, and they are both worried about what they've been seeing with me. So, where are they?" Erika wanted to know.

"Now, where else would we take them? When we called Nana this morning to let her know you are in the hospital, she insisted we bring them over right away instead of waiting until tomorrow. So, they are doing great. They couldn't wait to go," Tamarra finished.

"Have you seen the doctor yet? We talked with him yesterday," Lydia eased in.

Erika nodded her head yes and looked from one to the other. "Did he tell you that I was pregnant…with twins?"

"Yeah, we're really sorry about that. We were shocked. Why didn't you tell us?" Lydia asked with open curiosity.

Erika just stared at them both with a blank expression on her face. Was she hearing right? Had Lydia dared to speak for Tamarra, she noticed, grinning inside. She clasped her hands together as she decided to be truthful with them. "I didn't have a clue, and I am thankful that I didn't. I really would have been out of my mind for sure with all the other stuff going on."

"Okay… I guess we have that out of the way," Lydia announced, feeling a little awkward hearing her sister talk like that. "I am just so thankful that Tamarra was there when you needed help," she gave the woman a short tight smile.

So, that's what this camaraderie she sensed between them was all about—Lydia's gratitude. Well, whatever it was, she was fine with it, if it helped them to get along. "Lydia, I'm sorry. It's just that being pregnant was the last thing that would have entered my mind or that I needed to worry about on top of everything else right now. And if I had known, that would have been just another nail in my coffin of worry. At least that's how I see it right now."

"Didn't you miss your cycles?" Lydia quizzed.

"No," she said simply. And frankly, she hadn't. In retrospect, the past few months had been suspended in time, simply blurred together. Erika couldn't figure it out or recall her last period. "Can we talk about this some other time? My brain's on overload right now, okay?"

"We don't have to talk about it at all. It's your business. It's just that it was a surprise."

"Noted," Erika acknowledged, hoping that it would be the end of it. "I'll call the kids later and let them know how I am doing." Erika changed the subject.

Lydia got the message and followed her lead. "I am sure they are worrying Nana to death about where you are and what's happening to you. They have already given her their version of your drama. And all about your ride in the ambulance, which didn't reassure them at all. I suppose it is way too early for the doctor to say how long you're in for?" The intensity of the doctor's warm light brown eyes was still fresh in her mind.

"Yes. He said exactly that, and we'll see in a few days."

Then Tamarra voiced what Lydia was thinking. You have a mighty fine doctor assigned to you. But, to me, a stone fox is what he is. Enough to make a woman want to play sick for a while, I'd say."

She and Lydia fixed their eyes on Erika for a reaction that didn't come until Lydia spoke up. "Doc has my vote, but the sight of him every day would motivate me to get well quick. You know, get the doctor-patient thing out of the way 'cause it's a no-no." She lifted her eyebrows at a deadpanned Erika. "What about you? What do you think, or are your eyes impaired like the rest of you?"

Erika was barely able to stifle her weak laughter. "Cut it out, both of you. I just had surgery in case you two forgot. So don't try to make me laugh. It hurts too much," she reprimanded, amused to hear such flirtatious comments from them during their personal sufferings. She wasn't surprised at Tamarra because, as beat up as she still looked, her eyes seemed to light up around any good-looking man with brown skin. But Lydia was the shocker considering what she had been through with the Ash Man. "Yeah, yeah," she conceded. "He seems like a very nice and competent doctor."

"Do you mean nice, personality-wise, or nice, as in yes, I noticed that he is fine or good-looking?" Tamarra challenged.

They were going to make her laugh again if she wasn't careful, and she was not having it. Determined not to take their bait on this, she mumbled. "Come on and be serious for a minute," Erika pleaded, trying to turn the conversation in a different direction. "Lydia, I need you to do me a favor first thing Monday morning."

"Ahh," she sighed. Okay, give it to me." It was clear she was not ready to change the subject, just yet, so what could she do?

"Call Mrs. Z for me and see what's happening. I never got a chance to tell you that I found out something about Silvia in Foxmaine County that should be helpful for my claim."

"You went to Foxmaine County?" Lydia exclaimed in amazement.

"Yeah, led by the Spirit, I guess," Erika explained, anticipating her next unasked question. "I didn't find what I was looking for, but I got something that raises a few interesting questions."

Lydia thought of the call she was anxious to make on Monday morning as well to her credit union. "Speaking of Silvia, you won't believe something I found out. I don't believe it myself."

Erika described her adventure to Foxmaine County in detail. Hearing about her experience only excited Lydia more. After she shared her conversation with Miss Flo,

Erika lay in absolute wonderment at the magical turn of events over the past few days. The answer to her prayers were in the works even as she lay there. She knew it, could feel it, and her faith in the Lord's good work was magnified.

16

Lydia had several messages in her voicemail from Ashton, Benette, and the Credit Union. She questioned what it meant that they both had called and whether she should return Benette's call. If she dared to call Ashton, he would probably let her call go to his voicemail and call her back when he felt like it. Benette had asked for Lydia's number in case something came up, and she had reluctantly agreed. But she hadn't really expected to hear any more from her, especially not so soon. She never wanted her to know how Ashton had tricked her or that all this time she thought she was having an affair with a married man—her husband. Aside from that, Lydia left her to guess whatever reason she wanted for her reaction at their meeting. The sound of her voice on the message right after Ashton's gave the story, she told a sense of realism it did not have before, and Lydia really wanted to avoid them both. But she knew things were not quite over yet and that she probably was better off returning the call than not.

Benette's voice was upbeat on the phone. "Hey Lydia, I'm glad you called me back. I want to say I am sorry for upsetting you the other day with all that stuff about Ashton, and I hope you don't regret meeting with me." Her accent fluxed in and out.

"That's okay. You did me a solid. I'm more grateful than you know that you insisted on talking to me. I needed that stiff kick in the pants."

"In hindsight, I should've been more sensitive about how I said things, but it was difficult to know where to start." Benette sounded apologetic, not realizing exactly what she said that had rendered Lydia speechless as she talked up a blue streak.

"If that's why you called, be assured—you did just fine," she started, hoping that she would never really know. She had been too stunned to say much of anything.

"Not really, but I did want to apologize since we are talking. I need to share a few things that I think you should know."

"Benette…it's really not necessary since whatever friendship Ashton and I had is ended, even if he hasn't quite got it. But, since we're talking, okay, I'll bite," Lydia responded nonchalantly. She wondered how interesting whatever it was she had to say would be this time.

"Ashton has been pressing me for an answer to his ring. He claims that he wants to get married soon, so I just told him it was over between us for good. That I'm seeing someone else that I care a lot about, and I'll be damned if I wait for him to ruin things for me, like he's done in the past. Meeting with you gave me the courage to do that finally and I thank you."

"Oh boy…" Lydia exclaimed, unable to cover up her amusement. Ashton's non-marriage was breaking up. "That probably caught him by the short hairs."

"I guess. He didn't take the news well at all. Went into an egotistical fit and demanded the ring back, which brings me to the point you need to know. I ran across another one of his receipts, but he caught me this time and snatched it before I could get a good look at it. But I saw enough to recognize that it was from the shopping channel, and I don't know why I want to think that's where the ring he gave me came from, but I do."

Lydia burst into laughter at the idea. "Ashton orders from the home shopping channels?" she asked in disbelief.

"Well, he probably shops anywhere he can spend someone else's money. You know that's where his gold jewelry came from. The receipt looked a lot like the ones from a channel that I am quite familiar with myself." There was a smile in her tone. "And I hate to say it, but I have the feeling that he used your card number to order my ring. That's probably why it was so nice, because if you know him at all, he is not laying out that kind of money for anyone but himself."

Lydia most certainly didn't know that. She remembered Benette said she came across the receipt that must have been for the jewelry she allowed Ash to buy. "I hope you're wrong about that, because that really would be adding injury to insult. That would be a hell-of-a-thing to do to me on top of everything else," she spat out before she could catch herself. The ring she had immediately came to mind. That's probably where it came from as well, Lydia concluded, feeling herself sink to another level of disappointment she didn't even know existed for him. She couldn't bring herself to mention that Ashton still owed her money for a charge, and he had not even mentioned paying for it.

"I just thought you should know. But let me tell you what I did—he's frustrated as hell." Her tone turned more dramatic, and a short laugh erupted before she continued, "I told you that the apartment's still in my name, and he's pretty good about paying rent on time. Anyway, he tells me he got notice it's time for the lease renewal. Well, I am tired of him being there under my name, so the day after I followed him to your place, I gave the thirty-day notice. I think he forgot I can still do that whenever I want. Ashton's a real slickster."

Benette snorted. "I don't put it past him to call the rental office and try to work his charm. I already warned them about him, and the manager said they have a waiting list, so he doesn't think so." Her accent made the word "think" sound like 'teenk again'. "He only has a few weeks to find a place, and let me tell you, he is livid!"

She made no effort concealing her glee about Ashton's living situation, warning her that he might be hunting for a 'pless ta steh,' as her accent bent the words. She squealed with a child's delight.

Lydia was trying to tie the pieces together now. That was probably why he had said they needed to talk in his message. This conversation proved to be as enlightening as the first, and Benette's words of caution and warning were barely finished before the phone beeped, indicating another call coming in. Having the two of them on a conference call would have been a fitting finale to her wonderfully uplifting and empowering weekend, she thought sarcastically. His cell number appeared on the phone, so she thanked Benette for the update and switched over to hear his deep, sexy voice.

"Hey, babe, it's me. How are you?"

"I'm tired, Ash. That's how I'm doing."

"You got my message, didn't you?"

She thought about what Benette had said. "I got your message. But it's not a good time. Can we talk some other time? Besides, I was heading for the bathroom," she lied.

Now his attitude changed, and he came across a bit more forceful. "I can call you back in fifteen minutes," he announced and hung up.

She sat on the love seat staring at the TV but not seeing it while her mind flicked through several rather unrealistic scenarios of how to handle Ashton. *What to do next,* she wondered. Time was not on her side because she knew he would be calling back precisely when he said, in fifteen minutes, simply because she didn't want him to. And, sure enough, before she could get a strategy clear in her head, the phone rang again, and she knew who it was.

"Babe, Ashton." His words came slow and she detected a slur?

"My, aren't we prompt tonight. That's not like you. So, what's on your mind?"

"Nothing, other than missing you. I'm feeling kind of down right now. I've been having a hard time catching up with you lately. When I call, I keep getting that damn voice thing. Where've you been, anyway?"

There was tension in his voice and a more distinct slurring. He must be high, and she could certainly understand why, but on what she was not sure, since he favored smoking grass as much as drinking beer.

Was he seriously asking her where she had been? She knew it was all rapidly unraveling for him. This sure confident man had never questioned her whereabouts, but then again, he never had reason to. Lydia wasn't sure why, other than that he still owed her money, but she was not quite through with him yet. "I've been with my sister. Why? She asked harshly, knowing he did not deserve an answer at all, and hoped for a method to her madness for indulging him, though she still didn't know what it was.

"Oh yeah, she lost her husband. How is she holding up, anyway? I don't think I ever asked you that."

"Her name is Rikki. No, you haven't." Ashton had never asked about Lydia's family at all. "But she's just fine," she answered politely.

"Well, that's good. I'm glad." The quiet between them held an uncomfortable pressure that only Ashton seemed bothered by.

"So what about us?" he asked finally. "Are we just fine too? We still need to talk. Can I come over?"

"And leave your wife at this time of night. I wouldn't dream of it. Besides, I told you I'm through."

"Babe, you don't mean that. I'm still trying to make up and I'm more than willing, but that's hard to do over the phone. You get what I'm saying? Why don't I come over? I would like to be with you a while tonight."

Lydia was silent.

"Come on. I need to talk to you," he pleaded.

"It's late and I have a busy day tomorrow. What's your wife going to say about you going out this late, anyway?"

"It's not all that late, and I can be there in a few minutes.

And don't worry about my wife. I'll square things with her like I always do. So, how about it?"

It took everything she had and a little she some she was short of not to call him out for what he was: a lying son-of-a-you-know-what. But she managed to control herself. It was something she vowed to do more of. Keeping her cool, she stopped short of putting the whole matter to bed and blowing his phony cover.

"No, Ash. You think everything's okay because we're on the phone. Didn't you hear me say I'm tired?"

"What about the ring?" he interjected. "It fits; you like it—I know you do. I'll even bet you're wearing it now," he teased, trying to sound intimate.

"What about it? And why would I wear it?" she snapped abruptly, thinking about the ring Benette had as well.

"You took it, so I figured everything was fine."

"Yeah, you insisted on leaving it, so that's what you want to think. I hadn't planned on getting into all this with you tonight, but you want to know what I really think about that ring?"

"You know you like it. Just admit it," he coaxed.

"It looks nice, Ash, but what you saw was shock, not joy. Gifts aren't your usual style, and I'm used to getting very little from you. The whole thing comes across as suspicious. It would've been better if you hadn't bothered. I'm not interested in getting a ring from you. I'd have much more preferred the money this cost instead—to at least pay off that charge you still owe me."

"Oh, so now you're throwing that in my face."

This wasn't where Lydia planned the conversation to go. "Look, Ash, I've said more than I intended. I'm through talking."

Desperation crept into his voice, and his tone became harsher. "Wait a minute. Don't play games, okay? Don't play with me. If that's the problem, just say so, and I'll deal with it. I can bring your money over tonight and pick up the ring and return it tomorrow, if that's what you want. Whatever it takes to make everything alright between us," he responded, as if they were negotiating a deal. Maybe they were.

If what Benette said was true, she did not see how he could possibly give her cash he would get for the return of a ring bought on credit. But as long as she got her money, did she really care? "Yeah, that'll work for a start, but you will have to bring the money and pick the ring up tomorrow evening. Like I told you before, I'm tired," she reminded him. "And I am only asking for what you owe me, understand?" she stressed.

"Yeah, yeah, yeah. What time?"

"Around seven. I want cash or a money order, Ash. That would make me very happy."

Pieces of a vague idea started in Lydia's mind as they talked, but she was not sure where she wanted to go with it. So, it was a stretch to think that she could manage the outcome in her favor. She wanted to shove the fake marriage he so selfishly used to manipulate and con her with in his face and then down his miserable throat. If the truth, according to Benette couldn't break his unsavory hold on her, she was a hopelessly lost soul. And she certainly hoped that she knew herself better than that. But she was grateful for her contact with Benette and considered it the true wake-up call; she was sure it was meant to be.

The terrifying ordeal that Tamarra endured was a mindful lesson that meeting alone with Ash in her apartment at this point would leave her extremely vulnerable for what she wanted to do. A wise precautionary measure would be to have someone there whose presence might offer a measure of liberating finality to the whole matter. But who? She wanted and needed her money from him while he was willing to give it up. The call from the credit union popped into her head. Was it about something Ash had done? Be that the case, she could gladly arrange a parting gift of her own just for him. A little something extra…maybe as special as Benette's. She thought about calling her friend Sondra, who would probably be ecstatic about helping her out on this. As she explored possibilities, the idea of who she needed became crystal clear.

Tamarra arrived home after dark and cautiously searched her surroundings. She was only there now to pick up some things because she planned to stay at Erika's a few more days. Images of what happened and the gravity of it came crashing down now that she was alone, and she sobbed openly. She was also grateful that she had been with Erika and that the ambulance had come so quickly. She could not remember ever being so frightened, except when Dorsey was there the other night. The doorbell jarred her from her thoughts, and she was apprehensive about who might be there. She felt weak with relief when she saw Jaite's face through the large peephole.

The way Jaite positioned himself in the opened door with a hint of contempt in his serious eyes revealed the frustration he tried so futilely to suppress. Since her assault, he had worried, watched, and called repeatedly throughout the weekend. When she was not home and did not return his calls, he did not know where she was or what to think. Had the madman returned and she lay somewhere in the house badly hurt or maybe kidnapped in her own car? He had worked himself up to the point of trying her doors, peeking through the windows, and watching constantly for her car. He just wanted to know that she was alright.

"Hey," he said, looking into her still-bruised face. "I'm not getting into your business, but I have been really concerned about you." He ran his fingers through his thick hair. His eyes searched her face. He didn't know whether to be angry at her or to merely accept the relief he felt at seeing that she was fine. "Is that guy still giving you trouble? Is that why you haven't been home?" He tried to avoid sounding as if he was prying.

Though ordinarily it would never occur to her to explain herself for anything she said or did, she knew he deserved one this time. She owed him. She hoped it would replace the look of scorn on his face that he tried to hide with the one of gentleness she had become accustomed to. But his expressions and demeanor told her everything. Suddenly, it was all clear to her. She still felt just as embarrassed even now about what had happened as she had the other night, but for a different reason.

"Jaite, I am so sorry. Please forgive me. I should have guessed that you might wonder what happened to me or maybe even worry. I've been at my girlfriend's house, and my mind was on other things. I think you already know why, but as it turned out, she became ill and needed me. I feel really bad that I didn't consider your feelings in this mess and completely forgot about last night." She looked at him apologetically.

He stared at her blankly. She was making sense until she wasn't. It took a few seconds to register to him that she was talking about the party—the non-date they were supposed to have the night before.

"That's not why I'm here, and you don't have to apologize. I didn't expect you to go after what happened. You're all bruised up, and I know you must still be sore." He stared at her with a sympathetic expression. "I really feel bad about what happened to you." He looked as if he wanted to reach out and hug her or something. "I was just hoping like hell that maniac hadn't somehow come back."

"I left that night and fortunately haven't been around to know that," she smiled awkwardly.

He gently touched the area near her discolored lip where there was a small lump on her jaw where there was still some swelling. And she allowed it. "So, how are you… still sore?"

"Not as much. But I've been so busy with my friend that I haven't had a lot of time to think about myself. She's in the hospital, and has twins," she explained, motioning him in. "Can I get you something?" The smile remained on her face as she talked. "Come into the kitchen and have a cooler with me," she offered.

That he happened to be there in her time of need was still a point of amazement for her, and she wanted to hear all about it. But even when he explained that his friend's party was cancelled because of an emergency and he happened by to let her know about the change, she wanted to believe there was more to it than that. He explained that he wanted to catch up with her as soon as he could, so he watched for her car that night from his window and was aware of when she got home.

No one was more surprised than he was when he walked the short distance to her half-closed door and heard the disturbance. Although he hadn't noticed Dorsey's car outside and did not know the man by name, he guessed this was the guy she dated, the one and the same whose car was parked outside last week. From the little Jaite had already seen of him, this kind of behavior seemed right up his alley.

It had taken him only seconds to assess the seriousness of what was happening and react after he walked in unnoticed. Dorsey had gone completely off, and it was obvious that he was totally out of control. Adrenaline had surged though, his body at the sight of Dorsey hovering over Tamarra crouching helplessly on the floor of her own house yelling and crying out in pain. Profanity spilled from Dorsey lips as he grabbed at her clothing, pulling her from the floor with one hand while preparing to deliver another harmful blow with the other—a lick that never came because he was suddenly there.

The full force of his body upon her attacker came without warning. Still, Dorsey's reaction was pretty spontaneous for someone who was as high as he could be. Because of Jaite's surprise from behind, fortunately most of whatever drunken strength he had left was arrested. The two men struggled, jostled, and wrestled as he delivered short body punches. But a drunken Dorsey was really no match for Jaite, who was more than able to pull Dorsey along the narrow hallway toward the front door and put him out. It was the horrific garbage-smelling stench coming from Dorsey that plunged Jaite and his nostrils into near defeat. He was sure the man's systemic alcohol level had probably worked to his advantage in subduing him. Dorsey was a strong man. Once he had managed to calm Tamarra and taken a good look at her face, he knew that it was just as well that the party was cancelled because she would not be going anywhere except to get medical attention—but he never got the chance to tell her. Her face brightened as she heard his side of the story. She knew he understood why she might want her voicemail to intercept her phone calls for a while, even when she was home. But she should have known he would be concerned as a neighbor, as a friend, as her hero.

The explanation he gave for being in what she described as 'the right place at the right time' and 'in the right frame of mind' sounded logical and perfectly plausible. *But then, don't blessings usually do?* she thought. She knew they had been caught in a scary, vulnerable, and potentially dangerous situation and a higher power had been watching over her—perfecting Jaite's timing and maybe even his fighting skills. There was no way to know if Dorsey even had his gun in the car that night, though she felt sure he must have for his part-time job. After all, a gun seemed his weapon of choice, his rite of passage, and, in the wicked, crime-infested streets of Washington, D.C., aka Dodge-City—a name borrowed from the old Western territory reputed for frequent deadly gun battles—a common toy.

After another lengthy talk, Jaite finished the cooler and rose reluctantly from his chair. He was glad they had spent the time together, but he sensed it was getting late. They had been talking for a while. "Well, I should go. Maybe we can do something like this again sometime. I would like to make up for the party, if you'll give me another chance."

She felt a special debt of gratitude to him for his willingness to get involved, jeopardizing his own safety for her. She knew that in these days, even a person defending himself had to worry about repercussions and retaliation from the very people who attacked first, and she hoped Jaite wouldn't have any such worries for defending her. People in this town were known for violence over things far less important than what he had done—saving her from who knows what. In fact, many of today's youth chose to twist the basic act of self-defense against theft and verbal or physical assault into an act of defiance or 'dissing,' a misguided sign of direct disrespect—often punishable by death.

Tamarra was pleased at the concern still on his face and the relief in his eyes. She smiled at him. "Why don't we just see what happens?" she answered, feeling that this would not be a good time to make any decisions about it.

"Fair enough. And thanks for not blowing me off." He smiled right back.

She noted that his unexpected visit had lasted several hours. They had exhausted the subject of Dorsey and talked more about themselves. She had even mentioned her family and her mother's illness. Though she had not visited the hospital over the weekend, her parents stayed on her mind.

On Monday, Tamarra went to the police station to press charges against Dorsey and secure a restraining order. She was armed with Erika's handiwork—several in-your-face photographs—as evidence of her allegations. Still, she was willing to bet that Dorsey would be pounding on her door once he found out. She would try to brace herself for another possible episode with him because, as frightened as he made her, it was important for him to get the message: she did not want to be bothered anymore.

She was at work when the police called late that afternoon to follow up on her complaint. At the first mention of Dorsey's name, she thought he might be denying the charges.

"Ms. Wilson…this is Lieutenant Conway. I am calling about the charges against Mr. Dorsey Kimball. Breaking and entering, assault and battery. That sounds about, right?" he said in a tone more telling than asking.

"Yes, I did. I have a restraining order already. Is there something else?"

"No, Ma'am, not for you anyway. We've connected the name on your complaint with a victim involved in a serious accident over the weekend. I was one of the officers on the scene. When we checked his cell, your number popped up numerous times."

For half a second, Tamarra's heart stopped. "Yes?" Her word urged him on.

"A man identified as Dorsey Kimball with a D.C. address had a head-on collision several miles from your address."

"Oh my God! What happened?" she cried, afraid to ask if he was dead.

"He was DWI and crossed the median strip. When we checked his cell, your number popped up. The driver and passenger in the other car were both killed."

She knew that DWI meant driving while intoxicated and didn't need to have that spelled out for her. She guessed few drivers these days did, but she couldn't resist asking about Dorsey. "That's because he had pretty much been stalking me. What about Mr. Kimball?" she asked simply, trying to digest the surprise of it all.

"Ms. Wilson, that's why I called. This man has been hospitalized since the accident. The last I heard, he got bruises, broken bones… cracked ribs…you name it, as well as a serious back injury. Yeah…he got pretty banged up on this one. And they say he's d**n lucky to still be here even though there's a chance he might be paralyzed. In any case, he won't be going anywhere for a while, so he shouldn't be bothering you or anyone else for a long time."

"I'm sorry to hear about the accident," she heard herself say while she was thinking that *'what goes around comes around.'*

"Just wanted to let you know what happened and see if you still wanted to press charges. From the information you provided, everything is in order, and the charges look good, so it's your call."

The sympathy she wanted to feel wasn't there. *So, Dorsey was out of commission,* she thought. His luck had still been better than Braxton's. She thought silently for a few seconds before she answered the question.

"Yes, officer. I do."

17

Lydia had her suspicions about why a credit union representative might have contacted her, but she could not wait to find out for sure. Her payments were current despite Ashton's charge, and most of the balance was a result of his non-payment.

The credit union representative explained that they had noticed several charges recently that had exceeded her limit by a few hundred dollars. Though payments were up to date, they wanted to know if she could cover the excess. Lydia had abused her limit, which wasn't that high in the first place. It was her way of controlling her charges. Ashton's balance should've been all that was left. She stared at her last statement with a total disconnect from what the representative described.

"My limit is $2,500. I don't have a large balance on my charge."

"Yes, Ma'am. You had a balance of more than five hundred dollars before a recent charge made for men's jewelry totaling twelve hundred fifty dollars. We received your payment of five hundred dollars, but over the past few weeks, there have been additional charges for approximately sixteen hundred dollars. We wouldn't ordinarily bother this early for such a small difference, but we have become a lot stricter considering today's economic downturn and fraudulent activity. Your next statement will show the purchases. But I am sure we can work it out," she finished.

"Can you tell me what the charges are?"

"Ladies' jewelry from the Gold 'N Gems. Are you not aware of these charges?" the representative wanted to know. 'Do you have access to your account online?"

"No. And I don't do online for store accounts." *Benette was right on,* she thought, wondering how they were going to work this out since she knew who the perpetrator was.

She explained to the representative that the charges were made without her knowledge or permission and, other than being placed in "dispute status," wanted to know how she should handle the matter. This was not her bill, and she had no intention of paying it. She was advised to submit a written request to initiate an investigation regarding the validity of the charges, knowing where that should lead. Lydia did not want to admit her suspicions, regardless of how sure she felt, and have that on record. If things had worked out as Ashton envisioned, she would have accepted that ring, and he would be excused for misusing her charge card without permission. And all would be forgiven, although she wasn't sure how he planned on getting around Benette's gift.

That evening, Lydia answered her door first to her invited reinforcement she had decided on, or whatever you wanted to call it. She was very thankful to get her on such short notice. Her guest asked what Lydia's plan was and what specifically she needed her to do. When Lydia had no answer, she was mildly concerned. She assured herself that there was the main goal of getting her money, but beyond that, she would have to just wing it. The guest agreed to wait in the bedroom until Ashton left as a safety precaution, if nothing else. A short while later, there was another knock at the door that Lydia knew it was Ashton. Well, regardless of how things played out, she knew she would put an end to the whole matter tonight.

She watched him through the peephole for a few seconds before opening the door, thinking this was her moment of truth. Still feeling her way through a somewhat murky idea, she behaved as if she were ready for him even though her company expressed concern that she had no practical plan of action—that Lydia was just winging it while she was asked to stay out of sight.

"Hey, Babe…" He rubbed his hands together and blew on them when he entered her apartment, looking fit and lean in a black and gold Pittsburgh Steelers jogging outfit and matching cap. She didn't know he was a fan.

The ring box sat on the almost bare coffee table in front of the loveseat, where he was sure to catch sight of it immediately. At the other end of that same table, behind a small floral arrangement, there was another box.

"I wish you would stop calling me that. We both know that I haven't been your Babe for a while now. Call me by my name from now on, please." She was sick to death of hearing that humdrum, 'Hey, Babe' from his lying lips. It annoyed her that he never said her name anymore. She was beginning to wonder if he remembered what it was or his way of making sure that he didn't misspeak. She scooped up the tiny box, first thing and led him toward the kitchen.

"Hey…whatever you say, Babe—I mean Lydia. You're calling the shots," he grinned slyly. "Mind if I sit?"

She ignored the question. "Here it is. Just the way you left it," she announced, sliding the little box toward him.

He just stood there while she waited for him to take it. "I thought we were going to talk," he reminded, looking a bit disappointed.

"And I thought you were bringing me the money you owe me," she stared, resisting the urge to yell at him.

Their eyes locked as if they were engaged in a mental standoff that lasted only seconds but seemed longer. She didn't flinch or back down, like she guessed she might have in the past. He sighed heavily, making a sound akin to a baby snort, took the box from her outstretched hand and jammed it into his jacket pocket.

"How about a check?" he asked, grinning devilishly.

"Don't even try it. You heard me. Cash or money order…please," she added ever so politely.

"Alright, alright! I'm just kidding," he laughed with amusement. "I got it all right here." He dug into his pants, chuckling and shaking his head in amusement at her skeptical behavior.

"You remember how much you owe?" she asked seriously.

He responded by counting from a thick wad of folded bills. "No, not really, but I got enough here to take care of whatever it is." His eyes flicked up at her for confirmation as he laid ten one-hundred-dollar bills and counted out fifteen twenty-dollar bills onto the kitchen table. She picked up all of the money except two twenties. It was enough to cover his twelve-hundred-and-fifty-dollar purchase, plus a little extra toward the finance charge. "That's yours. Thank you very much, Sir. All I want is what you owe me…no more…no less."

"Hey, that's fine by me. I was just trying to be nice. But now that we got that squared away, let's get serious." He moved closer and was two seconds away from putting his hands on her.

Lydia knew that this chance to talk was part of the bargain she had made and felt obligated to go through the motions of listening despite the urge to just throw him out now that she had what she wanted.

"Yeah, go ahead. I'm listening."

"I miss you, Babe." He was struck right away by the cold look in her eyes that reminded him quickly. "I mean, Lydia," he corrected, reaching out for her again.

"Will you just speak your piece, please?" she spoke harshly, gracefully moving toward the other side of the table. The TV in the bedroom could barely be heard in the kitchen, but she wondered how much their voices carried. The idea of sitting made her nervous, like she wasn't as much in control as she wanted to be, but she eased herself into a chair just the same.

"Look, Lydia. You know I've been apologizing for more than a week now. And that's not like me, right? But I know I messed up big time, and just to prove how serious I am, I'm willing to do whatever you want to make things right between us again. Just tell me what you need, and I'll make it happen." His facial expression seemed to ask what more could she possibly want.

"First, I suggest you return that ring ASAP and get back whatever credit you used to get it," she encouraged, stretching her face into a hint that evidently went over his head.

"You've got your money. I'll take care of the ring, okay? Are you waiting for me to beg for things to be like they were before between us?"

"You just don't get it, do you? I have been gleaning crumbs from your table for years. I am a single woman and you're, what, a married man? Right?" she hinted with stretched eyes, silently begging for him to correct her, but of course he didn't. "We've become, shall I say, totally disconnected lately. Don't you think this would be a good time for me to get on with my life? You've had a good run with me and held my life up long enough, don't you think?" she asked as if the whole thing was his fault. "I either need somebody completely of my own or nobody at all." The bitterness was coming through now.

Here was a perfect opportunity for him to come clean about his relationship with Benette, even if he didn't dare admit his false marriage. She was interested in seeing if he would take the opening and go for it.

"I know. I hurt you. I got it," he declared eagerly. "But how many times do I have to apologize about your birthday? Come on…just say the word, whatever you want, and I will make it work somehow." He threw the ball back into her court; only she didn't want it now.

"No, I don't think you do. It is not about birthdays anymore. That's over and done. It's about me. You want the word, huh? Now, it's just 'say the word,'" she repeated in disgust. "And then what? Oh yeah, let me guess. You're ready to leave Benette, maybe even get a divorce if I say the word?" she questioned.

"Well, that's a thought. We haven't been getting along so hot these days, no way. I could see making that change. Give me a couple days to clear everything up, sooner if you want. Look, it wouldn't be no thing to me at this point if I know I got you by my side."

"That's very interesting," she feigned. So, you know that if you decide to leave, that's totally on you. Don't put that on me. And where would you go in that short time? You plan on renting a room or can you get an apartment that quick?"

Now Ashton took advantage of this opening. "Well, yeah, I mean, it would be my decision. And maybe I can rent some space kind of quick, right here in your spare room. So, how about that? We could really help each other out here." A sly, street-slick grin distorted his face again.

How about that indeed? she thought. He was more pitiful than she ever dreamed a man could be. "I will tell you how I feel about your idea. In fact, I'll do better than that," she answered, putting her finger in the air to indicate she had a bright idea. "I'll show you." She quickly retrieved the other box from its spot on the table. "There's someone here who can help me with that." She left the kitchen and finally signaled her guest.

Ashton sat there with his head hung, shaking it in dismay as if he already knew that he had missed his mark with her by a mile and didn't know how to correct his course. He could not imagine what Lydia was up to while he listened helplessly as she called out to someone he hadn't even known was there.

He stared in awe as Benette took a stance next to Lydia just inside the kitchen doorway, and together, they gave Ashton a patient, indulgent stare. The other box was in her hand. His jaws literally dropped in astonishment, looking as if he had trouble believing his eyes at the sight of this unlikely pair of women in the same room at the same time. He looked as if he had been touched with a stun gun or something.

"Hello, my dear Ashton. Surprise, surprise!" Benette sang out joyously. "Thees one's for ya, too." She moved toward him slowly. Her words were beautifully accented as she placed her box on the table and returned to Lydia's side. "It really is advisable that you return it immediately for the credit. We wouldn't want you to get into trouble with this debt," she hinted more strongly than Lydia had.

Lydia had a strange expression on her face. "This is how I feel about everything you have said." She and Benette folded their arms and waited for his reaction.

He stared at them in silence, completely dumbfounded and amazed at the unlikely sight of them together. He appeared to be just as floored as Lydia had been to hear Benette's story. He looked back and forth from one to the other, apparently reconciling what he saw, and no doubt questioning how this could possibly be happening to him.

His startled gaze was akin to that of a trapped animal. His confusion was obvious in his speechless stare and repeated back-and-forth glances, even before a loud, boisterous laugh erupted from him. Every time he looked at either of them, he would shake his head and double over laughing until he couldn't seem to stop. He laughed so hard, he almost choked a few times, and water streamed from his eyes. Weakened from shock and laughter, he pushed himself slowly from the chair and walked wearily toward them. They both moved aside for him to pass through to the living room and to the door like the beaten dog he was. They watched him open the door to leave while they did a victory fist bump.

He turned and stood at the door looking at the pair of them, with a wry smile on his face. "You two have got it going on for sure… and don't let anybody tell you any different. That y'all aren't all that," he said, espousing his slangy phrasing again. The expression on his face said that maybe he finally had a respectful appreciation for two fine and beautiful women that he had messed over and lost. He looked them over once more before he walked out of their lives.

EPILOGUE

Erika was apprehensive, yet, as always, impatient. She had barely settled back home and was hoping Ms. Z would call. This woman, she believed, had everything she needed to give her the best therapy for a speedy recovery and finally resolve Braxton's business. But as the days dragged on since her and Lydia's conversation with SITER, that tiny, devilish doubt muscled its way in, and she struggled to push it out.

The next day, when Lydia told her that the counselor was calling, Erika took a few seconds to build her nerve before timidly taking the phone, with Lydia waiting nearby. Only a few days out of the hospital and here she was, as sore as when she'd given birth to the twins. Fortunately, Lydia had taken time off work to stay with her, and Tamarra, now back home, came over to help. Erika listened to what the counselor had to say and her eyes misted.

"Mrs. Marselle, I am sorry about your recent illness. I won't take up too much of your time with this," she started.

"Hi, Mrs. Zimmermann. I'm glad to hear from you," Erika greeted happily.

"Well, let me just say…you and your sister did very well indeed. SITER and I thank both of you. There were more Silvia Rollins than you'd imagine listed over the years, and you two helped make a timely investigation possible. Otherwise, there's no telling how long it might've taken to run a thorough check. Probably much longer than you could stand, my dear." She gave a light chuckle.

"I'm thanking the Lord," Erika interjected, marveling at the blissful coincidence that Silvia was the daughter of Miss Flo, her sister's neighbor who had felt close enough to share personal details about her daughter. The old saying that God works in mysterious ways came to mind. This was proof enough.

"Are you ready for the real good news?" Mrs. Zimmermann asked rhetorically. "The bureau in Foxmaine County faxed confirmation that Silvia married another man long before you married Mr. Marselle. If she did that without the divorce, she claims they never got, the implication is bigamy," the counselor explained. "And under those circumstances, SITER is liable to report it."

Erika listened attentively with a big smile plastered on her face, not wanting to miss one single word. Lydia waited anxiously to hear the details of the outcome.

"Since Mr. Marselle remarried also," the counselor continued, "SITER has concluded that this amply supports the more-than-logical presumption of divorce. Under the circumstances, it is a decision the company has the prerogative to make."

"Yes, that makes perfect sense to me," she agreed, trying to signal Lydia with her eyes. *Certainly a lot more sense than what I'd heard before,* she thought.

"It is also the company's conclusion that this horrible mix-up came about because that one single document naming you as the current spouse was either misplaced or inadvertently destroyed. We are so sorry about that."

"So, everything is finally straight?" she whispered tearfully, grabbing her sister's hand.

"Yes, it is. Of course, you will need to make one more visit to sign your other paperwork."

"I can come this afternoon if you like."

The counselor laughed at Erika's enthusiasm. "Yes, I believe you could, but that won't be necessary. How's tomorrow? Then we can have everything ready, so you won't have to wait."

This was exactly what she needed to hear. She was more than satisfied with the early afternoon appointment they settled on. Tomorrow will be soon enough. The look on Lydia's face when she had offered to go in that afternoon told her that. Plus, she knew she might have a problem convincing Lydia to drive her that day.

The following day at the agreed-upon time, Erika was in the SITER office for what she hoped would be the last time. Both Lydia and Tamarra had wanted to be there for what had become a long, drawn-out and momentous occasion. She ignored the little soreness she still felt as she got dressed for this meeting. Nothing would have prevented her from making this trip and finally having a positive conclusion for these recent nightmarish months.

"Mrs. Marselle." She was greeted warmly by the well-dressed matronly counsel for what she expected to be the last time. Today, she could not help but notice how nice she looked in a stylish short-sleeved caramel-colored silk dress and matching low-heeled peep-toe pumps. She extended her hand and smiled happily at Erika. "It's nice to see you again under better circumstances." She appeared genuinely delighted that the matter had prevailed in Erika's favor.

"Thank you. It does feel much better this time around."

"Why don't we step in back so we can finish this up?" Mrs. Zimmermann advised, leading the way. "Everything is ready, and it shouldn't take long at all."

A joyous feeling engulfed Erika's entire body like a wave. It was so intense that it brought tears to her eyes, and she fought the temptation to hug the messenger, Ms. Z. This time, there was no anxiety attack, no headache, and no need for Tylenol, because all of her worries, aches, and pains were suspended at the sight of the paperwork neatly laid out, needing only the sweep of her pen—and not Silvia's.

The counselor had wasted no time postponing the fraudulent claim once Erika had called, and after Lydia's conversation, she was able to cancel it altogether. Her claim would be approved immediately after the paperwork was signed and express-delivered to the regional payroll and accounting office for expedited processing. The counselor also totaled Braxton's leave pay and shares without delay, and that check would be issued within days. SITER could not do any better than that by Erika at this point.

"One more thing," she announced, looking into Erika's jubilant face. "There's the matter of Silvia Marselle and what SITER views as attempted fraud. She submitted a signed claim for benefits that, as far as the company is concerned, were not rightfully hers and claimed that your entitlement was invalid. SITER is not inclined to let this go unaddressed."

Erika's eyes widened as she heard this unexpected turn, hoping that SITER wasn't expecting any action on her part. She didn't know why what the counselor was saying surprised her, but it did. Her first inclination was to feel sorry for the woman, and she caught herself. The euphoria she was experiencing was so strong that she was ready to forget the ugliness of what Silvia had attempted to do. She wanted to let bygones be just that, now that she had what was rightfully due to her and her kids.

"Well, it has taken forever, but I am satisfied that things have worked out as they should. I don't want to press charges or anything," Erika said clearly with an empathy that was second nature to her. "Mrs. Zimmermann, I am just so relieved that this is finally done," she whispered, almost pleading. "And I personally would like to leave it at that. I don't want to bring any trouble to anyone. It's done and over with as far as I'm concerned."

"I will be sure to pass along your position, but that matter may very well be out of your hands. In this particular situation, I believe the company will have a say," the counselor said decisively. "We feel that Silvia's attempt to defraud was as much directed at SITER as it was at you, and there are consequences for such actions."

Erika sat quietly. Silvia had lost, and Erika could accept that as just punishment or reward; however, she chose to see it for all the inconvenience that she had suffered through. But she was aware that this woman was Miss Flo's only daughter, and she did not want to repay the help Lydia's friend had given by encouraging a possible prosecution for her daughter.

"I understand. I guess I'm out of it now. You do what you must as long as you and SITER understand that I am done," she smiled calmly. "I have had all I can take."

The counselor smiled with understanding and admiration. "I assure you that I do." She rose first this time, indicating the meeting was over. "I'm not sure the company has decided yet, but your decision to let things go may help. I just thought you should know."

Erika recalled their previous meetings. "And I appreciate that," she said with finality, gathering her copies of the paperwork and extending her hand with a smile.

Her lighthearted mood was evident as she left the small building with her sister and best friend at her side, both eager to rush her back home to rest. But sore as she was, Erika couldn't rest until she got down on her knees to spend some time talking to her Heavenly Father. She gave thanks and praise for her blessings and renewed her commitment more than ever to her faith. The journey had been grueling, but prayer and faith had prevailed.

Later, the women chatted up a storm in Erika's room, obviously ready for some semblance of celebration. While Erika indulged herself with decaffeinated coffee, Lydia and Tamarra refused to deny themselves something stronger, cracking open Tamarra's wine coolers.

"The past few weeks have been crazy, like a bad trip, haven't they?" Lydia remarked.

"Is that how you'd describe what we've been through? A bad trip," Tamarra teased. "I sure wish I could've passed on that one," she exclaimed with sarcastic laughter.

"So could we all," Erika added. "But did we learn anything? Are we finally on a better road?" A mystical gleam flickered in her eyes as she looked from one woman to the other. "That's what it's supposed to be all about, right?" she questioned with a serious expression.

"Maybe," Lydia answered defiantly. "I guess we will just have to see about that, won't we?"

"Well? Erika shifted the attention to Tamarra. "What about you?"

Tamarra looked thoughtful. "I don't know. Maybe, like Lydia said…we'll see. I just know I'm not looking for any more a—whippings from anyone." Then she smiled tenderly at her closer-than-ever buddy. "Thanks for not saying…I told you so."

"And you? Since we seem to be taking inventory here," Lydia was speaking to her sister.

Erika just smiled peacefully. She knew that Braxton would have been proud that she had fought to ensure some financial security for herself and their children. And the last thing he ever imagined was that

Silvia would waltz in after his death and claim everything he had worked the past twenty-five years for, whether they were married at one time or not. Erika and the twins would get everything she knew they were entitled to.

"I expect that I will think about my life with Braxton all the time, continue to give the twins all the love I can, and move on with my life the best I can," she said simply. She had no choice, and there was no easy answer for how she would start over without her beloved Braxton. "You want to go to Dr. Feelgood with me for my check-up, or do you think I can handle the visit by myself?" she asked Lydia with an amused wink, and all three women laughed at Erika's ambiguous statement because only one doctor came to mind. Erika had made a follow-up check-up appointment with the Maryland office of the OB-GYN surgeon who had most likely saved her life.

THE END

www.ingramcontent.com/pod-product-compliance
Lightning Source LLC
Chambersburg PA
CBHW020104310726
48970CB00002B/476